A Ghostwriter's Guide to Murder

Also available by Melinda Mullet

The Whisky Business Mysteries
Single Malt Murder
Death Distilled
Deadly Dram
Died in the Wool
In the Still of the Night
Spirit of the Dead

A Ghostwriter's Guide to Murder

A Novel

MELINDA MULLET

NEW YORK

Books should be disposed of and recycled according to local requirements. All paper materials used are FSC compliant.

This is a work of fiction. All of the names, characters, organizations, places and events portrayed in this novel are either products of the author's imagination or are used fictitiously. Any resemblance to real or actual events, locales, or persons, living or dead, is entirely coincidental.

Copyright © 2025 by Melinda Mullet

All rights reserved.

Published in the United States by Crooked Lane Books, an imprint of The Quick Brown Fox & Company LLC.

Crooked Lane Books and its logo are trademarks of The Quick Brown Fox & Company LLC.

Library of Congress Catalog-in-Publication data available upon request.

ISBN (hardcover): 979-8-89242-142-3
ISBN (paperback): 979-8-89242-251-2
ISBN (ebook): 979-8-89242-143-0

Cover design by Mallory Heyer

Printed in the United States.

www.crookedlanebooks.com

Crooked Lane Books
34 West 27th St., 10th Floor
New York, NY 10001

First Edition: July 2025

The authorized representative in the EU for product safety and compliance is eucomply OÜPärnu mnt 139b-14, 11317 Tallinn, Estonia, hello@eucompliancepartner.com, +33757690241

10 9 8 7 6 5 4 3 2 1

To Mark, Katherine & Amanda.
You are my life, my loves,
and always my true north.
&
To Abby who always keeps the
faith no matter how long it takes.

Chapter One

On paper there are a thousand ways to kill someone you hate. Admittedly, some more satisfying than others, but as far as Maeve Gardner was concerned, any of them worked when it came to energizing her writer's brain.

This morning's scenario had been enormously satisfying. A man spread-eagled against a wall, his hands and feet strapped down tightly, his killer firing darts at him one after another with a practiced hand. What better way to kill one big prick than with a thousand little ones?

It was an invigorating warm-up, but Maeve still found herself staring at a blank screen, unable to begin any real work. Her gaze strayed out the window in front of her to the canal beyond. Autumn had arrived with a vengeance the week before, and there'd been a serious chill in the air. Cold enough to demand scarves and hats, but this morning the sun had unexpectedly burst forth again with renewed vigor and the last vestiges of summer were whispering to her on the breeze. With the sounds of the city no more than a distant murmur, Maeve could hear the water calling, and she was struggling to find a reason not to answer.

She glanced at her watch. It was still early—time enough for a quick jaunt. Getting to her feet, she was immediately assaulted by a black-and-white fur projectile with a roguish patch over his right eye. She steadied herself before giving the head a quick scratch and moving toward the hatch. Maeve was quite sure Captain Jack had been a lawless pirate in one of his former lives, and his disconcertingly blue eyes still spoke of distant seas and devilish adventures. He trotted eagerly behind her, his nose bumping the back of her knee to urge her along. She untied the moorings, made her way back to the stern to start the boat's motor, and then steered away from the towpath and out into the canal.

The Captain took his place at the bow like a figurehead of old, his ears blowing back in the breeze. From time to time, he'd glance over his shoulder just to make sure his first mate was still at the helm where she belonged.

They made their way past the neighboring longboats parked nose to tail, bobbing softly on their wake. An elderly man polishing the brass bell in pride of place on his deck waved a greeting as they passed by. The canalside was a fellowship of wandering souls living in the nautical equivalent of brightly colored circus caravans, an eclectic troupe of individuals who had run away from life on dry land to join London's urban armada. Not that permanent mooring fees were cheap, but compared to rent in the city center, they felt like a bargain. Vacant moorings were fought over, and the distance between existing boats, like legroom on airlines, had shrunk dramatically over the past few years. In some spots a person could literally walk for miles hopping from one boat to another without ever needing to step foot on shore.

Maeve turned her face to the sun and took in a deep breath. Economics aside, *this* was the reason she lived on the water. As

A Ghostwriter's Guide to Murder

Ratty would say, to simply mess about in boats was good for the soul. The idea of an existence without limits, the freedom to depart at will, the whiff of adventure in the air—you just couldn't beat it. On this particular morning, she felt like an explorer chugging down a jungle river as she passed Regent's Park and the zoo, listening to the incongruous sounds of lions and monkeys echoing faintly over the water. Up ahead the trees that lined the canal were starting to turn, transforming into soft yellows and deep oranges, leaving pops of impressionist color reflected in the flat gray-green of the canal water.

Maeve swung the rudder out to maneuver under the Park Road bridge, waving at the children who ran from one railing to the other to watch the Captain emerge on the far side. A floating house was always a novelty. When she told people she lived on a houseboat, Maeve knew they pictured one of those swank models that appeared on the telly these days, but the *Revenge* was none of that. She was a proper narrow-beam canalboat—ten times as long as she was wide—painted a pale yellow with vibrant royal-blue trim along the roofline. She looked like something out of a children's storybook, and Maeve thought she contrasted pleasingly with the red boat moored in front of her and the green one behind.

They cruised out as far as Little Venice before turning in the Paddington Basin to head home. The journey took up a chunk of the morning, but the fresh air had done her good. Returning to the mooring, she began the tricky maneuver of docking. Parallel parking a car was a skill; parallel parking your home was an art. Maeve worked the throttle and the rudder in the precise rhythm she'd practiced month after month and felt a profound sense of accomplishment as the boat responded to her cues, slipping into the berth without tapping her neighbors on either side.

With a last swing of the wheel, the *Revenge* cozied up along the line of tires that served as a barrier between the well-buffed wood trim of her hull and the stone of the canal wall.

As soon as she tied off, Maeve headed belowdecks to put the kettle on, the Captain barreling past her in his haste to be first to the tiny galley. There were times she wondered about the sanity of keeping a fifty-two-pound dog on board a 500-square-foot boat. Clearly the math didn't work, but she couldn't imagine her life without him, so the point was moot.

She tossed the Captain a treat from the jar on the counter and removed her mug from its home on the window ledge.

The dimensions of their living space demanded that there be a place for everything and that everything stay in its place. Of course, the Captain was the wild card. Never in one place for long, he began by flopping on the floor where the galley flowed into the sitting room, which also served as her dining room and office. She was forced to step over him twice before he breezed out again, heading for the deck. Maeve lunged for the pile of papers being swept from the table by his tail as he passed, while he remained happily oblivious to the destruction he left in his wake. Within minutes the sound of his teeth squeaking on the rubber of the closest dock bumper echoed down through the hatch.

"How many times have I told you that's not for chewing?"

Maeve felt compelled to say something, even though she knew he'd ignore her. For her own sake she tried to maintain the illusion of control, but in all fairness a giant rubber ring suspended at mouth height was too tempting, and in the Captain's defense, it did look exactly like an oversized dog toy.

She poured water on the tea bag in her mug and took four steps to commute from the galley to her office, sitting down

A Ghostwriter's Guide to Murder

once more to stare at the computer screen in front of her. *Right. Here we go.* Invigorated. Ready to start. She clicked her nails on the keys in front of her, willing the words to come—willing her fingers to begin spewing out the overrated pablum for which she was paid. Still nothing.

She leaned back and studied the line of index cards pinned to the wall in front of her, hoping her meticulous outline would provide inspiration. It didn't. She rubbed her eyes and wondered, not for the first time, why she'd agreed to take on this job in the first place.

Being a writer was a frustrating and lonely existence, but at least it was her own self-inflicted hell. Ghostwriting was proving to be far worse. She was spiritually inhabiting someone else's hell with all the requisite grief and none of the accolades. She'd known that in the abstract when she committed to the project, but she'd kidded herself that the extra money would somehow make it easier. It hadn't. She picked up her mug and blew softly on the steaming liquid.

Installment number forty-three of Harlan Oak's Simon Hill Mysteries was right there on the wall in front of her; why couldn't she wrestle it from the wall to the page? She blamed Harlan. To suggest that his body of work was comfortingly predictable would be a kindness. In truth, the man's novels were hideously formulaic, and that was the heart of the problem. It made them easier to construct but paralyzingly boring to write. The current gem had Harlan's protagonist, PI Simon Hill, pursuing yet another killer in his outdated and somewhat pedestrian fashion. The plot was laid out in detail, but there was no room to stray from the path into darker, more tortuous waters. That wasn't what Harlan's readers expected, and God knows she'd been

5

reminded enough times of the importance of giving the readers what they expected.

After all, Mercury Publishing wasn't in the business of being innovative. They were in the business of publishing moneymakers, and aspiring but unpublished writers like her were there to edit. Harlan for all his deficiencies was a big moneymaker. There was no sentiment in Mercury's decision to keep his series going; it was simply against their business model to stop thrashing a dead horse until it ceased spitting out money, even when the horse in question was diagnosed with early-onset dementia.

So here they were, in full role reversal. She wrote, he edited, confused enough as a result of his illness to be unaware that the words he was reviewing weren't his. She was nothing more than a conduit for his dated yarns—chugging along, channeling Harlan, and putting her own aspirations on hold. It was tempting to be bitter, but she knew it wouldn't help the situation. She straightened her shoulders and sat forward again, addressing the keyboard. In the back of her mind she could hear her father's voice. *Always look on the bright side of life, de dum, de dum, de dum, de dum*—the Monty Python refrain popped in unbidden at the end. She was writing, she reminded herself firmly, and she was being paid for it. That made her a professional writer, and that was a start.

Maybe a change of scene would do the trick. Maeve picked up her laptop and moved to the bow of the boat with the Captain, settling into a deck chair with a sigh. It was warm and she just wanted to bask in the unexpected sunshine, but the squeak, squeak, squeak of the Captain's teeth on the rubber tire was impossible to tune out. It didn't bother him—he could keep at it for hours—but Maeve could feel the skin on the back of her neck twitching.

A Ghostwriter's Guide to Murder

She rose and went to shift the Captain from his post. She knew he'd been working on the tire over the past few weeks, but she hadn't expected him to make any headway. As she chivied him off, she noticed a hole in the rubber bumper. The recycled lorry tires were huge and inches thick. How on earth had the Captain managed to make a hole? A hole that was nearly perfectly round.

She shifted him aside and knelt to inspect the damage. Poking her finger into the space, she was surprised to see a slit opening deep in the worn tread of the tire. Roughly four inches long, it appeared to be part of a larger split that had been repaired with glue at some point. Maybe she could repair it again. The last thing she needed was a bill from the Waterways Commission for damage to their dock gear.

Wriggling her fingers into the opening, she pried the edges apart, managing to make the space larger as the glue gave way. The Captain came to stand by her side, watching her work. She expected the inside to be empty, but instead she saw a plastic bag, thick and opaque like furniture wrap, firmly jammed into the hollow interior of the tire.

Pulling the rubber open as far as it would go, she forced her hand inside, grasping what felt like a soft brick tightly wrapped in plastic. She jiggled and pulled until the packet in her hand popped free. Peering inside, she could see several more just like it. Without thinking, she pried off the wrapping and found herself face-to-face with the Queen in all her youthful glory. A crisp new fifty-pound note sat on the top of the pile, and as she rifled through the stack, she watched a whole parade of sovereigns marching past.

Chapter Two

Maeve looked to the left and to the right and was relieved to see no sign of life on the towpath. Slipping back belowdecks, she returned with a large kitchen knife and sliced the tire open far enough to really see what was going on. In for a penny, in for a pound—a lot of them from the look of it.

"Hiya, Maeve." The shout came from the deck of the kelly-green boat off her stern. Flustered, Maeve dropped the knife and watched in dismay as it sank into the water between the dock and the side of the boat. It was her best carving knife. She stood up quickly, adjusting her face in an attempt to look unfazed by the sudden appearance of her neighbor.

"Rowan. How are you?"

"Just grand, dear, and you?"

"Ah, never a dull moment, you know." Maeve wondered whether Rowan had seen her messing with the bumper or if she'd just chanced to emerge from belowdecks. "Big doings today?" she asked cautiously, keen to limit the ensuing discussion.

"We've got a huge crop of rosemary that needs bringing in and drying. Just off to the allotment now."

A Ghostwriter's Guide to Murder

Rowan and her partner, Sage, the two Irish ladies berthed next door, fancied themselves as Wiccans. At a guess, Maeve would say Rowan and Sage weren't their real names. Odds were they'd be something boring like Sara and Maud, but they seemed to be reinventing themselves down here on the water, and who was Maeve to argue? As an inveterate spinner of yarns, Maeve liked to imagine them running from a mysterious past. She often wove backstories for them in her head, all of which involved them having cursed their enemies and fled to a life on the water. Always entertaining, but now was not the time.

Sage came abovedeck at that point and waved. She handed Rowan one of the large baskets she was carrying, and they headed off down the towpath in the direction of Rochester Terrace. Maeve suspected they hadn't seen her mucking about with the tire. The ladies were of an age where curiosity was no longer something they tried to disguise, and if they'd noticed, they'd have asked.

Once she was sure that they were gone, Maeve turned her attention back to the cut she'd made in the tire's tread. The initial hole looked as if it might've been made with a drill. She hadn't noticed it before, but then again, why would she? Working carefully, she reached inside and pulled out five more decent-sized packets, all wrapped in plastic and heavily taped against the elements. She had to admit the tire was an ingenious hiding place.

Emptying the space in the tire, she peered into the trees along the side of the canal, looking for the slightest sign of movement. Seeing none, she stuffed the bundles up under her jumper and retreated down through the hatch.

She spread the packets across the table and stared at them in wonder. How long had they been there? Surely no one would hide this amount of cash for very long, and certainly they wouldn't forget it. The Captain put his paws on the table and sniffed cautiously. He was disappointed that it wasn't food, but he continued to watch with interest. It was his find, after all.

"Should we open the rest?" she asked. "Just to make sure it's all the same?"

The Captain looked up at her with bright eyes, his tail wagging in circles. She was sure his vote was yes.

Maeve dug out a pair of scissors and cut along the top edge of the other five packs, verifying the contents and counting the notes as best she could.

Fifty thousand pounds, give or take. It was mind-blowing.

Whichever way you sliced it, it was a lot of cash that surely couldn't have come from anything legal. Money hidden in a tire by a canal wasn't from a win on the pools.

"What now?" she murmured aloud, scratching the Captain's head. The logical move would be to call the police. But she was quite sure that would be complicated. They'd ask a lot of questions she'd have no answers for. She could just put the money back where she'd found it and let the owner claim it when they were ready. Steer clear of the whole bloody mess. Probably the smart move, and yet a small voice in the back of her head poked at her—*finders keepers*. She thought about what she could do with fifty thousand quid. Get shot of Simon Hill, for starters. Take off on a new adventure. Change her name like the ladies. She'd always fancied Rosemary.

Come on, Maeve, her rational self chipped in, *how far would you get if you fled?* Fifty thousand sounded like a fortune, but it would take more than that to really escape. And did she plan to spend the rest of her life looking over her shoulder, afraid some criminal was searching for her?

All well and good to think about adventure, to write about it even, but to condemn her and the Captain to a life on the run? She'd never survive the stress of it all. She had to see the police. But her fingerprints would be all over the packs now. And she'd moved them. She'd learned enough from writing Simon to know that the police would not be best pleased.

Taking a damp tea towel from a hook on the wall, she scrubbed the plastic on the outside, handling the bricks now with the washing-up gloves. A little Fairy liquid should remove the prints. She looked at the packets once more and hesitated. Maybe she could keep a tiny one back? As she stood there considering the matter, the Captain tried to take the packet from her hand.

"No," she said out loud. "No. We're not keeping it. Someone would miss it, and it's not worth the risk." The Captain gave a soft whine. "I know, looks like I'm not as much of a pirate as you," Maeve said, dropping a kiss on the top of his head.

She rewrapped the plastic around the first stack of bills, then spent several minutes playing hide-and-seek with the strapping tape under the bench in the sitting area. Once the money was secured again, she put everything back in the tire where she'd found it. Time to call the police.

She picked up her phone. What would she say? *My dog chewed open a tire and found fifty thousand pounds.* She'd sound mad. She stuffed the phone back in her pocket. The story would sound more plausible if she and the Captain told it in person— at least she hoped it would.

Melinda Mullet

* * *

"And you say the money was right here?" Detective Sergeant Kevin Dixon was giving Maeve a harried look.

"Yes, in the tire. Lots of it, or at least it looked like a lot." She started backpedaling. "Not that I actually looked or anything."

"Well, there's nothing there now." The police officer let out a long puffing sigh, his cheeks inflating like a balloon.

For once, Maeve was at a complete loss for words. She'd wedged the packets back inside far too tightly for them to have fallen out. What had happened? Someone must have seen her, swept in while she was gone, and taken the cash. Why on earth hadn't she just brought the money with her? Instead, she was standing here looking like a complete idiot.

"I could do you for wasting police time." DS Dixon broke into her internal rant. "I have better things to do than drag out here over my lunch hour."

From what she knew of police procedure, this would normally be something for a uniformed officer to handle, but she'd been told they were short-staffed at the Camden Road station and she was getting an actual detective—as opposed to a fake one, she presumed. Was she supposed to be pleased to be accompanied home by a balding middle-aged man with an attitude?

While Dixon was asking her questions, his uniformed sidekick was poking around the dock, accompanied by the Captain, who seemed determined to keep an eye on this stranger in the ranks. To PC Morgan's credit, he was at least continuing to look for the missing cash. He'd already checked both tires that abutted the *Revenge* and found nothing.

A Ghostwriter's Guide to Murder

"Listen, you can't just play games with us," Dixon continued. "There's a lot of genuine crime about these days."

Maeve wasn't paying much attention. She was wrestling with more pressing questions: Was she having a psychotic episode? Had she imagined the money? Was it time to quit drinking Sage's tisanes?

"Might have something over here, sir," Morgan called. He pointed in the direction of a chunk of dark plastic floating in the water almost into the main flow of the canal. If it drifted much farther along, it would float off. It looked like a black carrier bag that had filled with air. Could it be more cash? Maeve was encouraged. If they could at least find *something*, the police might believe her about the rest.

Morgan peered down into the canal with marked concern. His face made it clear he wasn't keen to take a dip in the icy waters, and she couldn't say she blamed him. The canal was shallow but freezing cold and slimy with algae.

"I have a steering pole," she offered, pointing to the long brass-tipped wooden pole strapped to the side of the boat.

DS Dixon nodded. Morgan unhooked the pole and narrowly missed hitting his boss in the head as he swung it out over the water. "Two ends to that thing," Dixon muttered.

Morgan poked at the bag, causing it to bob and move a bit farther away.

"Try the other end," Maeve suggested. "It has a hook."

The pole swung about again, and this time both observers were forced to duck. Morgan finally found purchase on the upper corner of the bag and began the process of dragging it closer to the shore.

Behind her back Maeve crossed her fingers. *Please let it be cash.*

Morgan shifted his grip and pulled harder. The object in the water moved toward them, bobbing along on the surface. Not a bag after all, it seemed. More like a discarded anorak.

The object came nearer still. Maeve stood transfixed, gripping the Captain's collar in her hand, hardly noticing that she was no longer breathing as a hooded figure floating face down in the water bumped softly against the hull of the *Revenge*.

Chapter Three

Ashley Warren saw the police arrive. He considered going over to see if Maeve was all right, he *wanted* to go, but he was a coward. A coward who was putting his own needs first, in this case the need to remain uninvolved in whatever was unfolding on his doorstep.

He could see an exasperated Met officer questioning his neighbor alongside the *Revenge*. The man was gesturing animatedly at the dock bumpers, his face like thunder. If he was hoping to rattle Maeve, he'd be out of luck. She'd take no nonsense from anyone, even the police. He'd sussed that out from the moment they'd met. She was full-on warrior class—auburn hair streaked with copper lights, fiery hazel eyes. Every inch a fighter.

The senior officer was making no headway, it seemed, but neither was the uniformed PC he had with him, who was pacing up and down on the towpath, searching for something. Ash strained to hear what they were saying, but nothing came through over the hum of the tech all around him. Maeve looked irritated but not upset. *Leave this to her,* he told himself, *and get back to work.* It wasn't good to stop in the middle of a quest. Before the police arrived, he'd been happily worming his way into a client's stronghold through a series of back doors and secret tunnels they'd never known they had. Once he reached his goal, it would take only a few strategic keystrokes to repair the breaches, secure the system, and prevent his client's real enemies from invading. A win for them and a win for him. He liked being his own boss and working at his own pace, not to mention charging a small fortune for his highly specialized services.

He dropped the corner of the blind and moved away from the window, back into the dark interior of the boat. From the comfort of his gaming chair, he sat staring at the wall of screens in front of him. The glow of four monitors was the only light in the shuttered space. His hands reached for the keyboard before changing direction and hovering over the gaming controller.

As one of life's reluctant participants, Ash often felt rather befuddled by the day-to-day campaign of existence, and the odd activity on the dock was stressing him out. Gaming would soothe him; work would not. He took a calming breath and reminded himself that he was secure on the *King of the Red Lions*. The boat's name was a tribute to the sentient vessel in the *Legend of Zelda*, but unlike the digital version, his *Red Lion* had so far failed to enlighten its owner in any way. No explanations for the vagaries of his life, no suggestions about what he should do next. His boat apparently had no wisdom to impart, or perhaps it simply had no interest in his questions. He sighed and reached for the can of energy drink on the floor at his feet.

God knows he asked what to do about Maeve nearly every day. When the yellow-and-blue boat first arrived next door, he'd mainly been pleased that it would provide a solid buffer between him and the wacky Wiccans. The old women were odd and way too chatty for Ash's liking, quirky NPCs he steered well clear of.

A Ghostwriter's Guide to Murder

Maeve, on the other hand, was lovely. Ridiculous to think he'd been worried about the noise and the added threat of forced human interaction. One morning he'd run into her, literally, as they were leaving the Tesco Express. She'd simply laughed over his mumbled apology before falling into step beside him, and in the ten minutes it took for them to walk home, he'd fallen in love. Miserably, frustratingly, and completely.

It was hopeless, he knew that. She was a warm, vibrant, beautiful woman. He was a broken-down computer nerd. Her amused and generally buoyant view of the world made him feel that, in spite of everything, things could always be worse. He was a dour, depressive old sod, yet when he was with her, he wanted to do better. To be better. But it wouldn't matter. She'd never be interested in someone like him. He looked at his reflection in the monitor in front of him. It was a pale and uninteresting sight. The whole thing was ludicrous, but for the first time he was realizing what people were on about. There was no logic at play here; it was pure emotion.

Work could wait. Gaming could wait. He rose to his feet again, drawn back to the window. Back to Maeve. She was still standing on the towpath, stiffly clinging to the dog's collar. The police were huddled together, discussing something below them in the water. Maeve looked frightened and alone. He made up his mind to go to her and damn the consequences, but before he could move, he saw the Wiccans approach and bundle her away, clucking over her like a couple of broody hens. *Damn*. He'd missed his chance.

He continued to watch the action on the towpath, hoping whatever was happening was something minor, something that wouldn't end up involving him, but that hope was dashed when he saw a Scene of Crime team arrive. The police would be talking to everyone, him included. Even though he had nothing to say. He hadn't seen or heard anything. He'd spent the morning and the better part of the night before engrossed in a project, headphones on—as usual paying no attention to the world around him.

He continued to peer out underneath the blind, watching the police work. The specialist team moved into action with a practiced rhythm. After a few preliminary photos, a canvas cradle was slipped into the water, and he watched a body being winched up onto the canal path. The victim's head was covered by a hoodie and it wasn't possible to say if it was a man or a woman, but based on the bulk and the clothing, Ash's money was on a man. A screen was rapidly set up around the corpse, and soon there was no more to see.

Ash retreated into the dark, rubbing his chest to try to ease the acid reflux. He grabbed a couple of Tums from the bowl on his desk and washed them down with the dregs of last night's beer.

He'd dimly recognized the older of the two men from the Met. He'd never worked with him before, so there was a chance Ash could continue to fly under the radar for a little while longer. The uniformed PC wouldn't know him—too young. Maybe he'd get lucky and the new bloke would be sent over to ask the preliminary questions. If it turned out to be an accidental drowning, that might be an end to it. He tried to be upbeat like Maeve, but his own natural pessimism overtook him. In his heart he knew it was just the beginning.

Like it or not, his secret would soon be out.

Chapter Four

Maeve sat in the police station for hours, drinking cup after cup of tepid tea, yet inexplicably, she was feeling a bit better. She suspected it had something to do with the drink Sage had forced on her after the initial shock of finding the body in the river, a bitter and leafy-tasting brew that she'd assured Maeve would calm her nerves and bring clarity. Maeve wasn't sure about that, but she did feel less shaky.

The sight of the dead body—a man, she'd overheard them say—had upset her far more than she would've expected. Writing about a corpse was one thing; seeing one up close was another, not that she'd seen the face. They'd moved her away before the body was taken from the water, but still, it was horrible. She tried to picture the morning's colorful leaves reflected in the water, but all her mind would conjure was the darkly clad figure coming alongside her home.

The poor man, minding his own business one minute and dead the next. Had he simply fallen in and drowned? Maybe hit his head on something as he went? Or—Simon Hill's voice chimed in uninvited—*did he have something to do with the money in the tire?*

Melinda Mullet

The more she thought about it, the more she thought it would be too much of a coincidence if there *wasn't* a connection between the money and the dead man. If she wrote a story like that, it would be unbelievable, even for Harlan Oak's readers. Maeve had absolutely no experience with this kind of thing in the real world, and absurd as it was, she couldn't help wondering what Harlan's anachronistic sleuth would do under the circumstances. She'd been living inside Simon's head for a year and a half now, and too often lately she had found his voice echoing inside hers like a nagging relative.

How would this unfold in Simon's world? He'd start with a timeline. He always did. The ABCs of detection, he called it.

There *had* been money there when she left the *Revenge* at half past eleven to go to the police station. She was sure of that now. How long was she gone? Three-quarters of an hour, an hour at the most. In the meantime, someone had come in, removed the money, and left behind a dead body. If the dead man was the owner of the money, he was either appallingly careless to have fallen into the water and drowned while retrieving his money, or—Simon nudged again—*a person or persons unknown relieved him of the cash and then killed him.* The latter did seem more likely, but she had to think it would've been a risky proposition in broad daylight.

Stop complicating things, Simon, she muttered.

Her muddled thoughts were interrupted by the arrival of PC Morgan, who led her down the hall to a room where Detective Sergeant Dixon was waiting. They were joined by an officer who introduced herself as Detective Constable Ayesha Gray. Ayesha, she insisted magnanimously.

A Ghostwriter's Guide to Murder

"How long have you been moored along Regent's Canal, Maeve?" Ayesha asked, her tone oddly upbeat given the circumstances. It reminded Maeve of a news presenter discussing death in somber tones but with the shadow of a smile.

"Little over a year."

"Freewheeling kind of life," Ayesha chirped. "Must be fun."

"So far, but this'll be my first winter living aboard," she replied honestly. "I guess we'll see if the heat's up to scratch."

"Where were you before?"

Maeve couldn't fathom the relevance of her former residence. She looked into Ayesha's eyes, hoping for some clue about her motivation, but saw nothing except an unwarranted blitheness. The woman was enjoying herself. New at the job or annoyingly keen—it was hard to say which. Maeve wondered if she was being allowed to cut her teeth on the irrelevant player in this scenario. "I lived in a flat in Islington," she replied.

Ayesha kept taking detailed notes while Dixon leaned back in his chair and watched. "What made you decide to move?" she prompted.

"Personal circumstances."

Dixon's eyebrows rose. Not enough of an answer, apparently.

"Messy end to a relationship," Maeve elaborated.

"Then you and your ex weren't on good terms?" Ayesha responded.

"He was a cheating bastard," she snapped instinctively before registering that it was a cheeky question and absolutely none of Ayesha's business, even if she was new on the job.

"When did you last see him?"

"When we broke up—four months ago." Had it really been only four months since she stormed out of their flat? The time had flown. She sat back and looked at Ayesha. "What does this have to do with anything?"

"Just getting some background information. And after you broke up, you bought a boat?" she continued.

"No, we bought the boat together over a year ago. It was his party boat and my writing retreat." *Well, if that didn't just sum up a key problem in our relationship.* "Now I live on board full-time, and he parties elsewhere," she concluded.

"You also work from"—Ayesha hesitated, flipping through the file next to her—"the *Writer's Revenge*?"

Maeve shrugged. "I do these days. Hardly anyone goes into the office anymore."

Ayesha paused to make a couple of notes before engaging again. "Tell me some more about the money you say you found."

"I *did* find," Maeve replied.

"Wrapped in plastic and stuffed inside a tire?" Ayesha was now managing to look doubtful and superior at the same time.

"Yes."

"What made you think to look there?"

"I told him already," Maeve said, indicating DS Dixon. "My dog was chewing on the tire."

"Right, your dog found it," Ayesha finished without making a note in her book. Was that merely a ploy meant to make her uncomfortable, or did they really think she might be lying? The woman didn't break eye contact. "And you say you have no idea where this money came from?"

"I say it and I mean it." Words were Maeve's business, and she wasn't about to have anyone else put words in her mouth.

A Ghostwriter's Guide to Murder

"I have absolutely no idea how the money got there or where it came from. It's not my money, and it has *nothing* to do with me."

"Ever see anyone messing about with the bumpers?"

"No." Maeve clasped her hands tightly in front of her. *Breathe. You are the victim here, not the perpetrator.* "Besides," she added, "my dog would go mad if anyone came near the boat."

"You mean a stranger?"

Maeve nodded.

Ayesha leaned in. "What about someone you knew?"

"I'm not sure what you mean by that." Maeve didn't like the inference and felt the need to stall before offering more.

"Would the dog bark at someone he knew?" Ayesha reiterated.

"Not always, I suppose." She hated to admit it, but the Captain wouldn't be the most reliable watchdog if the visitor in question, stranger or not, came bearing food.

"Do you know your neighbors?"

"The ones on either side, and a few of the others to wave to. Liveaboards are a friendly lot."

"Tell me about the folks on either side of you."

"Stern side is a couple of older women. Keep to themselves mainly. Retired, I think." Maeve wasn't going to get into the Wiccans and their unconventional lifestyle. She had no desire to involve them, and she was sure PC Morgan had already spoken to them. "Bow side's a single guy—works in IT."

"Do you know his name?"

"Ashley something. Don't know much about him." She wasn't lying when she said she didn't know much about Ash, and she'd always felt he liked it that way. Let them talk to Ash if they wanted to know more. Whoever he was, it was his story to tell, not hers.

23

At that point the door to the room opened and another man entered. "Don't mind me, keep going." He made himself comfortable in a chair against the wall, watching the proceedings with a dispassionate eye.

"Note that DCI Bolton has joined us." Dixon directed the comment to Gray before wading into the questioning himself. "Permanent mooring spaces on the canal are expensive."

It was more of a comment than a question. "I suppose," Maeve replied, surprised by the sudden change of topic, but with someone who was clearly a senior officer present, Dixon was taking control from his junior. Where was this going? It was none of their business how the five-figure annual docking fee was paid. They didn't need to know that Gavin had prepaid two years' worth after landing a big project. She wasn't sure he'd even thought about the fact that she was taking advantage of the prepayment, but as far as she was concerned, he owed her.

"You have a guaranteed place along the dock. That space and no other," Dixon continued.

"Yes."

"Convenient if you wanted to conceal something close to your property but not on it."

So that's where this was going. "Are you trying to suggest the cash was mine?" Maeve met Dixon's eyes without flinching.

"Is it?"

"No."

"Did you know it was there?" Dixon was covering all the bases.

"Why would I come to the police to report finding money if it were mine?" Maeve challenged.

A Ghostwriter's Guide to Murder

"Maybe you were keeping the money for someone else—had a falling-out. It happens. Reporting your accomplice could be just a spot of revenge. A writer's revenge," he said with a faint smile.

"Proximity doesn't equate to guilt." Maeve knew that much from writing for Harlan. She glanced toward the man in the corner. His face remained impassive, as if he were watching a play. The proceedings must be so commonplace to him, but not to her. "Why aren't you looking into the man in the canal?" she demanded. "He's dead, and he seems a more likely connection to the missing money."

Dixon moved in closer to the table and pulled a photo out of the thin folder in front of him before sliding it across the table toward her, his eyes riveted to her face. "Do you recognize this man?"

Maeve stared at the postmortem picture. The face was ashen, and there was a bloody wound on one side of the head. She felt the bile rising in her throat. It was gruesome, and she did her best to convince herself that she was mistaken. She could be, couldn't she? She could feel the gaze of the man in the corner burning into the top of her head and Dixon leaned forward in an attempt to look into her downturned eyes. She knew it was a simple yes-or-no question and she was taking way too long to answer.

"Do you know him?" Dixon pressed.

She wanted to say no, but she couldn't.

She nodded. "It's my ex. Gavin Foster."

25

Chapter Five

Returning to the canal in the late afternoon, Maeve found Rowan and Sage firmly established on the bow of the *Revenge*, waving what looked like a massive spliff in elaborate circles. The smoke coming off it caught the breeze and flowed lazily along the length of the boat. The Captain watched from the towpath, sneezing occasionally, and he came running as soon as he saw her, proceeding to hide behind her legs and watch the goings-on with a wary eye.

"There you are, dear. What an awful to-do," Rowan said. Decked out in her usual style, she was wearing a long, flowing skirt in shades of pumpkin and aubergine with a lacy vest and a collection of crystal necklaces that rattled as she moved.

"We wanted to tidy up a bit before you got home," she explained. "White sage is best for getting rid of negative energy, and goodness knows you're in need of a good cleansing after this morning."

"Right," Maeve said. She was in need of something, but she'd been thinking more in terms of a stiff drink. She moved closer to the boat. "Sorry for all the upheaval, ladies." Not that

26

it was her fault, and in truth she suspected her neighbors were in their element.

"Not at all, dear. It's the departed one that had the rough go of it," Sage tutted.

Maeve knew she'd regret it, but she asked anyway. "How's that?"

"The lingering energy of the dead man was positively *throbbing* from being so violently torn asunder," Sage replied. "He couldn't have been departed for long when they brought him out of the water. We told all that to the police, but they didn't seem interested."

Maeve wasn't surprised; Sage's explanations could be quite fulsome.

"I tried to tell them that the human body is an open system. We exchange energy with our surroundings all the time—gaining energy and losing energy. When we die, the atoms and the energy that make up our physical form aren't destroyed." Sage was warming to her subject. "They can't be; that's basic physics. They're simply repurposed. The essence of a person's energy continues to echo through space until the end of time."

"Like glitter blown on the wind," Rowan added dreamily.

Maeve usually found it difficult when the ladies mixed science and mumbo jumbo, but for some reason, this time their ramblings touched a chord in her. The idea that Gavin's energy would linger provided an odd comfort in this tragic situation. His life had ended violently, and though she'd envisioned it happening time after time and even crafted some powerfully wicked prose to that end, she'd never expected or wanted it to actually happen. Her imaginings had just been her way of giving vent to her wounded pride.

What she needed now more than anything was a drink and a chance to gather herself. Rowan and Sage were trying to help in their own peculiar way, but she needed her friends.

"I really appreciate the cleansing, ladies," she said. "I'm sure it'll do a world of good, but if you'll excuse me, I need to take the Captain for a walk."

The Captain was pleased to be leaving. He liked Sage and Rowan, but their food was a bit odd and the smells that emanated from their kitchen weren't always appealing. The Anchor was much more to his taste. There would be sausage rolls there. He and the landlord had an understanding.

*　*　*

The Anchor was a far cry from the trendier pubs and bars farther along the canal in the hustle and bustle of Camden Town. There was no elaborate cocktail list that had to be called up with a QR code, and you had to look carefully to find the front door, hidden as it was down the side of the building away from the water. The thick mullioned glass limited the light inside, and it could seem rather old-fashioned and dim with its sturdy oak tables and candles dripping wax down the sides of empty wine bottles. Maeve fancied it as one of the Captain's pirate hangouts of old, but in reality, it had been a regular watering hole for the boatmen who transported goods on barges from the docks at Limehouse westward through the city and into the countryside. The stables out back, which had once housed sturdy draught horses used for towing the boats, had since been turned into two compact flats occupied by the pub's landlord, Paul Lane, and Maeve's friend India Davis.

A Ghostwriter's Guide to Murder

Pushing through the heavy door, she was relieved to see that the place was largely empty.

"Hiya," India sang out from behind the bar, where she was helping herself to a glass of wine and adding a tick to the tab hung on the wall by the till. "You've had quite a day," she said with slightly more enthusiasm than sympathy. "I'm dying to hear all about it, but I told Paul we'd wait for him. He's gone to the basement to fetch some more vodka."

"Gin and tonic, light on the tonic," Maeve said. Beside her the Captain gave a sharp bark. "And a sausage roll when someone gets a minute."

She settled into their spot. The short-side counter of the main bar faced into a small, even darker corner further obscured from the rest of the room by a shoulder-high wall. It was a micropub within a pub, and Maeve had dubbed it "The Nook and Cranny." To the extent the other patrons even knew it was there, they generally ignored it in favor of tables by the windows in the front, which at least allowed for some natural light. The Nook and Cranny had two barstools at the counter across from a small table with a lamp made from an old sextant. On either side were two ancient wing-back chairs, one of which was now occupied by the Captain.

Maeve took a deep drink of the gin and tonic India set in front of her and allowed the calm to descend as she watched Paul Lane approach from the direction of the basement stairs. He would have made a great eighties rock 'n' roller. Not a glam rocker but a brooding lead guitarist: taut and muscular with a barely contained energy, like a coiled spring waiting for release. His hair was close cropped, the vestiges of a stint in the Navy from what they'd been able to gather, but they knew little else about his past. He remained tight-lipped on that subject, and his reticence was like catnip to Maeve.

Sadly, she felt he wasn't a man who took a great deal of joy in his own life, but he was the perfect publican: serious-minded, soft-spoken, and a good listener. The kind of man who never needed to shout but was always heard. If you were in trouble, Paul was your man. He'd know someone who knew someone. Deeply dependable. Solid. At least that's the way she'd write him as a character. Of course, in reality people were rarely so cut-and-dry.

"Y'all right then?" he asked, affixing a measuring spout to the new bottle of vodka.

"Sure. I always wanted firsthand experience being questioned by the police. Can use it in a book at some point. Gritty realism and all."

India slipped out from behind the bar now that Paul was back and perched on the stool next to Maeve's. The Captain lay down in the armchair with a heavy sigh, waiting for his sausage roll, his head resting on the arm, his eyes focused unwaveringly on the source of the food.

"Come on, tell us everything," India insisted. "All we've heard is wild rumors from the grapevine, and I'm sure they can't be right."

"It was his fault," Maeve said, tipping her head toward the Captain. "He managed to chew his way through one of the rubber dock bumpers and unearthed a bit of cash."

"How much is a bit?" Paul prompted.

"Fifty thousand quid."

India gasped. "Damn. And you went to the police? I think I'd have kept it."

A Ghostwriter's Guide to Murder

"No, you wouldn't, and just as well I didn't." Maeve didn't admit the idea had crossed her mind. "When I came back with the cops in tow, the money was gone and there was a dead man floating in the canal with his head bashed in."

"Bloody hell." Paul reached for a glass and poured himself a large whisky.

"There's more." Maeve found it hard to say the words; somehow it made the whole nightmare more real, especially as it was now Gavin she was picturing floating in the water beside the *Revenge*. "The victim wasn't a stranger."

India pulled her stool closer and laid a supportive hand on Maeve's arm. "You poor luv. Who was it?"

"Gavin."

"Gavin?" India let her breath out in a long, slow stream. "Well, if that isn't a bit of karma right enough. The coven must be beside themselves."

"Rowan was cleansing the place when I left," Maeve admitted.

Paul had a puzzled look on his face. "Do the police think Gavin was attacked, or was it an accident?"

Maeve rubbed at her forehead, hoping to ease the dull ache. "I spent the afternoon answering questions about him and our life together and the money I 'claimed' to have found. Frankly, it all was a bit of a blur after I found out it was Gav. But I had a strong sense they didn't think his death was an accident."

On reflection, she realized that Dixon's questions to her were the kind she'd have Simon ask a suspect. She sat up quickly. Did that mean *she* was a suspect? Was that why Dixon's boss had joined them?

Her stomach clenched. *Bugger.* She'd actually called Gav a cheating bastard for the record. That was bad.

"A missing fifty thousand pounds does kind of suggest foul play," India mused.

"But Gavin?" Maeve shook her head slowly.

India reached for her wine. "He must've been up to something. Why else would he show up at the *Revenge* out of the blue? He hasn't been near the place since you left him."

"As far as we know. More to the point, where the hell would Gavin get that kind of money?" Even as she said it, Maeve thought about the docking fees, paid in advance. It *was* suspicious. She'd never really considered where that money came from. She should have.

"He was a plumber. They make good money if what I have to pay's anything to go by," India offered pragmatically.

Maeve downed her drink and passed the glass back across the bar. "He made good money, but never fifty thousand in *cash*."

"Not many folks have fifty thousand in cash lying about the place," Paul observed. "That kind of money says drugs to me. Probably to the cops too. And messing with that kind of shit *can* get you killed."

"I find drugs hard to believe," Maeve said. "That would take brains, and we are talking about Gavin here. *Gavin*," she stressed, "the man who once had to go to A&E because he hit himself in the head with his own wrench. If he's involved with something criminal, he's not in charge, that's for certain." She accepted the fresh drink Paul handed her and mulled the matter over. "I suppose he might've been stupid enough to try to run off with someone else's money and got caught. He usually overestimated his own skill and underestimated everyone else."

"Proper whodunit." India's eyes sparkled. Grim as it was, she was clearly enjoying the whiff of mystery.

A Ghostwriter's Guide to Murder

Paul retrieved the Captain's sausage roll from the toaster oven and cut it into bite-sized pieces. The Captain moved around behind the bar and sat looking adoringly at his friend. "Not yet, mate, too hot."

"Not quite like a murder mystery," Maeve said. "What you read in books is all fairly clinical. Focuses on bits and bobs of evidence. This was horrific. Watching a lifeless body being winched up out of the water like a drowned rat." Gavin's lifeless body. She forcefully pushed the image aside.

"Best not to dwell." Paul looked over as the main door swung open.

"Thought I might find you here," Ash said, making his way along the bar to the Nook. "The Wiccans told me you were back from the police station."

Maeve gave a weak smile over the top of her glass. She'd wondered when Ash would turn up. This morning's turmoil would've bothered him, but as she'd suspected, he couldn't resist getting the news firsthand and he knew where to come. She'd invited him for a drink once, to say thank-you for helping her recover a lost document and saving her endless hours of rewriting. She hadn't specifically invited him again, but once he'd found his way to the Anchor, he'd returned regularly.

Of course, Maeve knew the real reason he was there. He had a crush on India. None of the others talked about it, but as far as Maeve was concerned, it was transparently obvious. She didn't blame him. India had a quiet glamour about her. Short hair in finger waves around her head, cheekbones to die for, and intelligent brown eyes that never missed a trick. Of course, if he was ever going to be in with a chance, he'd have to step up his game. He was a man in need of serious help. The jeans and plaid

33

flannel shirts that were his standard uniform had all seen better days—as had the rest of him. His hair was still long enough to be pulled back into a short ponytail, but the hair on the top of his head was thinning, and it aged him. Like Paul, he was probably in his early forties, no more than five years ahead of her and India, but Ash could pass for fifty even on a good day. He had a slight limp thanks to a bike accident, he'd offered once. Bicycle, she'd wager. He wasn't cool enough for a motorbike.

Ash took a long pull on the pint Paul handed him. "I was afraid they might keep you overnight."

"I got lucky, I think," Maeve replied. "I suppose they talked to you too. Sorry about that."

"It's their job." Ash was clearly trying to sound blasé about the whole thing, but Maeve suspected the invasion by his former associates had thrown him off-kilter. He'd let slip one night in the Nook that he'd worked for the police in the past. Not a street cop; something to do with computer forensics, from what little he'd said. He refused to talk about his work for the police and barely discussed his current private-sector jobs, other than to say he was swamped. All she knew was that he was visibly uncomfortable when anyone came near the *Red Lion*, let alone the police.

"From what they were asking, it sounded to me like you're a person of significant interest," Ash continued.

Maeve leaned forward on her stool at that. "They said I was a person of interest?"

"Not in so many words, but they were questioning you at the station and looking for forensic evidence on the boat . . ." Ash trailed off.

"Just because the victim was her ex?" India asked.

A Ghostwriter's Guide to Murder

"You knew the victim?"

Maeve nodded. "They showed me a picture of the body and asked if I knew him, even though I think they already knew I did. It was cruel."

"They needed confirmation," Ash said quietly.

"But how did they figure out the connection between the two of us so quickly?"

"Social media," Ash followed on without hesitation. "You posted pictures of the two of you." He paused fractionally. "I'm sure you would've posted pictures."

"But I took them down after we broke up. *Immediately.*"

"Not gone if you know what you're doing," Ash said. "Data's never gone."

"So, what happens next?" India asked. "I mean, Maeve clearly has nothing to do with all this."

"They'll ask more questions, and they'll be taking a closer look at the body to see what it can tell them." Ash looked down, as if he'd suddenly realized how much he was talking. "I mean, I was never a detective or anything, but the procedures are pretty standard."

"This just gets worse and worse. Do you think you could ask around, some of your old mates maybe, see if you can find out what's happening?" Maeve asked.

Ash looked uneasy. "I don't really have contacts at the Met anymore. There's been a lot of staff changes at Camden Road."

"But you could try, couldn't you?" India placed a hand on his shoulder, and he looked up into her face.

"I'll ask around, but I can't guarantee anything."

Maeve was pleased to see that the nudge from India seemed to have done the trick.

"Look at the bright side. Maybe they're done with you," Paul said encouragingly. "You went to the station, you answered the questions. You have nothing to do with all this; by rights, that should be it."

The bright side. Maeve gave a thin smile. It was as if her father were in the room. Perhaps Paul was right and the worst was over. She'd done nothing wrong. She'd be fine.

They all looked at Ash, hoping for some sort of affirmation from the closest thing they had to an expert. There was a long pause before he finally turned to Maeve and said, "A man was found dead next to your boat. A man you knew. If I were you, I'd find a solicitor."

Chapter Six

If Ash's assessment was correct, she was far from out of the woods. The thought had Maeve up eating rum raisin ice cream straight from the carton at gone one in the morning. The Captain was keeping her company in the sense that he was watching every spoonful that went into her mouth as if it gave him physical pain to see the food disappearing one bite at a time without any coming his way.

"You can't eat ice cream," she said.

Well, maybe he could, but the ensuing intestinal disorders didn't bear thinking about on a boat this size.

Maeve had been mulling over India's words. What *was* Gavin up to, and why had he shown up out of the blue? It couldn't be a coincidence that he'd suddenly reappeared the day she found the money. How would he even know she'd found it—unless he'd been watching. The thought gave her a chill. Watching the money or watching her? He'd have no reason to be watching her, so the money, surely.

If she accepted the notion that the money she'd found had belonged to Gavin, where the hell had it come from? And why

37

hide it in a tire? It was a clever spot but hardly foolproof. She'd found it—well, the Captain had. A safe box or a lockup would've made more sense. She glanced down to find the Captain looking well pleased with himself, licking the edge of the ice cream carton hanging forgotten in her hand. She moved it out of range and reached for her glass of wine. The red wasn't mixing well with the dairy—maybe she should've gone with a white. Still, waste not.

Downing the rest of the glass, she considered whether Gavin had ever mentioned a safe box. To the best of her recollection, he hadn't. A lockup? The only thing he owned that had any value, at least in his mind, was a collection of Star Wars memorabilia. She'd insisted he get it the hell out of the flat when they moved in together. The memory was hazy, but she was pretty sure he'd said he was getting the lockup then. If he still had the lockup and the money was his, why not store it there? Probably lost the key. That would be just like him.

She sat up suddenly. Maybe that was why he'd been here. She'd found the key at one point, stuck inside a book Gavin had left aboard the *Revenge*. Safe from thieves, he'd said, and she'd just laughed. Still, a book wasn't a bad place for him to hide something. After all, *Gavin* and *book* weren't two words you'd readily put in the same sentence unless you were talking gambling.

She got on her hands and knees and rummaged through the bookshelves built in under the settee, finally finding what she was looking for. *Your Money or Your Life: 9 Steps to Transforming Your Relationship With Money and Achieving Financial Independence.* Had he? she wondered. Opening the book, she turned to the inside back cover. She was right, there had been a key, but it

A Ghostwriter's Guide to Murder

was gone. It had been held in place by a bit of white gaffer tape, making it almost invisible if you didn't know what you were looking for, but someone had peeled the tape back, slipped the key out, and pressed the tape back down. Maeve tipped the book into the light and could still see the faint outline of the missing key.

When had he reclaimed it? Before she moved aboard full-time, or maybe as recently as this morning while she was with the police? She shut the book with a snap. Gavin had always had that bad-boy appeal. Her bit of rough, India used to tease. But a serious criminal? The type that might have fifty thousand in cash lying about the place? No way.

Gav was hardly the brightest bulb in the box, and they hadn't had much in common. Incredible, really, that they'd lasted four years. What *had* she seen in him? Sex. The answer sprang vividly to mind. There was absolutely no complaint there. No doubt the reason she'd stayed as long as she had. But, apparently, she'd underestimated him. There must've been aspects to his life she'd completely missed. Now he was dead. She sat with that thought for a minute. Gav might've been a prat, but he didn't deserve this. Not the Gavin she knew, but what about this other Gavin? Who was he?

If she considered it dispassionately, he had changed some-what recently. He'd been more ambitious, more driven. Not just the stupid, cheating boyfriend: the one-dimensional character she'd painted in her skewed version of their relationship. How had the real story gone? Paul thought drugs. Gav had been anx-ious to make more money. Had he found a way to achieve finan-cial independence? Had he gotten involved with an illegal side hustle? Run off with the proceeds from some deal and hidden it?

39

Surely someone would've been after him if he had. She thought about the body in the water.

Someone *was* after him—and they'd found him.

That would explain the bashed head and the missing loot, wouldn't it? Simon's voice echoed in her head. Maybe it was being surrounded by her book notes, maybe it was because it was the middle of the night, but she could almost feel Simon Hill standing over her, whispering in her ear. She knew writers could be sentimental about their characters, treat them like family even, but Simon was adopted, for God's sake. He belonged with Harlan, not her, and yet she could feel him prodding at her. She was a suspect in a crime, so what was she going to do about it? He would be busy finding evidence that would clear his client. What would clear her?

Proving the money existed, and proving she hadn't stolen it, would be a start.

She licked the ice cream off the spoon with the tip of her tongue and threw the remainder of the carton in the bin. Pacing the length of the boat, she did her best to think as Simon would. The money belonged either to Gavin or to someone he'd stolen it from. If he'd stolen it, then it was likely whoever he'd double-crossed had found him, taken the money back, and killed him. The other option was that the money was Gavin's, some ill-gotten gains he'd hidden at the dock. If he was watching her and realized she'd found it, logically he'd come back sharpish to reclaim it before she could get the police involved. But then how on earth had he wound up dead in the canal?

She tried to imagine the scene in her head. Gav was accident prone. She doubted the police would be aware of that. Could he have retrieved the cash, then slipped and fallen; clobbered his head on the boat and wound up drowning?

The police's questions suggested they thought it was murder, but, if she was honest, tripping and falling into the river only to accidentally drown sounded much more like something that would happen to Gavin.

If that's the case, where's the money? Simon prodded.

He'd have dropped it, and it would've sunk, she snapped back. The thought made her stop in her tracks. If that were true, the money would be under the boat right now. The thought was appealing—not murder, just a mistake. On impulse she reached for her phone.

"Paul?"

"Maeve?" His groggy tone made her look at the clock on the wall. Almost two.

"Sorry, sorry, I didn't realize how late it was."

"You in trouble?" She could hear him stifling a yawn.

"Always, but not at this precise moment. Look, can I borrow some of your old dive gear?"

"My dive gear?" It sounded like he was struggling to follow the conversation.

"Yeah, I noticed it in the shed the other day when I came to drop off those boxes of books you said I could store."

"Why do you want my dive gear?"

Maeve explained her theory.

"Right"—Paul sounded like he was getting nearer to his usual self—"but it's hard enough to find anything in the canal in the daylight. In the middle of the night, it'll be impossible. Besides, I don't have any air in the tanks."

"That's all right. I just need the wet suit and the mask. I mean, the canal's no more than four feet deep near me."

"Can't it wait till the morning?"

"I'm sure the police are watching the boat. They'd see during the day, and I don't think they'd be happy."

"If they're watching, they're watching now." Paul had a habit of hitting the nail on the head, even when it was a nail you'd rather not see.

"I could slip in over the far side, away from the towpath. It's dark. They wouldn't be able to tell what was going on." Maeve stood, twisting a lock of hair round and round her finger. She was too anxious to sleep; she had to do something no matter how daft it might seem to someone else. "Look, if the money is there, it won't have gone far; it'll have sunk straight to the bottom. Quick down, quick up. You don't even have to involve yourself. I could just slip over and borrow your gear. All I need's the key."

"Day or night, no one goes down alone." Paul sighed heavily. "I'll have to be there, and as long as I'm there, I'm goin' in."

Chapter Seven

Paul wasn't completely sure why he'd bounced out of bed so quickly and was now lugging a large carryall stuffed with dive gear down the towpath in the pitch dark, but then again, who was he kidding? It was because Maeve was the one asking. There was something about that woman. She walked into the Anchor and it was like a cool sea breeze sweeping in. No matter what was going on, she kept her sense of humor. Even with a dead ex-lover on her doorstep, she was joking, not panicking. From the outside she appeared to be relatively calm, but Paul suspected that was for India's benefit. Something very sketchy had gone on with Gavin, something Maeve didn't deserve to be dragged into, and if he could help keep her out of it, he would.

He shifted the bag on his shoulder. Chivalry aside, if he was honest, he'd also been a bit bored lately. A midnight scavenger hunt was just the ticket. Shake things up—shake *him* up.

He didn't see anyone on his way over, and if the police were watching, hopefully they'd think he was responding to some sort of late-night booty call. If they opened his bag and found a rubber wet suit and a snorkel, they'd be sure he was.

He entered the *Revenge* through the galley and was greeted by the Captain jumping up to lick his face, almost knocking him off his feet.

"Sorry, mate, no sausages."

Maeve tried to drag the dog back toward the bed in the stern, but he was having none of it. "Thanks, Paul. I really owe you one."

He glanced at the empty bottles of wine in the sink, calculating that this might be a fleeting, booze-fueled notion. "Not sure this is the best tactic, but if you're dead set on it?" He looked down at her in the confined space to see if she might've changed her mind, but the pursed lips and the steady gaze told him she hadn't. "Right, well, shift over, then. Let me get into my gear."

Paul pulled off his jumper and the Def Leppard T-shirt he'd been sleeping in and discarded them on the bench seat along with the jeans he'd pulled on over his swim trunks. He stepped into the one-piece wet suit and pulled it up as far as his waist before sitting down to slip on a pair of neoprene booties.

The Captain gave him a good sniff, snorting slightly at the rubbery smell. Maeve leaned on the counter in the galley, watching with interest. He zipped up the front and pulled the hood over his head. He knew he looked ridiculous, and Maeve was struggling to keep a straight face.

"Let's get on with this." He spat into his mask and wiped the fluid around the glass as he moved toward the door.

"Is that for luck?" Maeve asked.

"Well, I'll need luck, but no, just keeps my mask from fogging up," he replied. "Grab the box torch out of my bag, will you?"

Maeve dug in the carryall and held up a light encased in a yellow plastic case. "This one?"

A Ghostwriter's Guide to Murder

He nodded and reached for it, hanging the light round his neck on a cord. "Stay in here. We don't want to draw any more attention to this little lark than we need to. If anyone's watching, they're less likely to notice me." He indicated the all-black rubber suit.

"If the cash packs are there, they should be about the size of a brick." She gestured with her hands. "Oh, and while you're at it, look for a large carving knife—between the *Revenge* and the wall."

She came as far as the door to the bow and stopped, watching from inside as Paul slipped over the side of the boat and stood, putting his mask on. It was frigid, and he could feel the water seeping inside his wet suit. It wouldn't take long for the layer of moisture trapped between the suit and his skin to warm to body temperature, but long enough to make him shiver violently as he sank down below the surface. The canal was no more than four and a half feet deep at this point, but the water was murky even in the daylight and filled with silt and algae that were immediately stirred up by his arrival. He took a couple of deep breaths through the snorkel before diving under and switching on the torch.

He'd spent years deep diving in the military, but it never ceased to amaze him how quickly you left the chaos of the world behind when you submerged, no matter how shallow the water. It wasn't exactly picturesque down here, but it was, as always, silent. Blissfully silent. Visibility was poor, but he could see the collection of rubbish that had been thrown in by canal walkers. Crisp packets and beer cans covered in a furry green slime. The packets he was looking for would look clean and new. He shone the light around, moving as little as possible to avoid stirring up more residue.

Allowing himself to drift outward slowly, he moved the light in a broad arc until he reached the other side of the canal. There was nothing. He moved to the surface and blew the water out of his snorkel with a practiced puff. Floating face down on the surface, he used the light to scan the floor of the canal inch by inch one more time. Still nothing. He hated to disappoint Maeve, but at least now she'd know.

Moving to the side of the canal between Maeve's and Ash's boats, he examined the wall carefully. The box light caught a glint of metal at the base of the wall, and he reached out a hand to touch it. It was a key. Its relative cleanliness suggested it hadn't been in the water long. And slightly farther along, he saw Maeve's knife. At least he wouldn't come back empty-handed.

He made his way back to the water side of the *Revenge* and stood, removing his mask and letting go of the light, dropping them onto the deck. Getting out of the water would be trickier than getting in. Maeve stuck her head out the door. "How's it going?"

"Take the Captain and move to the far opposite side of the boat. I need some counterweight."

She and the Captain disappeared. He waited briefly before hoisting himself up and flopping onto the deck like a fish. Rising only as far as his knees in order to remain unseen, he crawled into the galley, again coming face-to-face with the Captain, who licked his nose in greeting.

"Anything?" Maeve asked, handing him a towel.

"No cash, but here's your knife. Good thing Gavin wasn't stabbed to death or you'd have some explaining to do. And this." He handed her the key. "May be nothing, but at least it went in recently. Is it yours?"

A Ghostwriter's Guide to Murder

"No, not mine, but I think I know where it came from." Maeve stepped aside and pointed to the tiny shower stall. "I left you another towel, and there should be enough hot water for you to at least rinse off."

Paul slipped into the shower and shed his gear, the retained water from the canal flooding down the drain in a muddy brown rush as he stood under the showerhead. Toweling off, he realized he'd left his shorts in the carryall, and he stepped out to retrieve them with the towel wrapped around his waist.

Maeve handed him a mug of tea as he popped his head out, and he felt the welcome warmth flood through him. He caught her eyes taking in his bare skin, and he grabbed his bag and reversed into the shower stall once more. He didn't need her to see the scars on his back. It would only raise more questions and speculation on her part.

Maeve made a game of trying to guess things about his past. Looking for his deep, dark secrets. After a few drinks she'd regularly concoct stories—some humorous, some outlandish. They were entertaining but never anything close to the truth. All she or any of them knew was that he'd been in the Navy. He never talked about the search and rescue missions and certainly not about the combat side of things. He'd emerged scarred but in one piece—physically, at least. Emotionally was another question, but not one he cared to ask. It seemed self-indulgent. He'd tried a bit of online self-help, but it was a waste of time. He knew he'd left some part of himself out there in the ocean, and he often worried that the best of him was gone and what was left was just a hollow shell.

From what he'd read, the despair he felt was common and he should have every confidence that it would fade in time. His secret, if he had one, was that he no longer had any hope that it would.

When he emerged from the loo, she'd already rinsed and dried the key and was looking at it carefully under a light. "Well done. This was Gavin's." She spread a book out on the counter next to her. "I remembered he kept the key to his lockup hidden on the boat, but when I went to check, it was gone. Look." She pulled up the tape at the back of the book and showed him how the key he'd found lined up perfectly with the indentations on the gaffer tape that had once held it in place. "Same key. He must've retrieved it, then dropped it when he went into the water."

"Could mean he was planning to move the money in the tire."

"But someone took it and presumably killed him over it." Maeve sighed. "It's all I can think about. I was so hoping this wasn't what it seemed. Murder is so . . . so irrevocable. Now we have a killer and a victim and somewhere between them a story that has to come to light before we have any answers."

"I've seen what you do with Simon Hill. If anyone can reconstruct this story, it'll be you," Paul said.

Maeve looked startled. "You read Simon Hill?"

"Didn't used to—do now."

Maeve draped her arm around his shoulder and gave him a squeeze. "That's above and beyond the call of duty, just like this." She gestured to the dive gear strewn on the floor. "I suppose I wasn't really expecting to find the money. It was a long shot at best, but I needed to do something, and I couldn't think of anything else." She cocked her head to one side and gave him a mischievous look, the moment of darkness banished. "You had me worried there, you were down so long. How long can you hold your breath?"

A Ghostwriter's Guide to Murder

"A fair bit. Maybe four minutes."

"That's more than a fair bit. Now I have it," she said, a gleam in her eye. "You were a Japanese pearl diver, weren't you?"

"Japanese pearl divers are mostly women," he said.

"Then you were in love with a pearl diver. She promised she'd marry you when she finally found the great black pearl, but she died trying. Heartbroken, you trained to dive yourself and kept diving until you found the illusive pearl."

"Which I cashed in on a second-rate pub in Camden Town. Give me credit for a bit more gumption than that." Paul couldn't help smiling.

"Right, so maybe not, huh. Will you tell me if I get it right?"

It dawned on him that Maeve was always so full of hope. That was what drew him and others to her. She wouldn't understand a life without it. That's why she could guess as long as she liked; she'd never hit on his truth.

"*If* you get it right, I'll tell you."

49

Chapter Eight

Maeve had made her way through most of her first cup of coffee and was trying to rouse herself after a night of too little sleep and too much rumination. She saw the flicker of a blind at the window of the *Red Lion*. Ash must be awake already, or he'd never gone to bed. She wondered if he'd witnessed Paul's antics of the night before. She padded across to his mooring in sweats and a pair of worn sheepskin moccasins, unsure of her welcome.

Ash liked to keep people at bay emotionally and physically. She'd been on board but never inside the *Red Lion*. She'd peeped in through the hatch once—it was a wonder the vessel stayed afloat given the amount of hardware he kept on board.

She knocked on the side of the hull, and Ash stuck his head out of the door. He looked even rougher than usual. "Permission to come aboard?"

Ash came on deck, extended a hand to help her onto the narrow ledge on the side, and steadied her until she was settled in a deck chair at the bow. The Captain stood on the towpath looking up at Ash with almost human blue eyes.

A Ghostwriter's Guide to Murder

Ash hesitated. She sensed he wasn't really a dog person. "All right, you too," he conceded reluctantly before disappearing belowdecks and returning with a Lord of the Rings mug and a coffee press, which he extended to Maeve.

She held out her own mug gratefully.

"Restless night?" he asked.

"A bit. Too much thinking, I guess. Worrying that whoever killed Gavin might still be watching the boat. Worried I might be next—found dead and floating face down in the water."

"If you aren't involved in any way, and I'm presuming that you aren't . . ." Ash paused.

"Thanks for the vote of confidence," Maeve muttered before registering that Ash was continuing to regard her intently, waiting for more of a response. "No, I'm not involved," she insisted.

"Then I don't think you should be worried. There isn't any reason for someone to continue watching the boat. Presumably they have the money they came for and they've dispatched your ex. It's more likely that they're well away from here."

Ash was probably right, but it wasn't entirely comforting. "Do you think the police are watching me? They seemed suspicious about my story."

He shrugged. "It's their job."

That was a yes, then. "I had a theory late last night," Maeve continued. "Seems daft in the light of day, but if Gavin tripped and fell into the water, hitting his head as he went, it could've just been a horrid accident. If he did fall, then it's logical the money would've fallen with him."

"And it would still be sitting on the bottom of the canal," Ash said quietly.

He was quick, no doubt about that. "That was the general idea. I dragged poor Paul out of bed with his wet suit to take a look."

"Ah." For some reason Ash seemed to relax fractionally. "Find anything?"

"Not a sausage." At the word *sausage*, the Captain's ears pricked up. "No, dear," Maeve said, absent-mindedly stroking his back.

"Unlikely he just tripped, then," Ash concluded. "What if whoever took the money from your ex simply pushed him into the water to get away? If he hit his head as he fell, the money would be gone, but there might be traces of blood on the side of your boat or mine."

Clearly Ash's time with the police hadn't been wasted. He was well ahead of her. "They looked at mine, but I hadn't thought of yours." Maeve took a sip of her coffee. Ash's theory was interesting. If the money wasn't Gav's in the first place, he could hardly report it as stolen if it was reclaimed. The culprit wouldn't need to kill him to keep him quiet, he'd just need to escape. That would make Gavin's death manslaughter, not murder. She knew she was grasping at straws, but it would be slightly less repugnant. Either way, Simon and the police would be looking for indentations in the wood, stray strands of hair, or traces of blood on the side of the boat, and she should be too. "Can we take a look?"

"Sure." Ash rose and moved to the stern of the *Red Lion*, which lay no more than eight feet off the bow of the *Revenge*. He knelt down and examined the top and the sides of the hull.

Ash didn't touch anything, she noticed. He knew what he was about when it came to forensics.

A Ghostwriter's Guide to Murder

"Can't see anything," he said, finally pushing himself back to his feet using the roof of the cabin. "I know you don't relish the idea, Maeve, but I have to say this seems like murder to me."

"I know you're right, but I'm struggling with the idea that Gavin was so deeply involved in something that it would get him killed and I was blissfully unaware. Makes me feel like an idiot."

Ash wiped his hands on his jeans. "Could be a recent thing."

Maeve nodded. That might explain things. Trouble he'd found after she left. Maybe something to do with his new woman. "They carted off some of my stuff for examination. Any guess on when I might get it back?"

Ash looked out across the water. "Did they take your computer?"

"No, just the guide poles, hooks, and a few tools. Why?"

"That means they're just looking for physical evidence at the moment."

"You mean a murder weapon." Maeve stood on one foot, nervously tapping the other on the wooden deck. "Is it at least a good sign that they didn't take my computer?"

"I would say so, yes."

She wouldn't have suspected having an ex-cop around would be useful, but it seemed she was wrong. Her knowledge of police procedure began and ended in the 1950s. Ash was her link to the present. "Did they give you any other hints about what they were thinking when they interviewed you yesterday?"

"No. And no reason why they would." Ash seemed ill at ease. Perhaps she'd overstepped, or perhaps he knew more and didn't want to say. They walked back to the bow, and Ash drained the rest of his coffee. "You're welcome to sit out here and work if being on the *Revenge* makes you uneasy, but I have a client project I need to get back to."

He disappeared into the dark interior of the boat like an animal retreating into his cave. Maeve sat stroking the Captain's ears, watching the boat rise and fall softly on the water. The rocking motion was almost enough to lull her to sleep, but the Captain began to issue a soft, low growl from deep in his throat. It was a rare occurrence, and it made her sit up and look around. She saw a uniformed officer approaching down the towpath from the direction of Camden Market, accompanied by DS Dixon.

They'd be looking for her. She rose, hopped off Ash's boat, and walked back toward the *Revenge*. Maybe it was good news. Maybe they were coming to tell her they'd found the killer and she could relax. She stood on the towpath, trying to look calm and collected, wishing she was wearing something other than sheep slippers.

She attempted a smile, but it froze on her lips when she saw the look in Dixon's eyes.

She glanced toward Ash's boat, but there was no sign of him. She thought she saw the tiniest twitch of the blind, but it could've been her imagination.

DS Dixon stepped forward. "Maeve Gardner, you're under arrest on suspicion of the murder of Gavin Foster."

Chapter Nine

Once again, Ash watched the proceedings on the dock from beneath his bathroom blind. He saw Maeve leading the Captain over to the Wiccans and leaving him there before she was taken away.

He'd hoped he was right when he said the police weren't seriously considering her, but inside he'd known he was only being positive for Maeve's sake. When the police took the poles from the *Revenge* yesterday, he'd known they'd be sending them to forensics on a rush basis. Something must've come back with blood from the victim on it. He also knew that his police brethren could be quite lazy. If they thought they had what they needed to charge Maeve, they wouldn't be rushing to look further afield for a suspect. Always the easy way out. It was sloppy, verging on the negligent, but it was an ethos that permeated that particular Met unit—at least it had when he was at Camden Road.

Should he get involved? That was the question, wasn't it. Moreover, could he really be helpful if he did get involved? Staff changed so often he was unlikely to know anyone who had been there in his time, even though it was only a couple of years ago. When he left, he'd severed professional ties with the force. He had no desire to be reminded of the circumstances surrounding his departure. It probably would've been better if he'd upped sticks and moved, but in his deepest soul he was a hobbit and had no desire to stray from London. He'd lived here all his life, and even without rolling hills and small round doors, it was home.

He'd had a brief go at taking his house with him, cruising up and down the canals on the *Red Lion*. A free spirit, staying nowhere longer than a day or so, but he quickly came to the realization that he preferred his adventuring online. Questing far and wide on virtual missions gave him comfort, but his corporeal body longed to stay put. Close to his local Costa, within the delivery range of his favorite pizza place. Gone to ground but not gone. He'd hoped that being on the boat would give him the best of both worlds and allow him to remain somewhat off the radar. If anyone from his past came looking for him, he'd be hard to find. Digitally, he knew how to hide, but physically, yesterday had blown that sky-high.

The officer who came to see him hadn't recognized him, but as soon as he ran Ash's name through the computers, he'd surface. The former cop at the center of a colossal cock-up. The inquiries into the incident, his hasty departure. All of it would be there, and they'd discover who he'd been and where he was hiding. And soon enough his new friends would know about his failures too.

That was what distressed him most.

An instinct for self-preservation told him to run. Quickly. To get the hell out even if it was just for a couple of weeks. Head up the Grand Union Canal. Maybe only as far as Slough. Nothing too dramatic. After all, he'd bought the longboat to keep himself lithe and untethered. But he knew he wouldn't leave. There was work, for starters. He was in the middle of a tricky project, tunneling his way into a multinational brokerage firm's database. Their sensitive client information one short foray away.

But most of all there was Maeve. Her presence was like an invisible wall that kept him from straying beyond the boundaries of the game. Her eyes looking to him for answers, or at least reassurance. Reassurance he couldn't give. She was in trouble, and he wanted to save her, as if it might somehow change the way she looked at him. The police had her in their sights and it would take a lot to move her out, like someone wandering in off the street with a bloody cudgel and a confession. They certainly wouldn't be out looking for another suspect, not when they had a perfectly good one in hand.

The best help he could be right now was to try to unlock the weapons she'd need to fight. Did she know a lawyer? She definitely needed one now. He had no one to recommend, but he knew someone who did.

* * *

India ran a floating bookshop on the canal the other side of the Camden Market. Located across from the Crumb bakery and the Costa, the Book Boat was a popular stop with shoppers. There were long folding tables set out on the canalside with new and used books for browsing through. The children's books were kept in the rear of the boat, and the kids liked to clamber down the short flight of stairs to explore the interior.

Ash used to watch them from the outside seating at the Costa. He'd taken a look belowdecks once out of curiosity. The inside of the *Wayfarer* was painted with scenes from *Wind in the Willows*, with Ratty and Mole and Toad himself peering out from behind the pale-green shelves. Wispy clouds skittered along the length of the ceiling on a painted blue background. A pile of rainbow-colored cushions in the bow of the boat made a soft pit for reading while parents browsed in peace on the towpath or maybe even snuck off for a coffee.

Two Chelsea mums were bouncing babies in those front-pack things, and the sound of more children giggling came from the interior of the *Wayfarer*. Ash found India sitting in a folding chair at the far end of the book tables, knitting, and she waved as Ash approached.

"Not used to seeing you out in the daylight, Ash."

"Yeah, well." Ash could think of nothing else to say, so he came directly to the point. "They've arrested Maeve."

"What?" India was on her feet instantly, abandoning her knitting midstitch.

"They think she had something to do with Gavin's murder."

India looked around helplessly, bending to retrieve her ball of yarn, which had rolled precariously close to the water's edge. "How do we help her?"

"She needs a solicitor," Ash said. "Your brother's one, isn't he?"

India pursed her lips. "He is, but I'm not sure he does criminal cases."

"Call him. If nothing else, maybe he can recommend someone."

A Ghostwriter's Guide to Murder

"Right." India seemed to be relieved to have something specific to be getting on with.

"Watch the shop," she said over her shoulder as she pulled her phone from the pocket of her jacket and dialed, wandering away from her customers as she spoke.

"He's in court this morning," India said when she returned, "but his assistant promised she'd talk to him as soon as he came out." She pulled a tissue out of her pocket and blew her nose loudly. "The whole thing's mad. Maeve never killed anyone." She pulled Ash aside at the widened eyes of the mum browsing through the table of biographies nearby. "I mean, she was at the police station at the time he died, right?" Her voice had dropped. "What better alibi could she have than that?"

"She could've killed him, hid the money, and then gone to the police," Ash pointed out.

"But you don't believe *that*, do you?" India glared at him. "I know I don't."

Ash closed his eyes and made himself consider whether he was about to say he thought Maeve was innocent because he truly believed she was, or because he wanted her to be. It came as a shock to realize he didn't really care one way or the other. If Maeve killed someone, it would be for a good reason, and he'd support her no matter what. "No," he said finally, "No, I don't think she killed anyone."

"Right. Then what are we going to do about this?"

Ash always felt slightly intimidated by India. He appreciated that she was a straightforward, no-nonsense type. He could handle that; in fact, he preferred it—less social confusion that way. But she was also a natural-born organizer, and when her gaze fell on him, he felt somehow even more inadequate than usual. He

59

was desperate to help Maeve, but when put on the spot, he had absolutely no idea what they were "going to do about all this."

"You know more about police procedures than the rest of us put together," India insisted. "How long will they keep her? Hours? Days? And will they put her in a cell with a load of hardened criminals?" India frowned at the thought.

"How long they keep her will depend on whether they're just questioning her or whether they formally charge her," he said.

India nodded slowly. "That's the kind of information we need. Someone like you knows what's what."

Ash felt better for India's encouragement. "And no, she won't be held in a cell with others. Camden Road's fairly comfortable, all things considered."

"Can we see her?" India asked.

"'Fraid not. Unfortunately, from the outside there really isn't much more we can do for her right now other than getting her a good brief."

India clearly wasn't satisfied. "I'll find her a solicitor, but there has to be something else we can do. What did you do when you worked for the police?"

"Broke into suspects' phones and computers," Ash admitted. "Checked into their financials and looked to see what their social media presence might tell us. Anything to do with peoples' digital lives, really."

"Then that's what you need to be doing now," India insisted.

Ash looked up quickly. "I'm not spying on Maeve."

India sighed in exasperation. "Not Maeve, you daft man. Gavin Foster. You need to find anything you can on him. Who he worked with, who he socialized with—all the things the police might ask about."

A Ghostwriter's Guide to Murder

"Okay, but some things I could do as a cop would be illegal now."

India regarded him with her hands on her hips. "Somehow, I don't think legality's a burning issue when it comes to those high-paying corporate clients of yours. You telling me you're not willing to be a bit flexible with what's 'allowable' for Maeve?"

"No. I mean, yes. I mean, you know I'll do anything I can for Maeve," he finished lamely.

"That's what I thought." India smiled. "See what you can find while I keep hassling that brother of mine. And let me know if you hear anything more."

As he walked away, Ash felt slightly less inadequate than usual. He had a skill set, and it did make sense to tap into it. Truthfully, he'd looked at Maeve's social media shortly after she came on the scene. He'd idly run a search on Gavin Foster, curious to see what kind of man appealed to her. It had been an exercise in self-flagellation. Foster was tall and good-looking. Of course he was. Ash hadn't registered much beyond that and the slightly comforting revelation that Foster fixed bogs for a living. India was right, though; it was time to take a deeper dive into the life of Gavin Foster.

This was a real-world quest to save a woman in distress. It was time to unlock their best defensive weapons, and for a change, he might actually be one of them.

61

Chapter Ten

Maeve sat in the bare whitewashed cell for what felt like days rather than hours. The place smelled of antiseptic and bleach, which was reassuring in its way, but it was also giving her a headache. Everything had been a bit of a blur since she'd heard DS Dixon say the words you heard all the time on the telly. She'd never thought those words would be aimed at her. She wasn't guilty, but clearly they had some reason to think she might be. She was aware that she didn't have to say anything, but she kept hearing the words *it may harm your defense if you do not mention when questioned something you later rely on in court.* What a ridiculously convoluted sentence. As an editor she'd have red penned that at once. Was that supposed to make things clearer to you in an already stressful situation?

She looked down and saw her hands shaking. She clasped them together and squeezed until her knuckles turned white. What would she say when they questioned her? It would depend on what they asked, wouldn't it?

Simon would revisit her relationship with Gavin. What she knew about him and why she might want him dead. Simon

62

A Ghostwriter's Guide to Murder

would be gentlemanly. Discreet in his questions but often asking for information he already had just for confirmation. Would it be the same here? Arresting her was one thing, but they'd have to have significant forensic evidence to make anything stick, and given that she hadn't actually bashed her ex-lover over the head, it wasn't likely they'd have that. *Come on, be calm, be positive.*

She jumped as the door to the cell was opened by the same uniformed officer who'd accompanied Dixon to arrest her.

"They're ready for you." He led her down a narrow corridor to a bleak little room in the rear of the station. A long, thin industrial lighting fixture hung over the lone table—not a flattering light for anyone, and DS Dixon looked even grimmer under its influence. He didn't have the look of a healthy man. His eyes were a dull shade of brown and his skin was pale. Not an outdoorsman, she'd warrant, and not a healthy eater from the look of the chocolate wrapper and energy drink can he dropped in the bin as she entered.

At the table in the center of the room, DC Ayesha Gray sat looking the picture of health. Robust, though some less charitable might think of her as stocky, Maeve would guess. Did that make her the brawn of the duo to his brains? She'd been enthusiastic before, but none too savvy.

DS Dixon gestured to a chair at the table opposite Gray, who had a file in front of her and was operating the audio recorder. Maeve had nothing to hide, but somehow the machine made her uncomfortable. They all identified themselves for the record.

"We'd like to start by going through your movements yesterday one more time," Dixon said. Gray pulled out a notepad and sat poised to write. Gone was Ayesha the buddy cop; Dixon was in the driver's seat now. "What time did you allegedly find the money in the tire?"

"As I said before, late morning. I'd taken the boat out to give it a bit of a run. I came back and made tea and was settling down to work.'

"And that's when you found the cash," Gray prompted unnecessarily.

"Yes." At least they seemed to think the cash was real now. She wasn't sure if that was better or worse.

"How did you determine it was cash?"

She debated how to proceed, but the full truth seemed like the better option. If they'd found the cash and found her fingerprints on it, she'd need to explain why. Maybe that was why she was here.

"I went to see if I could repair the place where the dog was chewing, and I noticed there was something inside what should've been an empty space."

"And how did you know that what you were looking at was cash?"

"I was curious, so I cut the tire open a bit more and removed a couple of the plastic-wrapped packages."

"A couple?" Dixon echoed.

"All right, all five of them."

"And through the wrapping, you could tell it was cash?" Dixon asked.

"Not clearly." This was not going as well as she'd hoped. "I opened one of them and saw what was in there."

"Just to be clear," Dixon said, "you opened the packages and touched the cash."

Maeve nodded.

A Ghostwriter's Guide to Murder

"For the recording, please."

"Yes. I did."

"How much cash was there?"

"Roughly fifty thousand pounds."

"And then?"

"Well, I knew I needed to report the find, so I sealed the packages back up and returned all of them to the tire before coming to the station. I figured you'd want to see everything as it was when I found it."

"But it was too late for that, wasn't it? You'd already tampered with the evidence." Dixon scowled. "You say it was late morning when you found the cash, and yet your initial statement to the police was at thirteen fifteen. Surely it didn't take you that long to restore the cash to its hiding place."

Should she confess she'd had a good think about just taking off with the money? No. That level of honesty would be counterproductive. "I had a bit of work to finish before I left. I figured it had been there a while. No rush, right?" She tried to sound casual but sensed Dixon wasn't buying it.

"Did you speak to anyone during that time? See anyone?"

"No."

"You didn't reach out to Gavin Foster to tell him what you found?"

"No. Why would I? We weren't even on speaking terms."

"Finding a large stash of money might just open up the lines of communication." Dixon tipped his head and watched her closely. "I think you did call him and he came right over. I think you had an argument about the money. You grabbed a steering pole from the side of the boat and cracked him over the head with it before dumping him in the water."

"No." Maeve was emphatic. "I told you yesterday, I haven't seen or spoken to Gavin in over four months, and besides, I had no reason to think the money might be his."

"Yet his body was found floating in the water next to your boat." Dixon opened the folder in front of him. "And forensics tells us that only your fingerprints are on the steering pole that was taken from your boat yesterday."

"I was using it to steer the boat when I took it out in the morning; of course my fingerprints would be on it. And your man was wearing gloves, so his wouldn't be." Maeve was getting impatient. It felt like Dixon was being purposely obtuse.

"We also have evidence that suggests the pole delivered a lethal blow to the back of Gavin Foster's head before he was deposited in the Regent's Canal."

"That may be so, but it wasn't by me." Maeve leaned forward. "Someone must've come by the boat after I left. Maybe someone was watching the boat, waiting to collect the cash. They could've been wearing gloves too. Killers do, I believe."

"We know that Gavin Foster had prepaid for that dock space for a period of two years," DC Gray popped in. "Was that particular tire a standard drop for cash?"

"How the hell would I know?" Did they really think she'd be stupid enough to blunder into a trap like that? Gray had been watching too many cop shows on telly. Maeve didn't even allow Simon to juxtapose questions that way. Well, not too often anyway.

Dixon shot Gray a quelling look. "You were in a relationship with Gavin Foster for four years. Lived together for at least half that time. You can't tell me you have no idea what his business dealings were." Dixon was switching tracks, shifting the focus to Gavin.

A Ghostwriter's Guide to Murder

"He was a plumber."

"A self-employed plumber, and you're an editor at a second-tier publishing house. That won't get you a large canalside flat in Islington. Not on your salaries."

Maeve suddenly felt panicky. They'd had a good deal on the rent from an older woman who had no idea what the place was worth, but would the police believe her if she tried to explain? Not likely. Moreover, Dixon's prodding dragged to the surface the questions she'd been obsessing over—who had Gavin really been? And had she actually known him at all? She felt like she was treading water in the sea and at serious risk of going under. She'd hoped the simple truth of her answers would be enough, but the police weren't sounding convinced. They were trying to pin Gavin's murder on *her*. She raised her chin defiantly and looked at Dixon full on.

"That's it. I'm done. No more questions. I want a solicitor."

Chapter Eleven

❧

Ash stared at the man laughing back at him from his screen. Too good-looking by half in spite of the scar running along his jaw-line. The scar was probably what women found so appealing, a physical manifestation of the air of mystery that sparkled in his eyes. It put a disembodied hero of the ethereal world like Ash right out of the running. A complete nonstarter. Women would throw themselves at a bloke like Foster and he'd catch. Ash would have thought Maeve had more sense than to get involved with the likes of Foster. But love, and he supposed even lust, weren't matters for rationality, as he was learning firsthand.

Foster seemed to spend a lot of time on various beaches in Spain with his mates. Lots of drinks and a few random women, attractive enough in a page-three kind of way. Ash noticed that Foster posted regularly to Instagram, but none of his pictures were real-time shots. Smart enough to ensure that anyone inter-ested in him would know only where he'd been, not where he was at the moment.

The man was a self-employed plumber, with an interesting police record. Pulling it up had been a breeze. In fact, slipping

A Ghostwriter's Guide to Murder

in though the back door of the Police National Database was far easier than it ought to have been. Ash wondered if the Met was aware of how big the hole was and how much it needed patching—but that was an issue for another day.

Gavin Foster had been pulled in a number of times between 2011 and 2018: pub brawls, traffic tickets, even a negligible possession charge. All fines paid and Bob's your uncle. Not the cream of society but hardly a criminal mastermind. His record for the last twelve months was more interesting. He'd been stopped twice crossing the channel from France, searched, questioned, and released. Questioned in connection with an extortion charge and again in relation to a stabbing outside a pub in Lambeth. No formal charges. In fact, he'd never spent more than a few hours in custody. His solicitor would turn up—same guy every time, Mark Elliot—and he'd be out within the hour. A top-drawer solicitor, way beyond the financial means of mere mortals like Foster.

Someone had to be paying to keep Foster out of trouble. Likely a bigger fish who was ensuring he didn't get caught in the police net. Why? Certainly not out of the kindness of someone's heart. Was it because Foster was being useful, or maybe out of a fear that Foster might get chatty? If it was the latter, that meant Foster must've known things worth discussing. That alone could've made him a target for elimination in some circles.

Ash took a quick dive through the press. Newspaper archives were less reliable but often fruitful. Foster's plumbing business had subcontracted to a company called Dawson Construction on a series of commercial developments south of Wapping. That had been twelve months ago, but just recently a number of lawsuits and countersuits had been flying over a part of the project called the Waterfront. Residents of the posh flats were complaining, reasonably enough, that when they rolled out of bed to head for their posh jobs in the city, they were landing in pools of mucky water from a rash of broken pipes. In the end more than half the flats were affected, major repairs were being undertaken, and Dawson Construction, needing a scapegoat, appeared to be throwing Foster to the wolves.

The thought brought a faint smile to Ash's lips. Seemed ol' Gavin had overreached himself. Not enough experience to take on a project the size of the Waterfront. He'd faced a skill check and apparently failed—epically. Not only was it a reason he might have found himself in deep trouble with some powerful people; it was a fail by Mr. Perfect that warmed Ash's heart no end.

Chapter Twelve

"I'm sorry, madam, no one is allowed into the custody suite except the detainee's solicitor," the desk officer repeated.

"This gentleman is Ms. Gardner's solicitor"—India gestured to her brother Julian standing slightly behind her—"and I am his clerk. His *senior* clerk."

The officer shook his head. "I'm sorry, madam. Mr. Davis may go in, but I must insist that *you* wait out here."

India wasn't about to be kept from seeing Maeve in her hour of need. She pulled herself up to her full height, standing eye to eye with the junior officer and turning on the look that had quelled many a lesser man. "Are you suggesting that I don't *look* like a legal clerk?"

The subtle insinuation of discrimination did the trick.

"No, madam, of course not." He looked over his shoulder nervously.

"Right. Then we're Ms. Gardner's legal *team*, and we demand to see her now."

Behind her India could feel Julian squirming. He hated it when she made a scene.

As they were led through the locked door behind the main desk, Julian hissed in her ear. "I wish you wouldn't do that. You undermine my professional standing."

"You worry too much," she countered. Julian was the first of her siblings to get a professional degree, but in many respects, he was still the insecure teenage boy working in their parents' Caribbean restaurant near the Elephant & Castle. Even now as a respected solicitor, he hated to draw too much attention to himself. She could never understand why. To be fair, his self-confidence probably hadn't been helped by their mother's insistence that posh-sounding names would give her children a leg up in the British system. Names like India, Julian, Jemima, Willa, and Clarence had given them all more than their fair share of negative attention at school and beyond.

"You worry too little," Julian mumbled as they cleared through security. "I really don't know that much about criminal law. I'll do the best I can for you, but . . ."

"You'll remember enough from uni to fake it until you can figure it out," India insisted. The boy had always needed a bit of a poke to get him going.

They were led into a small meeting room and sat in uncomfortable folding chairs waiting for Maeve to be brought along. India was pleased to see the look of relief on her friend's face when she saw her visitors.

"They said my attorney was here, and I had no idea what they were talking about." Maeve sat down, giving them both a weak smile.

India squeezed her hand across the table. "Maeve, this is my brother Julian." She gave him a lingering side eye that said *embarrass me and you'll regret it.* "Ash said we should get someone

A Ghostwriter's Guide to Murder

in to see you as soon as possible, and this was the best we could do on short notice."

Maeve shook hands with Julian, ignoring India's slight, and said, "Thank you for coming."

"I presume they questioned you this morning?" Julian asked.

"They did."

India reached into her bag, pulled out a notebook, and began to take notes as Maeve gave an outline of the earlier questions and her answers.

"Doesn't seem like much for them to go on," India observed when Maeve had finished. "I mean, obviously Maeve's fingerprints would be on everything. It's her boat. Isn't that what you call circumstantial evidence?"

"Yes," Julian said with a trace of impatience. "And without witnesses they'll have an uphill battle making it stick. If they're suggesting that you argued with Gavin, then there should've been a witness somewhere. Sound carries on the water. Do you have neighbors that would've been around?"

"Yes, both sides, though not sure how much help they'd be."

"I'll still want to see their statements." Julian paused for a moment. "What can you tell me about Foster's friends and coworkers? Anyone around on a regular basis? Anyone he used to get into trouble with?"

"He had three childhood mates he spent a lot of time with. They were on the darts team together at the local pub."

"Name of the pub?"

"Is that relevant?" India thought her brother was grasping at straws.

"Do you want me to do this or not?" Julian snapped.

India held up her hands in surrender.

73

"They hung around a place called the Bell up near Emirates Stadium."

"Was that still his local?"

"I couldn't say for sure." Maeve shrugged. "But probably. It was near enough to the flat in Islington, and from what I hear, he's moved the new woman in there."

Julian looked at Maeve with something akin to an apology in his eyes. "Do you know her name?"

"Vicky something. She runs a tattoo parlor near the Seven Kings Tube station. I didn't want to know more than that."

"Not important. I'm sure the police'll have spoken to her," Julian continued, making his own notes now. "Can you give me specific names for any of his mates?"

"Jimmy something, and one of them was Roy, I think, but they all had stupid nicknames. Anyone who knew the dart team would know their names."

"What was the dart team called?"

Maeve rolled her eyes. "Darty Deeds. Gavin was a big AC/DC fan."

"Any work associates?"

"Associates? No. The only person I knew of was a man involved with his latest construction project. Commercial developer named Ross. Before we split, Gavin gave him my name and I wrote some promotional materials for the project. Fluffy stuff, but it paid really well."

Julian made a note, then paused for a moment as if not sure what to do with that information.

"Come on, then. What's next?" India prodded him in the ribs with a well-placed elbow. "How do we get her out of here?"

A Ghostwriter's Guide to Murder

Julian scowled at his sister and turned back to Maeve. "My suspicion is that they're just fishing at this point. Questioning you to see if they can get more solid evidence or, better yet, a confession. If not, they'll have to let you go. Remember, there's a difference between arresting and charging. They may've arrested you, but I don't believe they have enough here to actually charge you with murder."

"That's something, at least." Maeve rubbed her temples with the tips of her fingers. "How much longer will I be stuck here?"

"They can keep you for up to twenty-four hours. If they have additional evidence, they can apply to keep you longer. That'll be the first indication of how serious they are. Best-case scenario is they find a lead to the real killer and release you without prejudice."

"And in the meantime, we just sit and wait? What good are you, man?" India heard her Caribbean heritage slip in softly as she berated her brother.

"I'm an immigration lawyer," Julian snapped. "I'm doing the best I can under the circumstances."

"And I really appreciate it," Maeve cut in, clearly trying to forestall further friction between the members of her legal team.

India snorted. "What would Mama say?" She sat back and crossed her arms. Julian had always been a mama's boy. He waved a hand in her direction as if to erase the words from the air between them.

"If they want to question you again, Maeve, I'll come. In the meantime, I'll hang on to these notes, and if they decide to pursue matters, I'll have some inquiries made. Unfortunately, I'm in the middle of a complicated trial right now and I honestly can't afford to sink too many resources into this if the police end up finding a better lead and taking off in another direction."

"Do you think they'll find another suspect?" Maeve asked.

"If they're investigating this properly, then yes. You say you're not guilty, then by definition, someone else is, and with any luck they'll find them."

"And if they don't, we will," India interjected forcefully.

Maeve was led away by the PC outside the door. She smiled cheerfully as she left, but India knew it was just a brave face.

Julian put his things back into his briefcase and rose. "Don't make matters worse by sticking your nose in, India."

She spun back to face him. "Don't you start tellin' me what to do. I'm going to help my friend if I can. And you should be ashamed for not getting that poor girl the hell out of here."

"I did all I could do for now. If they try to keep her longer than twenty-four hours, then I'll do some research and figure out where we go from here, but I'll have to start charging you at that point."

India gave him her most disdainful look, unwittingly the spitting image of their mother. "Just you try."

Chapter Thirteen

India sat perched on her usual seat in the Anchor, listlessly eating peanuts one by one from the dish Paul had brought her. She'd read somewhere recently that the key to losing weight was to eat more slowly. The key to losing weight was to eat less, she knew that, but she'd go with slowly for now. Slowly but steadily.

"How did it go with your brother?" Paul asked from the other end of the counter.

She popped another peanut in her mouth. "Let's wait for Ash. He said he was coming."

If Paul found the request odd, he didn't say so. India was stalling. She needed time to formulate an answer to Paul's question. How had it gone? It was hard to say. She had to admit Julian went to the police station with hardly any argument at all. He'd spoken with Maeve just as she'd asked, but he'd done nothing, and he hadn't seemed all that keen to do more. Instead, they'd adopted a wait-and-see approach that was all wrong as far as she was concerned, at least while Maeve remained behind bars. And she knew Maeve wasn't reassured. She could see it in her eyes despite her attempts to remain cheerful. There had to be something more they could do. She hoped Ash would have an idea.

As if summoned by her thoughts, Ash arrived, shaking the rain off his jacket and hanging it on a hook by the fruit machine. Paul handed a packet of crisps across the counter to a man in a garish orange jumper and hastened down to their end of the counter. The two men looked at India expectantly.

"How was she?" Ash asked.

"Anxious." India gratefully accepted the glass of wine Paul handed her. "I mean, you would be, wouldn't you? They haven't really told her what's going to happen next, but from the questioning, it seems Gavin was hit with a barge pole. Maeve's barge pole. Naturally, her fingerprints are all over it—only hers, mind. Now the police are trying to establish that she was the one who wacked him on the head."

"What did your brother have to say about the situation?" Paul asked.

"He said we should wait and see what happens next. No point throwing too many resources into investigating—his words, not mine," India stressed, "if they ended up not pursuing any charges."

"And Maeve was okay with that?" Ash asked.

"You know Maeve, always upbeat, but inside she's not happy, I'd say. Though I didn't get a chance to talk to her alone."

"It's mad," Paul said. "Why aren't the cops looking for the real killer? He has to be out there, and I'm no expert, but the longer they wait, the harder it'll be, right?"

He and India turned to Ash in unison.

"I hate to say it, but they don't have a lot of incentive to look further afield." Ash looked embarrassed and continued to speak while staring down at his worn trainers. "They have an easy answer in front of them, so why make more work, and they're desperately short-staffed." He glanced up and quickly back down again. "It's no excuse, I know."

Ash looked so deflated India didn't have the heart to take her frustrations out on him, tempting as it was.

"Are the police trying to locate the money?" Paul asked.

"The police theory is that Maeve found it and called Gav. He came over and they had a row, then she killed him and kept the money."

"That's ridiculous," Paul said. "Wherever the money ended up, it's not on or near the *Revenge*."

"Maeve mentioned you took a dip last night." Ash flashed a genuine smile that India realized she'd never actually seen before. "Hats off to you, mate, for freezing your whatsits off."

"What did I miss?" India looked back and forth between Paul and Ash. She hardly thought of the two of them as proper mates, but here they were, keeping some kind of secret from her.

"Maeve thought Gavin might've slipped and fallen. An accidental death," Paul explained. "If he did, he'd have dropped the money on the way down. The police never really looked."

India grimaced. "But nothing, I presume."

Paul shook his head. "Nothing."

"Would've been nice, though, wouldn't it? Simple, easy answer." India took another drink and turned back to Ash. "What have you found out about Gavin?"

"Basics of his police record. Mostly minor stuff. No criminal convictions, but it's worth noting that he has an amazingly slick lawyer for a plumber. He's been questioned several times recently yet always released lightning quick and without prejudice."

Melinda Mullet

"Sounds like the kind of brief Maeve could use," India said.

"Do you have a name for this bloke?" Paul asked. "Maybe India's brother would know something about him."

"His name's Elliot. Mark Elliot."

"I'll see what I can find out." India made a note.

Ash nodded. "I trolled through the press databases as well and saw Foster got in over his head on some of his recent contracting work. A lot of lawsuits. Could've been the start of bigger problems. I'll keep digging."

"What about his personal life?" Paul asked.

"Nothing that jumped out."

"According to Maeve, Gav's passion was darts," India offered. "He plays—played—for the team at his local along with his best mates."

"That could be something," Paul said, perking up. "Where's his local?"

India thought for a moment, trying to remember what Maeve had said. "The Bell in Islington," she said finally.

Paul pulled out his phone and searched. "Not exactly a swank establishment, but the dart team's good. They've won a load of awards."

"They're called Darty Deeds," India offered. "Ever heard anything so daft?"

"Team names with puns are always popular." Paul glanced around the meager crowd in the Anchor. "I can go over to the Bell lunchtime tomorrow and have a chat with the owner. See what he can tell me about Gavin."

"You'll need to be very careful," Ash said. "You don't know who the killer might be, and you wouldn't want to tip him off."

A Ghostwriter's Guide to Murder

"I'll tell them I'm looking to start a darts team here at the Anchor." Paul looked across at the well-worn dart board hanging forlornly in the corner. "Nothing in their league, mind, but everyone has to start somewhere."

"Worth a try," Ash said.

"Maeve mentioned that Gavin had moved the new girlfriend into their old flat," India said. "The one he left Maeve for."

"What's this woman's name?" Ash asked.

"Vicky something. Maeve didn't know the last name. Can't you pull that up from somewhere? If we find out who she is, I could pay her a visit."

"I'll add it to the list." Ash made a note on his phone.

"But one thing at a time," Paul said. "Let's try his mates first."

India threw back the remainder of her wine. They were just like Julian—*hurry up and wait*. Typical men, focusing on one thing at a time, and Julian not focusing at all. It just wasn't good enough. Maeve was facing a murder charge, not a parking violation. If they were going to be any help, they needed get a move on. It was time to dive in headfirst, not faff about in the shallows, and if they wouldn't, she would.

81

Chapter Fourteen

Reveling in her sudden freedom, Maeve emerged from the station into the crisp morning air and headed straight for the Roasted Bean. She was in desperate need of a decent coffee and a breakfast sarnie. Something solid to wash away the unpleasant taste of the cop shop's morning brew. She ordered and settled into a table for one in the corner by the window looking out across the canal.

She'd been held for just twenty-four hours, a good sign by Julian's reckoning, but she still only felt a measured sense of relief. She hadn't slept the night before, her bizarre predicament looming large in her mind. How could this be real, and what would happen if they ended up charging her? Julian thought it unlikely, but then again, who'd have thought she'd be in custody in the first place? If they charged her with murder, her career would be over, her reputation ruined. She'd read stories of things like this, but she'd never thought it would happen to her.

As the tears pricked at the back of her eyes, she tried to force herself to embrace the positive aspect of the experience—it would be tremendous fodder for her writing—but she couldn't

A Ghostwriter's Guide to Murder

summon any enthusiasm for the idea. Incarceration was something she never wanted to face again, not even for the sake of her art. It was soul destroying.

Her food arrived, a greasy, comforting, carb-laden feast accompanied by a heavenly flat white. She could feel body and soul reuniting, and she picked up her phone to text India and Paul to let them know she'd been released. She received a quick thumbs-up from India but no further reply. Busy? Or maybe they thought the worst was over now. She wished she shared their optimism, but she was in a right proper mess, and from the way things were going with the police, it looked as if it was going to be up to her to claw her way out.

Leaning back in the booth, she tuned in to the voice of Simon rattling round in the back corner of her mental attic. *You didn't kill Gavin, so who did?* If she had any hope of answering that question, she'd have to revisit Gavin's life—a trip she wasn't anxious to take. She needed to think like Simon, ask questions of those who might know what he'd been up to the past few months. But who would that be? She'd never had much to do with his friends. She could reach out, but talking to his mates would look suspicious to the police, and they'd likely draw the wrong conclusions.

Who else did she know with a connection to Gavin? The other woman sprang to mind, but she wasn't going there unless things got dire—well, more dire.

The only other person was this Ross bloke, the developer Gav was working with who'd been looking for a writer. He'd accepted Gav's recommendation, so they must've known each other fairly well.

She sipped her coffee and searched her emails, finally coming up with his full name: Malik Ross. She'd drafted a proposal for the man and sent it in. He'd obviously been happy, because he'd paid up promptly and then asked her to write the text for a series of brochures. He was planning a themed leisure venue based on the James Bond franchise. According to Gavin, immersive entertainment venues were all the rage these days. Punters paid good money to pretend to do something they weren't actually doing, like virtual reality skiing, car chases, and space adventures. The notes she'd been given on the 007 Experience called for an eighteen-plus area for vodka martinis and Bond girls as well as a gambling space called Casino Royale. She'd drafted appropriately tantalizing text for the brochures, but Ross hadn't asked for it yet, so it was sitting in an email waiting to be sent.

Ross must've gotten to know Gav from one of the commercial construction projects he'd worked on in the last year or so. Would Ross know anything about what Gavin was up to? Maybe, maybe not. It was an incredible long shot, but she honestly couldn't think of anyone else. Shooting off an email with a load of random questions wasn't an option, but maybe she could drop by his office on the pretext of asking his input on the brochure materials. If he proved to be chatty, he might shed some light on the subject, and if he didn't, at least she'd be able to get paid for the work she'd done. Either way, she had to try something.

* * *

When Gavin told her Ross was a real estate developer, Maeve had pictured a high street office with a secretary and a back room full of red-lined architect's plans pinned haphazardly to the walls. She wasn't prepared for the sweeping panorama of the Isle of Dogs that greeted her from the reception area on the twenty-fourth floor of a newly built office complex. Malik Ross

A Ghostwriter's Guide to Murder

was clearly a force to be reckoned with in the real estate business. If Gav was hanging out here, it was no wonder he'd started to fancy himself as a player.

Suddenly her plan seemed laughable. There was no way this man was going to meet with someone walking in off the street, even someone who was already doing work for him. Especially as rumpled as she was from a night in the nick. Why hadn't she gone home to change? She started to back out of the door she'd entered through, but it was too late. The receptionist had already clocked her.

"Can I help you?"

The voice was well modulated and suited the surroundings. "I, um, well, I'm here to drop off some brochure materials for Mr. Ross."

"Certainly." The woman held out a perfectly manicured hand. "I'll make sure he gets them."

"Actually, I had a couple of things I wanted to clarify with him before I finalized."

An equally perfect pair of brows arched disdainfully. "Did you make an appointment?"

"No. I didn't think to."

"Then I'm sorry, you'll have to call for an appointment and come back."

"We're out of water in the gym again, Rachel," a voice called from down the hall.

"Fresh bottles were just delivered. I'll bring you one," Rachel replied, jumping to her feet.

"I'll get it," came the reply, nearer this time, and a man entered, dressed in a running kit with a towel draped around his neck. "Sorry, didn't know you were busy." He glanced her way. "Did I have an appointment on the books?"

85

"No, sir."

Maeve took a deep breath and stepped forward, holding out a hand. "Maeve Gardner. I'm working on the 007 brochures for you, and I had a couple of questions. Sorry for just stopping by . . ." She gestured lamely at their grand surroundings. "I didn't realize."

"Ah, Gavin Foster's"—he hesitated—"friend. Nice to meet you. I'm a bit of a mess, but I can spare a couple of minutes if you don't mind all this."

He gave a lazy smile and seemed well aware that most women wouldn't mind "all this," as he called it. Ross was fit and he knew it. Attractive in his own way but trying too hard, if you asked Maeve. If she met him in a club, she'd run a mile, but as it was she followed him down the hallway, looking at the framed renderings of prior projects that lined the walls. She recognized the Waterfront. Gavin had been involved in that. In fact, he'd been putting in long hours on it before she left. Maybe that was the root of his newfound ambitions. He'd been given a significant role on the project, and Maeve had wondered at the time if he was walking before he could run. Was that where he'd met Ross?

Ross gestured to a chair across from his massive desk and settled himself in his own plush leather chair, his back to the spectacular view behind him. "I was sorry to hear about Gavin. He was a good lad and a valued member of the team."

Maeve wasn't quite sure how to respond to this. She wouldn't have expected Gav to be part of a man like Ross's "team," and truth be told, he probably wasn't. From the looks of him, Ross was the type who spit out platitudes without thinking, but his desire to be seen to be solicitous might come in handy. "Yes, he

A Ghostwriter's Guide to Murder

was a good guy and so proud of all the work he'd done for you." She gave a slight sniff and looked down, as if holding back a tear or two. "I just can't imagine how this could've happened. I mean, he was hardly the sort to be involved with anything nefarious, was he?" As leading questions go, it wasn't brilliant, but she would've allowed Simon to ask it.

"I'm sure not," Ross said unhelpfully.

Maeve looked across at Ross with what she hoped was a helpless but beguiled gaze and plowed ahead. "He was such a fan of yours." She thought Ross would like the tribute. "Always talking about what an amazing instinct you have for business. I mean, I can see that with the James Bond project. Dead brilliant."

"Well, I thought of him a bit like a son." Ross smiled. The flattery had hit the mark. "I'd even say he learned everything he knew about business from me. Not the plumbing part, of course, but the finances. You could say I was a kind of mentor to him."

"He'd certainly been aspiring to dizzying heights recently," Maeve threw out.

"Tough game, real estate, especially in a city like London." Ross turned slightly in his chair, looking out the picture window behind him. "Takes a certain kind of man to make it in this game, and don't you kid yourself, it *is* a game. A rough one."

"Oh, I can see you've clearly risen to the very pinnacle in your business," Maeve gushed, trying not to gag as she did so. She rose from her chair and walked over to the floor-to-ceiling windows. "Looking out here, you must feel like a king surveying his kingdom," she said.

Ross rose and came to stand next to her. She could smell the mixture of drying sweat and Penhaligon's. "It's not easy to run an empire. A lot of balls in the air all at the same time, if you know what I mean. You gotta keep track. Know when to charge ahead and know when to cut your losses."

Maeve wondered if they were still talking about Gavin now, or was the man just spouting out his general business philosophy? "Gavin had a lot of balls in the air when I knew him," she offered lamely. Actually, Gavin always had a lot of balls, in the air and otherwise.

Ross continued to look into the near distance as he spoke. "Like I said, Gavin was a good bloke, but he still had a lot to learn. There are always temptations in this business and opportunities to make mistakes, especially when you're getting started. It takes time to learn who you can trust and who you can't."

A warning light was flashing on Maeve's mental dashboard. She had a strong sense the man beside her shouldn't be trusted. Had Gavin known that, or had he been oblivious, blinded by the trappings of wealth and power that were all around them? Could Ross have had a connection to Gavin and the money? She'd need to tread carefully, but Simon would never forgive her if she didn't pursue this line of inquiry. "Gav could be a bit naïve businesswise," she admitted. "I worry that's what got him killed. Trusting the wrong person, I mean." Maeve could see Ross's face next to her reflected back in the glass. She looked carefully for any trace of malice or even regret but saw only indifference.

"Come on, as long as you're here, let me show you the project you've been writing about." Ross led her over to an easel on the opposite side of the room, which supported a six-by-five-foot artist's rendering of the 007 Experience. "Gavin was excited about this project," Ross said. "Shame he won't get to work on it, but maybe we can name a cocktail after him or something."

A Ghostwriter's Guide to Murder

Ross smiled broadly, as if he'd offered an enduring monument to his recently deceased plumbing contractor. Instead it was an empty gesture by an empty man. Maeve suspected that Gavin was just one of the many little people in Ross's world. Interchangeable like Lego pieces, their only function was to support the creation of his next lavish vision. Gavin's death was of no more consequence to Ross than losing a shipment of fixtures. Everyone was replaceable. And once they were replaced, life went on as normal for Malik Ross.

Chapter Fifteen

Paul exited the Tube at Drayton Park, pleased to be out on a bit of an adventure. He hadn't realized how much he'd missed the rush of adrenaline and the lure of uncharted waters. Ahead of him, Arsenal's home stadium loomed up like a massive industrial complex, churning out winning players but too often lately mediocre seasons.

His path led him away from the arena and its dismal memories, along an alley behind the Co-op, and round a corner to the Bell. The paint on the sign over the door was fading, and the place certainly did nothing to invite strangers in off the street on a whim.

Inside, the Bell was a real old-fashioned boozer. No fancy menus, no candles or flowers on the tables. There was a *Ladies* and a *Gents*, prominently marked—no nods to sexual ambivalence here. Many years ago the walls must've been white, but decades of cigarette smoke had turned them a dirty shade of tan and the sour smell of stale tobacco still rose from every soft surface in the room. Four dart boards took pride of place on the far wall, facing into clearly marked throwing lanes. They were the only things in the room that looked new and well tended.

A Ghostwriter's Guide to Murder

A beefy man with a bushy mustache looked up from behind the bar. He had the racing pages spread out across the counter and didn't look pleased to be disturbed from his studies. According to Ash, this should be the landlord, Brian Burkes.

"Pint of bitter," Paul said.

The man nodded and retrieved a glass from behind him.

Paul pulled out ten quid and laid it on the counter in front of him. Based on the ambience, it should more than cover the bill, but in this city, who knew. "You Brian?" he asked.

The man didn't pause in filling the glass. "Who's askin'?

"Paul Lane. I'm a friend of Gavin Foster's."

Brian looked up from the tap, his eyes narrowed slightly. "And 'ow'd you know Gav?"

"He had a boat docked over near my pub. Used to pop in from time to time, and we'd talk darts. He was trying to get me to start a team of my own."

"Hmm." Brian looked neither impressed nor especially bothered.

"Gav always said I should talk to you. Meant to get on it sooner." Paul thought about Arsenal's most recent loss, hoping it would make him look sufficiently gloomy. "But time gets away, and now . . ."

Brian slid the beer across the counter. "Gav was a grand player. Heart and soul of the Darty Deeds."

Paul took a pull off his pint. It wasn't half bad. "Never dreamt I'd be opening a memorial darts corner, not for someone so young." He wished he'd given a bit more thought to how this conversation was going to unfold. It was harder than he thought to question a slightly hostile stranger without being too obvious. He picked up his beer and wandered down to the end of the bar to look at the

Melinda Mullet

trophies displayed in a recessed nook. "Impressive record your lads have. Mind tellin' me how you got the team going?"

Brian paused for a moment but seemed to decide the question was harmless enough. "Jimmy started the team. He and Gav were best mates from way back. They brought in Roy Boy and the Machine." He pulled a photo off the mirror behind the bar and passed it over the counter. "That's the lads at the championships in Majorca two years ago."

For a moment, Paul continued to stare at the names on the trophy in front of him, committing them to memory. Gavin Foster, Mac "the Machine" Toliver, Roy Malloy, and James Bishop.

"Did they play abroad often?"

"Often enough. League stuff and friendlies. Still had a dozen matches left for the season." Brain tipped his head toward the schedule pinned to the wall.

Paul took a subtle snap of the sheet with his phone. The team had had matches in Poland, Spain, France, and Denmark already this year. They were scheduled for Germany, Portugal, and Spain again in the next four weeks. Handy if one of the team was carrying drugs. Would they still be able to go now, without Gavin at the helm?

He turned back to Brian. "Will the team replace Gavin?"

"That's no easy thing. Can't just grab any old sod off the street."

"No replacin' our Gavin." The voice came from behind Paul, startling him. A man of indeterminate age had just entered from the street. His face was deeply lined, but it was hard to tell if it was from a rough life or a long one. His bright-orange vest had *Dawson Construction* emblazoned across the back. He stood at the counter, ordered a bap and a pint, then dumped his hard hat

92

A Ghostwriter's Guide to Murder

on a table by the window. The name *Dunn* was written on the back in Sharpie.

"Watchin' Gav play was like magic," he said. "Never missed. Could pop it wherever 'e wanted near every time."

The lunch rush was starting, all regulars it seemed, and Brian's attention was diverted. The crowd was mostly steel-toed boots and high-vis vests. Paul looked around the room. He was good at reading people, and he'd need to watch his step here. He was a strange dog on this pack's home turf, and an outsider here was enough of a novelty that several groups of men were already looking his way without enthusiasm. A few quiet words from Brian over the bar, and the level of animosity seemed to drop a notch or two. But not enough to be considered welcoming.

Taking a seat near the window, Paul made eye contact with Dunn before speaking. "Sad thing, Gavin's death," he remarked. "Real loss to the game."

"It's a right tragedy's what it is." The older man shook his head. "Never seen a better player in all my years." Dunn turned to look at him full on. "You knew Gav?"

"We used to bond over darts." God, where had *bond* come from? he thought. India's touchy-feely shit was rubbing off on him.

"You any good?" Dunn demanded.

"I can play, but nothing like Gavin. I'm just starting a pub team in my own neighborhood. Organizing, mind you, not playing." Paul was struggling to sound casual. He wasn't one for prying into other people's lives and God knows he wasn't one for talking about his own, but if they had any hope of helping Maeve, he needed to try.

93

Dunn rose and pulled two wooden boxes down from a shelf near the boards. "Come on. Let's 'ave a go in memory of Gav. Quick game of cricket, any order."

Paul followed him over and picked up the box of darts Dunn had left for him. It would be the one with the wonky flights, he was sure of that.

"Fancy a bit of a wager?" Dunn was doing his best to seem offhand. "Gav was always one for a flutter. But then you were a friend, you'd know that."

The statement was almost a challenge, and Paul knew he needed to put up or shut up. "Sure, why not."

"Twenty quid?"

Paul conceded with a dip of the head before allowing Dunn to win in the contest for who went first, hoping to soften him up.

"Got your team settled?" Dunn asked as he made his first shot.

"Not yet. We'll set tryouts soon, see who shows up." Paul threw the best of the darts in his hand and watched it fade to the left, landing in the pie segment above the 15. He could correct for that. "Is that how Gavin put his team together?"

"Nah, Gav 'ad 'is boys from the start. Been playin' together since they were lads. Knowin' who you're with makes a difference when you play as a team. Takes trust."

Was that on and off the boards? Paul wondered. "Guess they all had flexible jobs like Gavin to be going on the road so much." He knew it was an odd remark, but he didn't know how else to draw out information on the rest of the team.

"Aye, well, Jimmy and Roy Boy worked with me at Dawson. Management's good about lettin' the lads go for league stuff and all."

A Ghostwriter's Guide to Murder

"And Gavin worked for himself, right?"

"An' for Dawson too. We'd been using 'im more and more. Gav was becoming quite the posh businessman."

Paul hadn't spent much time with Gavin; still, he'd never have thought of him as posh or a businessman. Things must have changed lately. "What about Mac Toliver?" he prompted. "Does he work for Dawson too?"

Dunn chuckled. "No one really knows what the Machine does. If you ask, 'e'll just say 'e's got family money."

Paul looked round in surprise as he pulled his darts from the board. "A toff?"

"The Machine? Gawd no. Grew up on the streets. 'Andy with 'is fists an' good at keepin' a secret. Qualifies ya for any number of things, don't it."

Paul was quite sure it did but had no idea what that meant in this case. "And the Machine"—he hesitated slightly at the use of the nickname—"he was good mates with the rest of the team?"

"The Machine was like a big brother—always kept an eye out for the other three."

Brian approached with Dunn's sandwich. "Best be careful there. Don't call him Dunn and Dusted for nothing." As he spoke, Dunn closed the nineteen in a single shot.

Brian leaned against the bar close to the boards, watching and listening. Maybe keeping an eye on Dunn, who'd been surprisingly chatty. Paul sensed he wouldn't get much more out of Dunn now. He'd managed to compensate for the drift of the darts and shot a triple seventeen, and Dunn followed with an easy triple eighteen.

"Ya got some skill there yourself, lad. Startin' to think I'm the one being 'ustled," Dunn said.

Paul smiled. "Nah, just lucky." No need to mention he'd been champion three years in a row on the *HMS Churchill*. "Being good takes more practice than I have time for."

It was down to the final bull's-eyes now, and Dunn already had one in hand. "What'd ya say your pub's called?"

Paul hadn't intended to give that much information about himself, but conversation was a give-and-take; besides, he suspected they'd be able to find out easily enough. He paused to take his shot. "The Anchor," he said finally, watching the dart find its mark.

Dunn took a shot and hit the bull without hesitation. One more and he'd win. Paul wasn't going to push his luck. He picked the dart with the worst flight and let it go. It hit the pie just above the center, as he intended.

Dunn gave a satisfied smile. "Main thing, son, is you can't cave in under the pressure. You'll never win in life if you can't 'andle the pressure."

Dunn's dart made a clean bull's-eye.

Pressure was one thing Paul knew about, and this little outing had proved it was something he could still handle, and that pleased him. He laid twenty quid on the table and drained the rest of his beer. Winning was something he wasn't sure he'd ever manage to do in the grand scheme of things, but he had managed to put names to Gav's friends. Friends who'd known him for years. Friends that, with a bit more prodding, might shed some light on how he got to be "posh" and how he came to such a grim end.

Chapter Sixteen

India had spent most of the prior evening paging through a book of Victorian botanicals until she'd found what she was looking for. A delicate pen-and-ink rendering of a climbing rose. You could almost smell its fragrance, and in her own mind she was sure it was a delicate peach color. Heady and intoxicating. She'd read about women like that in her books. Enchanting, beautiful, the kind of women who made men weak and were always in the middle of some exciting adventure.

She loved their stories, but her own life seemed paralyzingly dull by comparison. She longed for adventure, yet adventure wasn't going to just land in her lap. She'd have to go out and find it, and Maeve's predicament was just the push she needed to get her out the door.

She put the book in her bag, then requested an Uber to get her across town. It wouldn't do to start an adventure on the Tube packed in like a sardine on the Northern line.

Her driver's name was Kev, and his girlfriend had just left him for a podiatrist. It never failed. She attracted every battered and bruised soul within a ten-mile radius, and all of them felt free to unburden themselves at will. She listened patiently, offered a few well-meaning platitudes, and had Kev drop her near the Seven Kings Tube station. He seemed a bit more sanguine as he sped off, but she wasn't sorry to be shot of him.

She'd spent a good hour on Google turning and enlarging the streets surrounding the station until she found what she was looking for: the Ink Spot. A small establishment between a dog groomer and a betting shop. The only such establishment within walking distance run by a woman named Vicky.

A bell tinkled as she came through the door, and a woman poked her head around a curtain from the back room. "Allo."

"Hi." India thought the woman looked a bit surprised. "I have an appointment for eleven o'clock with Vicky."

"India, right? You caught me making a coffee. Want one?"

India considered her churning stomach and said, "No thanks."

"Come on in then and 'ave a seat."

In spite of her loyalty to Maeve, India thought Vicky looked rather nice, not at all the harpy they'd envisioned. Course it was Gav who'd strayed. Vicky was likely just as much a victim in her own way as Maeve. *Win 'em in a crap shoot, lose 'em in a crap shoot,* her Auntie Adele used to say.

Vicky came to join India, giving her a reassuring smile. "Do you know what you're looking for, or do you want to browse through some samples?"

India dug in her shoulder bag and opened the book to the picture she'd found. "Can you do something like this? I mean, will it show up on a darker skin like mine?"

"Course it will. Anyone who tells you it won't don't know what they're doing, luv." Vicky sipped her coffee and looked closely at the picture. "Where's it going?"

A Ghostwriter's Guide to Murder

This weighty matter had absorbed a great deal of India's attention the evening before. She'd had a momentary fancy about her belly or her inner thigh, but as sexy as that seemed, the thought of the pain and prolonged personal exposure to a stranger had finally convinced her that her left tricep was the way to go.

Vicky disappeared behind a screen to make a transfer pattern and brought it back for India's approval.

"That's lovely."

"Right size for ya?"

Suddenly the drawing seemed rather large. "Sure." She strung out the word. "That should be fine."

Vicky gave her a stern look. "No *should be* about it. Make absolutely sure it's right before I get my pen involved. No regrets."

"Could you maybe make it a tiny bit smaller?" India didn't want to be brazen; she just wanted something tasteful, something that felt like her.

"Course we can do smaller. Now's the time to ask."

The machine in the back cycled again, and Vicky returned with a smaller version.

"Lovely."

"Right, then. I'm gonna get you prepped." Vicky pulled out a wad of cotton wool and doused it in alcohol. "I take it this is a first for you?"

India nodded, then shivered as Vicky wiped the alcohol over her upper arm. She was starting to feel a bit woozy. She usually did when she was nervous. It was silly, really. She'd have to move past it if she was going to be dancing outside the box on a regular basis.

Vicky placed the transfer on her arm and then peeled back the shiny paper to reveal a perfect purplish version of the flower snaking its way up her arm. India was tempted to stop there, but she'd come for an adventure and to talk to Vicky for Maeve's sake. Backing out wasn't an option.

"Take a look in the mirror over there and make sure that's what you're after."

India rose unsteadily and moved closer to the mirror, holding on to the table next to her. "Perfect." She turned right and left, examining the illustration. "Ever have anyone chicken out at the last minute?"

"A few, but not many. Some as should 'ave given it a bit more thought and didn't, but that's the way with folk, innit?" Vicky began to set up her equipment, removing several needles and tubes from sterile packages. India felt that was a good sign.

Once she had everything laid out, Vicky lifted her pen and hovered over the design transfer. "Right now, 'ere we go. Slow, deep breaths," she instructed, pausing until India complied. "The pain'll ease after the first minute or so."

India could only hope she was right, but no matter what her head said, she still tensed as the needle pierced the skin. It felt as bad as she'd imagined it would. A burning sensation, a sharp pain, but India tried to distract herself by formulating the questions she wanted to ask Vicky. She wasn't going to go through all this pain and come away with nothing but a tattoo to show for it.

She worked to unclench her teeth. "How long have you been a tattoo artist?"

"Almost eight years now. Used to be a manicurist back in the day, and then I got my first tat." Vicky smiled fondly at the memory, pushing up her left sleeve with the wrist of her right hand to display a compass. "Me mum always said I never knew which way was up. Compass was a bit of joke."

"It's lovely."

"Truth is, you either 'ate the sensation or you love it."

India was definitely falling into the former category. She inhaled deeply, then exhaled, making herself focus on Vicky's words.

"I don't mind the pain," she went on. "You 'ave to just embrace it, you know. Let it wash over you."

India nodded, unable to speak for the moment.

"Pain lets you know you're alive." Vicky stopped for a moment and wiped her needle. "I've bin at this location for nearly six years now. Nine months ago, this bloke walks in to get a dart on his bicep. 'Ad the most gorgeous skin I'd ever seen, and trust me, I've seen all sorts."

India hummed encouragingly.

Vicky was bent closely over India's upper arm, but she paused as she looked up. "It was like working on a perfect canvas. Could 'ardly keep me mind on what I was doin'. By the time I'd finished working on that glorious arm of 'is, I was all in, and so was 'e." Vicky gave a sad smile.

India couldn't help making the mental calculation that nine months ago meant it was a full five months before Maeve found out and dumped Gavin's arse.

"We started seeing a lot of each other. I was sure 'e was the one. 'Ad this done for 'im." She stretched the neck of her T-shirt down and showed off a heart-shaped dart board with a dart stuck smack in the middle.

"Sounds like the real thing," India managed through partially clenched teeth.

"It was. I tell you, I could've drawn a mural on that body, worked on it every night for the rest of me life and never got tired." Vicky trailed off, brushing a tear from the corner of her eye with her sleeve.

"Oh, you poor dear, what happened?" India was counting on the newness of the trauma inspiring additional confidences.

"Two days ago, I 'ad the police at our door sayin' that someone'd cracked 'im over the 'ead and killed 'im. Broad daylight an' all."

"That's terrible," India said, genuinely saddened for the woman.

"Life is pain," Vicky repeated.

At the moment, India had to agree. "But murder," she said, exhaling mindfully. "That's awful. Do the police know who did it?"

"Gawd knows. They were askin' questions about 'is ex, but I don't buy it. She was some posh bitch. Cold, you know. Doubt she'd 'ave 'ad it in 'er. I'd a killed for Gav, but I didn't," she added quickly.

"You don't have any idea who might've killed him?" India asked.

"I kept me nose out of Gav's business. I didn't need to know wot 'e was up to when 'e weren't with me. Curiosity killed the cat an' all."

Seemed Gavin Foster had been blessed with two regrettably incurious women in his life. Two women who now had no idea why he was dead.

"'E was well connected. I know that much," Vicky continued. Her tongue was peeking out of the corner of her mouth as she focused on a tiny rosebud on the edge of the design. "But some of the lads that 'ung round 'im at the pub were a bit rough." Vicky looked up. "Wouldn't want to be alone in an alley with 'em."

A Ghostwriter's Guide to Murder

India looked at her wide-eyed. "Do you think one of them could be the killer?"

"Don't know what to think." Vicky dipped the needle in a dish of fresh water and wiped it off with a cotton bud, sniffing slightly.

"You must miss him dreadfully. Why didn't you take some time off to regroup?"

"Time's money. Besides, it 'elps me to keep busy."

"Tell me some more about your man, then. I love a good romance, and I've got a bit of time on my hands." India tilted her head toward the work in progress. "What did you like to do together?" she prompted.

"We used to go to Spain every six weeks or so for a little break. Bit of business, bit of vacay. I love the sun and the sand and the sangria. Little slice of 'eaven for me. I look dead pasty without a bit of sun and not just from a tanning bed. Not the same, is it."

"Sounds lovely."

"I'd drawn that for 'im. Was going to ink it next week." Vicky gestured to a picture of a deserted beach framed by a rocky shoreline tacked on the wall with a pushpin. "It was our special place. We was talkin' about movin' out there permanent like. Gav was lookin' to buy an 'ouse by the sea. I was all for it, I mean, I can do what I do anywhere. Folks love to get a bit of ink on 'oliday."

How was Gavin affording a beach house in Spain? That would take a lot of money, much more than fifty thousand. Where was it coming from? Since Vicky was a part of this plan, maybe she would know more about it than she knew about Gavin's business. "Isn't beach property pretty dear in Spain?"

"Nah, ya get a lot more for your money there than you do 'ere. Besides, Gav'd come into a bit of money."

"An inheritance?"

Vicky looked up from her work, the pen poised in midair, and India realized the question must've sounded a bit odd. It was hard to subtly question anyone about money. "I was just thinking about his family," she backtracked. "They must be devastated."

Vicky set the needle back on its track. "Didn't really 'ave any family. Not anyone 'e was close to anyway. Only me. Mostly 'e was just keen to ditch the rat race, take it a bit easier. 'E'd bin savin', and if you can, well why the 'ell not. Life's too short."

India wanted to pry more into the source of Gavin's funds, but pushing harder would only look strange. If the money wasn't an inheritance, was it stolen, or was it money he'd earned illegally? They'd all agreed—*legal* money would be in a bank. Maybe Ash had found out more. Her train of thought was disrupted by the tears that were now rolling unheeded down Vicky's cheeks.

India put her free arm around the woman and did her best to offer some comfort, in part because she felt for Vicky but also because she didn't fancy someone carving into her skin with blurry vision. Adventure was one thing, but permanent disfigurement wasn't part of the plan.

Chapter Seventeen

Ash abandoned his client work the moment Paul's text came through and started checking into the men of Darty Deeds. Roy Boy Malloy had a record as long as your arm, running the gamut from public urination to driving under the influence to assault and even transporting stolen goods. Jimmy Bishop had embraced a similar career trajectory. Neither was a serious criminal. They were the men who supported criminal operations: the bag men, the runners, the muscle. They'd gone quiet of late, at least for the last couple of years, unlike Foster, who'd continued to attract police attention.

Mac "the Machine" Toliver was more complicated. Several Grievous Bodily Harm charges as a younger man and even a charge of possession with intent to distribute roughly five years ago. The latter seemed to have died on the vine—a bargain with the police or the CPS (Crown Prosecution Services), Ash suspected. However, the name of the arresting officer struck Ash as significant: a senior officer on the Met's drug team. If he'd been watching Mac Toliver, it meant the man wasn't a minor player like his friends; he was running with the big dogs.

Ash rose and went to make himself a coffee. He'd purposely not seen or spoken to any of his colleagues from the police force since the day he walked out of Camden Road nearly two years ago. Just one lone gaming partner, a bloke on the drug squad he'd played with for years. By mutual accord they didn't engage in small talk and spoke of nothing but the game. Ash had managed to avoid seeing any of his former coworkers—until last week, that is. At the time, Ash hadn't thought much of spotting his gaming mate at his local Costa on a weekday, but finding a dead body in the canal so soon after did raise a red flag. Was the drug squad watching Toliver's friend Gavin Foster for some reason? Had Toliver dragged Foster into something dangerous and managed to get him killed?

Ash inhaled deeply and blew the breath out through his lips in a steady stream. Only one way to find out. If he was going to continue to help Maeve—and of course he was going to help Maeve—he'd have to reach out to his former colleague.

Ash turned to his gaming console and fired up *Legend of Zelda*. It was tempting to jump in and start playing, but instead he sent a direct message to Doctor Permadeath.

Ashes2Ashes88: *Getting a bit of aggro this end. Need some answers.*

He waited and leaned over to the minifridge to find a yogurt. As he ate, he watched the screen, hoping to get lucky. It was always a gamble whether a player was online or not, but the diehards were usually watching the screen even when they weren't active. Chucking the empty plastic container into the bin, he saw the message pop up.

DoctorPermadeath: *You've been MIA. Thought you were camping elsewhere. Mission question?*

A Ghostwriter's Guide to Murder

Score. He reached for the keyboard to his right.

Ashes2Ashes88: *No. Business.*

DoctorPermadeath: *Off-line.*

Ash sat back and stared at the screen. Did that mean the Doctor was going offline, unwilling to talk about anything but gaming? It had, after all, been their only communication over the past two years. Or did it meant that he wanted to talk offline? Ash barely had time to take a sip of coffee before a message appeared on WhatsApp from the Doctor.

> *Good to see you resurfacing, mate.*
> *You've been missed.*
> *Not a soul at Camden Road these days*
> *that can match your skills.*

Ash grimaced.

> **Ashes2Ashes88**
> *Epic fail on my last skill check.*

> **DoctorPermadeath**
> *Bollocks. You're the best forensic IT specialist we ever had.*
> *These new kids do the bare minimum then sit on their arse*
> *waiting for you to tell them what to do next. No initiative.*
> *No willingness to take a risk.*

Taking risks was highly overrated in Ash's experience, but he hadn't stuck his neck out to talk about himself. He was here for Maeve.

> **Ashes2Ashes88**
> *Saw you at the Costa in Camden Market*
> *the other day. What's up?*

DoctorPermadeath
Should've said hi.

Ashes2Ashes88
Thought you might be working.

The Doctor seldom used his real name even at work. His initials were MD, and he'd always been known round the station as the Doctor. In his line of work, it was always good to maintain some level of anonymity. The Doc was part of an elite drug squad, not the serious crimes division where Ash had worked. Ash respected the Doc. He was a brilliant gamer and a solid cop, one who wasn't prone to idle gossip especially when it came to his cases. Ash knew he couldn't be coy if he hoped to get any useful information. He moved the keyboard onto his lap and started to type.

Ashes2Ashes88
What can you tell me about a bloke
called Gavin Foster?

DoctorPermadeath
Blast from the past.
Hasn't crossed my radar in years.

Ash tried again.

Ashes2Ashes88
What do you remember from back in the day?

Maybe something in Foster's past would provide a clue as to where and when thing started to go wrong for Maeve's ex.

DoctorPermadeath
Foster used to work for a bloke named

A Ghostwriter's Guide to Murder

Erik Stenson. A low-level flunky.
Not worth our notice. But Erik, he was
a right nasty bugger. Got himself killed
in a turf war with a drug gang from
Albania about 4 years ago. Alliances
shifted in the neighborhoods. Stenson's guys
were on the outs. Ito Osami took over.

Even Ash knew who Ito Osami was. A ruthless drug dealer and a real player in the local criminal scene. He'd taken over the London market four years ago, not that that was unusual. Changes at the top of the drug trade were like the regular cycling through of prime ministers with a bit more blood and a bit less invective, but Osami had proved to have longevity. He was still on top and looked to be staying.

Haven't heard boo from Gavin Foster since, the Doctor concluded.

Ashes2Ashes88
He was found dead in Regent's Canal
three days ago.

DoctorPermadeath
Was he now.
. . .
What's your interest?

Ashes2Ashes88
Body was basically floating in my back yard.

DoctorPermadeath
If there's anything to find, you'll find it.

109

Melinda Mullet

Ash did his best to express nothing more than a mild professional curiosity. He always preferred online conversations, no face-to-face contact, but he had to admit that it did present its own complications when it came to expressing the subtler nuances of questioning.

> *That's just it. Not much to see. Foster's been pulled in several times in the last twelve months. Released suspiciously quickly with the help of a pricy brief.*

Ash paused, then added,

> *Like someone still working for a drug boss.*

DoctorPermadeath
All I can tell you is he's not part of the local drugs trade. Not now anyway, and if you're not selling drugs on my patch, I'm not looking for you. Got enough to deal with.

> **Ashes2Ashes88**
> *You must hear things around the shop.*

DoctorPermadeath
Try to steer clear of your old side of the house. Department's a mess. Dixon's the best of the lot, but it's a low bar.

> **Ashes2Ashes88**
> *Didn't really know Dixon in my day. Thought it was odd they assigned a DS to the case. Murder's usually a DI.*

A Ghostwriter's Guide to Murder

DoctorPermadeath
*Don't have the manpower. They've been trying
to replace the last DI for over a year.*

        Ashes2Ashes88
        Who's supervising in the meantime?

DoctorPermadeath
DSI Bolton.

        Ashes2Ashes88
        *Jason Bolton's a DSI? How the hell did that
        happen?*

Ash remembered Jason Bolton as an officious little prat. Petty, domineering, and fatally unimaginative.

DoctorPermadeath
*Right place right time. And he's the master of
toadying to the divisional heads. He's got Dixon
and the whole crew over there running around
like chickens with their heads cut off.
Perpetual state of upheaval.*

The friction between Drugs and the Criminal Investigation Department was clearly still ongoing, and the Doc wasn't crossing the divide.

        Ashes2Ashes88
        Sounds like you're well out of it all.

DoctorPermadeath
*Don't envy Dixon. All Bolton cares about
is whether the department looks good on paper.*

The Met's all about your clean-up rate these days.
How quick you get cases off the books.
Bolton gets a lot of pressure from the top,
but we all do. There's a new divisional
head over both Drugs and CID.
Real hard ass about the numbers.
Everyone's being judged.
Results, results, results.

Ashes2Ashes88
Where'd he come from?

DoctorPermadeath
Up North. And he's a she.

Ashes2Ashes88
Bet that's going down well with the lads.

DoctorPermadeath
You know it, but the women are chuffed
as hell. Think it means more promotion
opportunities coming their way,
but so far I don't see any sign of it.

Ash was eager to move the conversation along. His concern was Maeve, not station politics.

Ashes2Ashes88
If Bolton's so keen to have his clean-up
rate look good, do you think he's willing
to accept the obvious on the
Foster killing and not dig further?

A Ghostwriter's Guide to Murder

DoctorPermadeath
If it keeps his desk tidy—hell yes.

That didn't bode well for Maeve. It was ludicrous to think that the police needed incentive to find not just a suspect but the right suspect, yet in this new age of policing, it seemed they did.

Ashes2Ashes88
A lot of cash in the Foster case—fifty thousand.
Surely they can't just brush that aside?

Ash waited, but the reply was slow in coming this time.

DoctorPermadeath
Whatever Bolton says goes. All I ask is that they steer
clear of what we're doing on the drugs side of the house.
We've got several delicate operations in play, and
you know better than most what interference can do.

Ash tried to shrug off the reference to the cloud under which he'd left Camden Road. As long as he had the Doc's attention, he was going to try another avenue.

What about a guy named Mac Toliver?

DoctorPermadeath
You think he's connected to Foster?

Ashes2Ashes88
They're mates. On the same darts team.

DoctorPermadeath
Then Dixon will be looking at him.

113

Ashes2Ashes88
He's not.

DoctorPermadeath
How do you know?

Ashes2Ashes88
*Because they've arrested Foster's ex-girlfriend.
The woman who reported a stash of money
hidden on the dock near the body that has
since mysteriously disappeared.*

DoctorPermadeath
*And your connection to
the ex-girlfriend is?*

Ash could almost see the smile on the Doc's face.

None.

He'd shot that back so fast he knew it looked suspicious.
He quickly added

*She's a neighbor. They've wasted
no time latching on to her, and of all
the people in Foster's life I'd say
she's the least likely candidate.*

DoctorPermadeath
*I trust your judgement, but I'd be careful.
Don't wade in too deep. You have no idea what
Dixon and his crew may be up to. Could be
their end game involves a bigger fish than Foster.*

A Ghostwriter's Guide to Murder

Ash had the distinct feeling he was being warned off the subject. The Doc's evasiveness on the Toliver subject hadn't escaped him. He'd touched a nerve somehow.

Ashes2Ashes88
And what about the ex-girlfriend?
She's not a big fish.
She's just a minnow minding her own business.

DoctorPermadeath
Circle of life, mate, circle of life.

Chapter Eighteen

As Maeve finally made her way home along the towpath, she could see Sage sitting with her legs dangling over the edge of the *Valeria*'s bow. When she caught sight of Maeve, she scrambled to her feet by way of her hands and knees, her prodigious bum in the air. It was a quite a welcome home.

"There you are, pet. Y'all right?" She stopped at the top of the ramp leading off the boat and stared at Maeve. "Your aura's flamin'. Coo, I've never seen it like that before. Bright red and pulsing. You're usually much bluer."

Maeve didn't comment, as it would only extend the conversation about auras further. "I'm fine," she replied. "Just exhausted."

Hearing her voice, the Captain came streaking from belowdecks, jumping off the side of the *Val* and running at her full bore. She braced herself and gave in to the exuberant greeting. She needed that rambunctious storm of unconditional love and affection. Up all night in the nick and then a jaunt over to the Isle of Dogs; she was knackered.

A Ghostwriter's Guide to Murder

"Can we get you a drink?" Sage offered. "I have a new thistle wine if you'd like, or we can get you a bite to eat. Rowan's cooking just now."

"Thank you, no." Maeve hoped her lightning-quick response wasn't as rude as it felt. "I need to grab a shower." She wanted to wash the police station off her, not to mention giving the old aura a scrub.

Dragging the Captain back to the *Revenge*, she found a receipt on the table where her computer had been. The police had come aboard and taken her laptop while she was in custody. That could not be a good sign. She wondered what the police thought about the index cards pinned to the wall in front of the table. The basic outline of book forty-three included a drowned body, a disemboweled corpse in a hot air balloon, and a murder made to look like suicide. As she thought about it, she broke out in a cold sweat. Even worse, on her computer they'd find the warmup executions of Gavin preserved in a folder called *Perverse Justice*. Could she look more like a killer if she tried? She felt the panic rising inside her and had to force herself to strip off and get in the shower.

The Captain was refusing to leave her side, and as she stood under the trickling water, she could see him sitting with his back pressed against the glass door. She was glad he was there, yet she still felt alone. She didn't want to be rude to India, but she thought her brother Julian had been bloody useless. He hadn't really seemed to care much about her situation one way or the other. It was possible he was certain that the police didn't have enough evidence to charge her, but Dixon and Gray had made it abundantly clear that she was their prime suspect. What if they didn't bother to look for anyone else?

Was she being framed by Gavin's killer? If so, why? Proximity? Convenience? She had no idea, but she was damn sure this wasn't over yet. The shower began to run cold, and she stepped out to dry off.

Her visit to Malik Ross had been eye-opening but not as helpful as she'd hoped. If anything, she'd left with more questions, not less. Changing into clean jeans and a loose-fitting jumper, she opened the cupboards, but it was Old Mother Hubbard in there. She'd been heading for the shops when the police showed up, but all that had been swept out of her mind in the ensuing chaos. She looked over toward the *Red Lion*, but there was no sign of life. It was gone five now. Ash was probably at the pub with India and Paul.

Her stomach rumbled loudly, making her mind up for her. Locking the door of the cabin, she and the Captain headed back down the towpath toward the Anchor in search of solace and sustenance in equal measure.

* * *

Walking through the door of the Anchor, Maeve heard a squeal of delight from India, who leapt from her barstool and rushed over to give her an enveloping hug.

Paul poured her a large glass of red wine and handed it across the bar as soon as she was in range. Ever the man with the answer.

"Tell us absolutely everything," India said as Maeve made embarrassingly short work of the first drink.

The Captain put his paws up on the counter beside Maeve and eyed Paul, who leaned over and ruffled the top of his head. "Sausage roll coming up," he said.

"Make that two," Maeve said. "And one of those nice pasties as long as it isn't chicken." Paul reached back for the bottle of red and put it on the counter next to Maeve. She picked it up and carried it to the armchair, followed by Ash, who settled into the other chair.

India turned on her barstool to face the chairs, Paul leaned across the counter, and everyone looked at Maeve expectantly.

The Captain had perched himself precariously on her lap, demanding her attention, and she had to make him lie flat before she could see her friends' faces properly. "I honestly don't know what to say. India probably already told you that they're trying to draw a connection between Gavin's activities and me, but I had no answers for them. Looking back now, we were together for four years, lived together for nearly two, and I'm ashamed to say I had no idea what he got up to."

Maeve thought back on her relationship with Gavin. It was like reliving a car crash in slow motion. There was darts. A lot of darts. And late-night sex. A lot of that too. As a lover Gavin was exciting, but as a man he was pretty dull, which was why she'd never bothered much. She was bored by his daytime self. Maybe she should've been afraid instead. "We never talked about anything of substance," she admitted. "It was a pretty one-dimensional relationship, if I'm honest."

"Even after four years?" India's eyebrows arched toward her hairline. "That's proper impressive."

Maeve ignored her, still thinking about their lack of communication. "He never encouraged confidences, and I suppose that was part of his charm. He was mysterious. In hindsight, I should've asked more questions. I just didn't."

She poured more wine into her glass, splashing some on the Captain's back, but he didn't seem to mind.

"Well, he wasn't in the drug trade these days, if that's any comfort," Ash offered out of the blue.

Maeve looked at him over the Captain's bulk, and he flushed. "And how do we know this, Ash?"

India came to Ash's rescue. "It's my fault really. I felt bad that Julian wasn't more help, so I encouraged everyone to start poking around a bit on their own, and you know how good Ash is at research."

Ash looked more disconcerted by the praise than the attention.

Maeve looked at each of them in turn. "Then you all believe me when I say I didn't kill Gavin?"

"Suspect you'd have been well within your rights if you had," Paul said. "But no, we don't think you killed him." They all nodded solemnly.

Maeve felt the tears threatening. India's loyalty didn't surprise her, but Paul and Ash—it was overwhelming and such a relief to find that she wasn't alone in all this. She had friends. An odd little band of souls, but genuine friends. The kind of friends willing to try to help a woman being framed for murder. And whether it was the wine or the dog draped all over her, Maeve felt a sudden surge of warmth toward them all.

"We've been busy already," India said, her enthusiasm barely contained. "Ash dredged through the dark web or wherever it is that he goes, and you're just in time to hear what he found."

They all turned toward Ash, who took a healthy swig of his beer before beginning. "I did try trawling around online, but I kept hitting dead ends, so I reached out to an old friend at the Met. He's with the drug squad, not CID, so this murder isn't really his department, but I asked about Foster. Apparently, he used to have some connections to the local drugs trade back in the day, but he stepped away after the man he worked for was

A Ghostwriter's Guide to Murder

killed. Scared straight, my friend thought. He hasn't been involved for years."

"Smarter than you seemed, then, you daft bugger," India said, tipping her glass skyward.

Ash nodded. "When I mentioned that Foster had been questioned by the police several times in the last year but let off right sharpish, my contact suggested Foster might be working for someone influential outside the drug trade; someone protecting him."

"Did he say who that might be?" India asked.

"No, but logically a recent associate. Someone with an interest in seeing that Foster wasn't getting chatty about their business."

"I might have a candidate," Maeve said, suddenly feeling better about her visit with Ross. "Like I said, I almost never got involved with Gavin and his work, but over the past twelve months he seemed to have become, I don't know, more ambitious, I guess. Taking on commercial projects: bigger jobs, more money. I didn't really pay much attention, but then about six months ago I was approached by a real estate developer. Bloke named Malik Ross who wanted help writing a proposal for a new entertainment development. He said Gavin had referred him to me."

"Gavin?" India frowned.

"Yeah, I guess I should've asked more questions, but things weren't so hot between Gav and me at that point. Plus this guy Ross was paying really well for a dead easy job, so I grabbed at it before he changed his mind."

"Did he say how he knew Foster?" Ash asked.

"Said they'd worked on some projects together. I didn't push it. He must've been happy with the work I did, because he

121

contacted me again a few weeks ago asking if I'd do some brochures, and I said yes."

"What's he like?" India asked.

"Never met him face-to-face until today."

"You went to see him?" India looked concerned. "Was that wise?"

"Probably not the smartest move, but when I left the station this morning, I felt no one was looking for the truth. Certainly not the cops. It was down to me to find someone who might know what Gav was up to. What he might have done to make someone angry enough to kill him."

"What did he say when you turned up out of the blue?" Paul asked.

"Thank God I didn't know what I was letting myself in for or I'd never have had the nerve to go. Big swank offices on the Isle of Dogs. He's clearly done a lot of development projects in the city. No wonder Gavin was enthusiastic. He was onto a winner there with Ross handing out assignments."

Ash caught her eye. "What did he have to say about Gavin?"

"Claimed he'd been a bit of a mentor to Gavin, but I got the sense that was just him bragging. He's that kind of guy. Cocky and full of himself. Wants everyone to think he's the man. He said Gavin still had a lot to learn, like who to trust in the real estate game."

India looked puzzled. "Did that mean Gavin was supposed to trust him as opposed to someone else?"

"Presumably." Maeve took another drink. "But he also hinted that Gavin had made mistakes, but when I asked if those mistakes might've gotten him killed, he switched the subject so fast it would make your head spin. Tried to distract me with the plans for the project he had me writing about."

Paul handed a plate over the counter with the sausage rolls and a beef pasty. "Judging by the outcome, the money seems to have been a mistake," he said.

"That's for sure. I also came away with a sense that Gavin was moving up in the world a bit. Not just your bog-standard residential jobs anymore. I think it might've been easy for him to get in over his head, especially if he was trying to keep pace with the likes of Malik Ross."

Paul passed a second bottle of wine across the divide. "Real estate moguls don't hire plumbers directly. There'd be a general contractor. Two of the lads from Darty Deeds, Roy and Jimmy, work for a company called Dawson Construction. Gavin, too, occasionally. I picked that up when I went over to the Bell at lunchtime. Might want to see if any of this bloke Ross' projects are being done by Dawson." The final part of his remarks were directed at Ash.

"Foster's definitely connected to Dawson," Ash confirmed. "He subcontracted on a huge project for them down by the river called the Waterfront."

Maeve nodded. "I saw the renderings for that on the wall in Ross' offices."

"Ross was the developer," Ash agreed. "However, Foster seems to have landed in way over his head. Facing lawsuits and all sorts."

"That could be the mistake Ross was alluding to." Maeve blew on a bite of sausage before popping it in the Captain's mouth.

"Certainly a strong contender. I also checked on the fourth member of the darts team Paul told me about—Mac 'the Machine' Toliver. My drug squad mate got very evasive when Toliver's name came up. Didn't want to talk about him. If I had to guess, I'd say Toliver's on his radar for something."

"Drug running, perhaps?" Paul pulled out his phone. "The lads from Darty Deeds are back and forth to the Continent regularly. The team's schedule was on the wall at the Bell, so I took a quick snap." He handed the phone to India, who passed it in turn to Maeve and Ash.

"They get around a bit, don't they?" said India. "Interesting that Spain's on the list several times." India paused for a moment, and Maeve could've sworn she was purposely gathering everyone's attention. "From what *I* learned today, Gavin claimed he'd come into some money." She paused for effect. "And according to the girlfriend, Vicky, he was thinking of buying a place in Spain and retiring."

"You spoke to Vicky?" Ash leaned forward. "How did you find the girlfriend?"

India swallowed the rest of her wine and extended the glass to Maeve for a refill before slipping the cardigan off her left shoulder and baring her upper arm. The edges of the tattoo were still pink, and she flinched as she moved. The three friends stared at her, gobsmacked.

Ash finally let out a low whistle.

"Well, bugger me," Paul said as Maeve dumped the Captain off her lap and stepped over to get a better look.

"That's gorgeous. You really did that just to talk to Vicky?" Maeve could feel the tears coming on again.

India looked embarrassed. "Well, I've been thinking of getting one for years, but yeah, going to Vicky today was for you."

Maeve collapsed back into the armchair. "You are too much."

A Ghostwriter's Guide to Murder

"Not just me," India added hastily. "Between us we'd rival your Simon Hill, wouldn't we?"

"Absolutely, but this is real life, not a story." Maeve's excitement at her friend's willingness to step up for her had momentarily blinded her to the implications of involving other people in her situation. "Look, I appreciate all that you guys have done. You've been amazing, but you can't keep on like this." Misery might love company, but she was potentially putting her friends at risk. "If Gavin was killed for the mistakes he made, the last thing we need is for the killer to get wind that an ex-copper and his friends are nosing about in his business. It's one thing if I become a target, I'm already knee-deep in this, but I won't risk that for you lot."

"We're being careful," India replied.

"If the killer can follow my digital trail, it'd be a miracle," Ash said quietly.

Given Ash's overwhelming reticence, Maeve had to think he must be quite brilliant at what he did for a living to say anything at all.

"You're the one that needs to say out of this," Ash continued. "If you start digging around, you'll only look more suspicious to the police."

You must keep digging, Simon piped up from the background. For a change, Maeve wholeheartedly agreed, but she wasn't going to argue with Ash; she knew he meant well.

"We all appreciate your concern," India said, looking at the other two, "but like it or not, we're in this. And not just because it's the most interesting thing to happen around here in a long time."

"Amen to that," Paul said.

"But because we care about you, and we don't want to see you get hurt. You're the one that cheers us up and reminds us it could be worse. This time it's our turn. Let us help you."

Maeve looked down to hide the tears that were now rolling down her cheeks. She had to admit her own sense of optimism and resilience had taken a huge hit over the past forty-eight hours and she'd found herself teetering on the brink of hopelessness. It was a place she hadn't really been before and didn't want to go now. Her heart swelled with gratitude for the people around her.

"Right, that's settled, then," Ash said. "Come on, India, what else did you get from tattoo woman?"

"Mostly I focused on the money, but she did say that Gav's friends were a bit of a rough lot. When I asked her if she thought one of them could've killed Gavin, she said she wouldn't put it past any of them."

"Fifty thousand quid could be a fair bit of inspiration," Paul noted.

"Maybe he took one of them along to fetch the money and they saw an opportunity and took it," Ash mused.

"In broad daylight?" Paul said. "Why not wait till later and somewhere more private?"

No one had an answer for that, not even Simon, Maeve noted. Which was odd, because usually the drunker she was, the more she heard from him.

"Still a lot of questions to be answered, but Maeve's free, and you have to admit we've got more to go on now than when we started the day," India said. "So, what's the next step?" She turned to look at Ash expectantly.

Put on the spot, Ash blanched and looked down at his shoes. India seemed to realize she'd made him uncomfortable and

A Ghostwriter's Guide to Murder

stepped back in. She had a knack for relating to him, Maeve thought.

"We need a game plan," India said firmly. "We're agreed that Gavin's got himself involved in something a bit shady. Made mistakes, maybe trusted the wrong person."

"The missing piece being who was the wrong person?" Maeve said. *Dig deep into the man's connections,* Simon murmured in the background. *The more unsavory the better.* "Malik Ross seems like a contender to me," Maeve said aloud.

India nodded in agreement. "He's got money and power."

"And stealing money from the boss would be a big mistake if you were found out," Paul added.

"Right, "Ash said. "I'll start by seeing what else I can find out about Ross."

"Meanwhile, I'll try to come up with another reason to head back to the Bell and talk to the dart's crew," Paul said.

"What about me?" Maeve asked. "I can't just sit here while the rest of you run around after me."

"You're coming with me tomorrow," India said. "I think it's time you got some new legal counsel. And I believe I know just the man."

With that, Simon fell silent—content for the moment.

Chapter Nineteen

❧

Ash was having trouble pinpointing the exact moment when Ross went from being a bookie and two-bit loan shark, known on the street as Malik the Man, to reinventing himself as Malik Ross, full-blown real estate mogul overseeing his empire from the Isle of Dogs. It seemed to involve the purchase of a derelict warehouse in Ealing a few years back, which he renovated into posh flats and sold for a whacking great profit. From then on, he appeared to have the golden touch, selling and buying as if he had a crystal ball. Sailing past zoning-panel requirements with minimal or no public hearings. He was always slightly ahead of his competitors when it came to planning permission and poised to take full advantage of changes in the law.

A charmed life of sorts, but as Ross became more of a presence within the real estate markets, he also became more of a target. Critics alleged that his mandated low-income housing offerings were substandard—*human warehousing* according to the *Times*, *hoteling* in Ross's vernacular. Dismal, cramped, poorly ventilated spaces that only added to the misery of the poor sods

A Ghostwriter's Guide to Murder

who had to live in them. Constructed, it seemed, with second-rate supplies and talent provided by Dawson Construction.

Dawson had a wildly convoluted ownership structure, with numerous holding companies and subsidiaries. But at the bottom of the pile, in a Jersey registration, Ash found MTM, Ltd. Malik the Man was the de facto owner of it all. He set up a spreadsheet comparing the projects Dawson Construction had completed over the past four years with Ross's real estate ventures, and as he suspected, the overlap was more akin to an eclipse.

Gavin Foster was likely up to his neck in it all, providing shoddy work to keep costs low on Ross's wretched developments. If Ross was willing to take advantage of the poor, what else was he willing to do? Perhaps murder a cheating associate.

The construction business was notoriously unscrupulous, and real estate development was often equally dodgy. Bribery and corruption were considered standard business practice. Of course, Malik Ross could be legit, but based on his past exploits, Ash was sure he wasn't.

If it was easy to make that kind of money legally, everyone would do it.

Ross would be successful because he was covering his tracks effectively, no doubt with the help of a team of professionals willing to do whatever he asked for a price. Ross's lawyers Hutton, Wallace & Stoat had a steely reputation, mostly servicing white-collar offenders, although notably a few high-power criminal types as well. Surely not a coincidence that junior partner Mark Elliott was the attorney of record for Gavin Foster. From the outside it looked like Ross was paying to keep Foster out of trouble, but why?

Ash looked at his watch and was mildly surprised to see it was nearly three in the morning. It had been a productive four hours, and it felt good to be playing to his strengths. Since coming home from the Anchor, he'd been glued to the screen in front of him, so he forced himself to rise and stretch the kinks out of his lower back. He ought to stand more often, but he never thought about it until it was too late. They said being sedentary was the next great health crisis. At least there was some comfort in knowing what was likely to kill him.

Ash climbed up on deck and took a deep breath of chilly air. He was awake. Tuned in to what was happening around him. He'd given up on the headphones, determined to be more responsive if Maeve needed him. He looked over at the *Revenge*. It was dark. Maeve would be asleep in the stern after the amount of wine she'd consumed, the Captain curled up at her feet. He wondered if she was worried about being alone. She needn't be. They'd look out for her. Him and Paul and India.

India had stepped up earlier to take charge when he was at a loss. She was good at that. Organized and inspiring. Everyone had their marching orders and knew where they were heading next. Sometimes all it took was a little push to get a team going in a multiplayer game. He realized that was how he thought of them all now. They were a team embarking on a quest together. A quest to prove Maeve's innocence. India was their mage and their healer. Paul their soldier, and as always, Ash was the ninja. Not the showy strengths of the soldier class, but every bit as lethal. Ash's attack was subtle and considered. The keystroke as mighty as the sword.

And Maeve, she was their bard, their storyteller. There was power in her words. God knows they'd already tied him up in

A Ghostwriter's Guide to Murder

knots. Every time he laid eyes on her, a cocktail of nausea and euphoria washed over him, proof of his abject capitulation. She could convince him of anything, but in this case she didn't have to. He was already marching willingly into battle as her champion.

Chapter Twenty

Maeve woke to find India standing at the foot of her bed. Or was it the angel of death?

"On your feet. Let's get you looking respectable."

Maeve sat up gingerly, her head still thick from the night before. The additional bottles of wine had seemed like such a grand idea at the time. "Where are we going?" she managed to croak out before the cotton wool in her mouth silenced further speech.

"We talked about this." There was a trace of impatience in India's voice. "We're going to interview a proper solicitor. And you need to at least look presentable if not actually innocent."

Maeve found a glass of water on the floor next to the bed and drained it before responding. "No way I can afford some swish lawyer."

"Didn't say we were going to *hire* him, did I? Just interview him." The Captain had vacated the bed and was leaning on India's legs as she scratched his ears. "Come on, we've got one hour, and from the looks of you you're going to need every minute of it. I'll get coffee. You work on a shower."

A Ghostwriter's Guide to Murder

By the time Maeve had allowed all the available hot water to trickle down on her head and made her way to the top deck, she looked better but felt decidedly worse. Her head was throbbing, and she'd had to apply a bit of peachy-colored eye shadow to her cheeks to enliven her features in an attempt to look less like one of the victims in Simon's stories. She'd followed the coat of makeup with four aspirin and a large glass of water.

"There she is," Rowan said. She'd pulled up two deck chairs and was sitting on the towpath with India, drinking a cup of herbal tea from a handmade mug. Maeve settled herself gingerly on the edge of the *Revenge*'s deck with her feet propped up on the canalside, gratefully accepting the coffee India handed her. She sat staring into the inky depths, allowing the steam from the cup to warm her face.

"All that black's not doing much for your chi," Rowan observed. "You look like a cat burglar."

"I didn't have the strength to coordinate anything this morning. Black slacks and a black turtleneck were as respectable as I could muster."

"Didn't think you could look any paler, luv," India noted, "but that's done it all right. Might get you a sympathy vote from the lawyers, but I'd like them to think you're going to survive until the trial, if there is one."

Maeve leaned her head against the side of the boat. "I'd say survival's fifty-fifty at the moment." She took a drink of the black coffee and felt her stomach lodging a complaint. "Why are we seeing these lawyers?"

"Because Julian was a right prat when he came, but mostly because this lawyer's done a great job over the past year keeping your Gav out of the nick."

"He's not my Gav," Maeve corrected.

"Fine, but Ash wants to know who's paying the fees to keep Gavin out of trouble, and more importantly, why. Besides, if he's that good, maybe he can help you too."

"Was this Paul's idea?"

"No. We all agreed to it. Even you, though I wouldn't be surprised if you don't remember."

"I'm not sure it was a good idea. What exactly are we supposed to say when we waltz in there?"

"Keep it simple. We'll say Gavin recommended them."

Maeve thought this was a dubious premise. "He recommended them from beyond the grave?"

India rolled her eyes. "No, before. Why would they know that you parted on bad terms? Not the sort of thing you rush out and tell your solicitor, is it?"

"I suppose."

"Come on then, get that coffee down you and let's go."

Maeve did her best, but she had to concede it wasn't great.

"Wait. Before you leave"—Rowan rose to her feet—"we have to fix you up a bit." She trotted back to the *Valerian* and returned with a turquoise wool coat over her arm. The coat was heavy and floppy and smelled strongly of weed. She draped it over Maeve's shoulders, and India smiled and nodded.

"Splash of color. Just the ticket."

* * *

When they arrived at Hutton, Wallace & Stoat, they were ushered into a large conference room designed to intimidate both competitors and clients alike. Maeve suspected it was easier to present a massive bill if you did it overlooking the spread of the

A Ghostwriter's Guide to Murder

Thames with the London Eye turning slowly in the distance. It seemed Ross and his attorneys shared an affection for visual intimidation.

They sat cooling their heels for a good fifteen minutes before the door was opened by a man in his late thirties. His fake tan was artfully showcased against the stark white of his shirt. An impeccably tailored suit and a fashionably thin tie completed the look. Even as a junior partner he had the appearance of a man who was doing exceptionally well for himself.

"Mark Elliot." He shook Maeve's outstretched hand and sniffed slightly, glancing around to see where the smell was coming from.

The jacket was a nice touch after all, Maeve thought, stifling a grin. Elliot was now looking decidedly confused, plainly wondering what he was getting himself into.

"Please sit down. Of course, before we begin, I'd like to convey our most sincere sympathies on the loss of your friend."

"Thank you."

"I presume you've had a letter from Mr. Stoat's office."

"Ah, no, should I have?" Maeve was disturbed to find she'd already lost the thread of the conversation and they'd barely passed the pleasantries. All she could think was that she'd change her name if she'd been born a Stoat. You really didn't want people associating solicitors with weasels.

Elliott allowed his brow to furrow ever so slightly. "You're not here about the bequest?"

"No, we were here looking for legal representation," India replied. She leaned forward to catch Elliot's eye.

"What bequest?" Maeve demanded.

"Mr. Foster listed you as a beneficiary in his will."

"Me? Not Vicky?"

"You."

"What on earth did Gavin have to leave in a will?" Maeve asked.

"He left you his share of a boat you jointly owned and the proceeds of a life insurance policy."

Now Maeve was completely confused. "Why would he do that? Not the boat, I mean—the insurance. Was it some token thing from the union?"

Elliot opened the file and pulled out a sheet of paper. "No. An individual policy. Global Life Insurance, and the proceeds are just slightly north of two hundred fifty thousand pounds."

Beside her India let out a small gasp.

"That's just not possible. Gavin shopped at Primark and used to argue over the price of a pint if we strayed into the wrong pub." Maeve felt a rush of nausea wash over her. Suddenly the coat felt stifling, and she slipped it off her shoulders. "He certainly wasn't the sort to pay premiums on a life insurance policy, and if he did, there's no way he'd leave the money to me. There must be a mistake."

"Mr. Foster was quite judicious with his finances."

Elliot was absolutely po-faced. He'd missed his calling as an actor. Maeve was certain he knew more than he was letting on. Surely Gavin hadn't taken out insurance because he'd suddenly become Mr. Responsible. Had he? Maybe he'd actually read and digested *Your Money or Your Life*? Or maybe he'd learned more from Ross about finances than she'd thought.

"I'll be happy to discuss the process with you further, but first, what was it that inspired you to seek our counsel, Ms. Gardner?"

"You've always done such a good job for Gavin," Maeve said. "*He* never got stuck in jail overnight."

"And you have?" Elliot had jumped immediately to the salient point. There was no way he was going to be distracted or to give any details about his client. It would be unethical. They'd been foolishly optimistic in coming to question the man. *But you did learn something crucial,* Simon piped in from the sidelines.

Unable to restrain herself, India blurted out, "She was arrested for the murder of Gavin Foster."

Elliot leaned back in his swivel chair and studied the two of them from the far end of the table. Maeve couldn't tell whether the news was a surprise to him or whether he was simply wanting to hear the words from her.

"I was taken in for questioning."

"Formally charged?"

"No, but I was told not to leave the area."

"I see. This makes matters considerably more difficult. Naturally, we would be unable to represent you, as it would be a conflict of interest for the firm in general and me in particular. And, of course, if it is ultimately determined that you were responsible for the death of our client, the insurance company would not pay out."

Things were happening way too fast for Maeve's taste. Normally the idea of getting a quarter-million-pound windfall would've been thrilling, but to cash in, she'd have to prove she wasn't a killer. Something that should be easy given that she wasn't, but Simon continued to poke at her. *How can you prove it?* Maeve took a deep breath and tried to steady her hands. "So, what happens now?" she asked.

Melinda Mullet

"We wait and see," Elliot said. It was the second time she'd heard that in as many days. The standard legal assessment, it seemed, no matter how posh the firm.

Elliot gathered his papers together and rose before opening the door and standing well back to allow them to pass through.

"I will say that you're on the right track seeking counsel." His eyes narrowed fractionally as he looked down into her face. "Of course, you'll have to look elsewhere, but I'd do it quickly if I were you. It's not going to take the police long to realize you have a substantial new motive for wanting to see my client dead."

Chapter
Twenty-One

Paul had just taken a large bite out of a vindaloo he'd tried to warm in the microwave when the door to the Anchor opened. Why was it always scalding on the sides with an icy pocket in the middle no matter how much you stirred it?

He looked up at the three men who'd entered the pub. The leader was dark eyed, dark haired, and absolutely massive. He managed to make the room look smaller by his mere muscular presence. Paul quickly calculated that the cash drawer was nearly empty, which was good news for him, but if the men were expecting more, things could turn ugly quickly.

He put down his fork and placed a hand on the fire extinguisher under the counter just in case. "Sorry, lads, kitchen's not open."

"You Paul Lane?" the leader of the group asked.

Paul was good at the semaphores that emanated from others. Always had been. Muscles wasn't asking a question—he knew who Paul was already, so no point in lying. "I am."

"We hear you was a friend of Gav's. Funny we never met," said the bloke in the Arsenal scarf.

"Well, not a close mate, but he'd stopped by here a few times. We used to talk darts. Told me I should come see 'im when I was ready to start a team of me own."

"He's dead and suddenly you're all about darts?" It was Muscles again. The Darty Deeds crew at a guess, though they were apparently in no hurry to introduce themselves.

"'E's bin on my mind—you know how it is when someone passes. Thought it'd be a nice memorial like." Paul found himself echoing the language of the men in front of him. Was he trying to seem more like one of them? He wasn't sure it'd save him if things went sour, but he thanked God he'd bought a new dart board and already set it up on the far wall. It gave his story a vague air of truth.

Arsenal wandered over to the board and picked up a handful of darts from the tray next to it and fired away. Clean to the center. "Right odd our boy was just down the canal 'ere when 'e got killed." Thwack. Another bull's-eye. "Bin visitin' you, 'ad 'e?"

"Had a bit of a barney maybe?" the skinniest of the three added. He'd been silent so far. Paul wasn't quite sure what he brought to the equation. Not a fighter, he'd guess, just a spotty-faced kid, but looking into his eyes Paul realized he could well be older than he seemed, or at least he'd seen a lot in his time.

"Hadn't seen Gavin round 'ere in months." Paul did his best to keep his voice calm and even. If they thought *he* had something to do with Gavin's death, that suggested they weren't involved themselves. What would Maeve make of that?

"Gav was killed almost in your backyard, and then you show up sniffin' round at the Bell. I think you know a bit more than you're sayin'." Arsenal retrieved his darts from the board and turned back toward Paul.

Asking questions at the Bell had clearly tipped off the lads, and they were here to see what he was all about. He'd need to tread carefully.

"Police seem to fancy his ex–posh bird as the killer," Muscles said, moving closer.

"They've let her go," Paul said. "She had nowt to do with this. Wasn't even at home when 'e was killed." They'd have no reason to believe him about Maeve. He needed a distraction to get them looking elsewhere, a grenade of his own to lob into the mix. He wondered if they knew about the missing money. "She'd gone to tell the police about the money she found when he was killed."

All three men turned and looked at him. Arsenal threw a dart back over his shoulder. It still landed in the middle ring.

Muscles' eyes narrowed. "What money?" He moved toward Paul, who continued to be very glad of the bar counter between them.

"Wads of it," Paul said. "Stuffed inside one of the dock bumpers by Gav's boat. When his ex came back with the cops, the cash was gone and Gav was face down in the drink."

"Where'd 'e get that kind of dosh?" The skinny lad directed the question to Muscles. It was as if Paul weren't there for a moment.

"Quiet," Muscles snapped.

Paul could tell the balance of power had shifted ever so slightly. He had information they didn't. Paul met the eyes of all three men without flinching and made a quick calculation of his odds. Arsenal and Skinny would be easy, but the big guy would be a serious problem. He hoped it wouldn't come to a fight.

141

"We figure Gavin came back to claim the cash and someone was waiting for 'im," Paul elaborated. "Nasty business," he added. "But 'is ex was more shocked than anyone. 'Adn't seen or 'eard from Gav in months, and suddenly there 'e was." Paul waited. Muscles was considering his words, and the other two looked to their leader for the way forward. "Don't you 'ave any idea who the killer was?" Paul prodded. "You're 'is mates."

"A few ideas, but that's our business." Muscles seemed to suddenly come back to the here and now. "Not sure why I should believe you"—he studied Paul cautiously—"but for some reason I do. Maybe 'cause me old man was Navy too." He nodded toward the small naval flag stuck into a jar of pens behind the bar.

Paul would take what he could get.

"Make you a deal," Muscles said. "You play Roy Boy here on the board. If you win, we're good. If Roy wins, well, we might just have to make a bit of a mess."

Finally, a name for the spotty-faced kid. The other two were clearly Jimmy and the Machine, and he had no trouble sorting which was which. Paul was suddenly thankful he'd thrown a few practice darts since yesterday's trip round the Bell. Seemed he was about to face the Darty Deeds crew head on, but what better way to follow up with these men who he was sure had tales to tell about Gav.

Roy Boy pulled his own darts from a pouch in his back pocket. Paul reached under the bar counter and grabbed his arrows before making his way to the throwing line.

Roy Boy threw first with his left hand, scoring a seemingly effortless double twenty. Paul threw next, aiming for forty but coming away with just twenty.

A Ghostwriter's Guide to Murder

Paul retrieved the two darts and handed Roy his to lead off play. Muscles gave them each 301 on the chalk board, and the game began with Roy shooting two double twenties and a treble. His number dropped to 161.

Paul stepped up and took a deep breath. Focus, balance. First shot was an errant nineteen followed by two double twenties. If he could hit his stride, he might just be able to hold his own. He'd been good once. Very good, he reminded himself.

Roy stepped back to the line and waited for Paul to retrieve his darts. This time he let loose a rapid-fire explosion. The kid's role in the group was suddenly crystal clear. He was a natural. He made scoring look as easy as breathing. Second leg gave him two triple twelves and a double twelve and he hardly seemed to look at the board at all. Muscles reduced his score to 65, leaving him an easy checkout.

Paul would have to pull out the stops to catch up. He placed a triple twenty followed by a double twenty and tailed off with a double eighteen. He was now at 66. In the running at least. Roy stepped up and hit a quick twenty followed by a five. All he needed now was a double twenty and he'd check out with a clean 0.

Paul started to back toward the wall with the display of rowing oars. Not his weapon of choice but needs must. He watched Roy Boy turn from the board and flick the dart over his left shoulder. Cocky little sod, but he was so good he'd make it. Paul was preparing for the worst, but then came the sound of metal on metal as the tip of the dart nicked the wire rim and clattered to the floor. Roy turned and looked at his downed soldier in surprise. Suddenly, Paul was in with a chance.

He shot a sixteen and then aimed for the bull. Fifty points would check him out with a clean 0, leaving Roy with 40 points on the board. He watched the dart fly like it was in slow motion. It headed unerringly for the center, but just before it made contact with the cork, the Machine reached across and knocked it away. Paul should've known he wouldn't be allowed to win against this lot.

Planting his feet, Paul faced the man as he approached, calculating the few moves available to him. The Machine placed his great bulk right in front of Paul. He wasn't looking down far on Paul, but slightly. Enough to give him superior leverage.

"Brian said you were a good player," he said quietly.

Paul frowned, thrown off by the shift in energy.

"If you can beat Roy Boy here, you've got balls. How'd you like to fill in on the team until we can find a permanent replacement for Gav?"

"I, er . . ." Paul wasn't sure if this was a legitimate invitation or more of a command performance. Either way it would be hard to refuse, an honor really.

"Well?"

"Yeah, why not. Get me some experience with the League before I start my own team." Paul suspected the Machine was just hoping to pump him for information about the case as it progressed, but he'd told the crew he'd look for a way to find out more about Gavin's darts team, and this was a golden opportunity. One they couldn't waste.

"Right. Saturday lunchtime at the Bell," Jimmy said as they headed for the door. "Welcome to Darty Deeds."

Chapter Twenty-Two

India sat waiting for the others on board the *Wayfarer*, listening to the rhythmic lapping of the water against the sides of the boat. Paul had texted to say the Anchor was off-limits for some reason, so they'd agreed to rendezvous at the Book Boat after closing time. It would be snug with four adults on board, but that wasn't India's main worry—Maeve was. She'd hardly said a word on the way back from the solicitor's office. The unexpected bequest from Gav had floored them both. Maeve knew it made her look even more guilty than she already did, and yet there was nothing she could do about it.

Paul arrived first, ducking in through the hatch, looking out of place amidst the child-sized beanbag chairs and the stuffed characters that decorated the bookshelves lining the boat. India pointed him to the large rocker at the rear that she used when she was reading to the kids and went back to catch the electric kettle. Maeve arrived next, accompanied by the Captain, and already things felt quite tight. Maeve stacked four kids' beanbag chairs into a pile and flopped onto them like a bird in a nest, pulling the Captain onto her lap. She buried her nose in his fur until all India could see was a pair of wide frightened eyes.

"Is Ash coming?" Maeve asked through the fluff.

Paul looked up from his phone. "Said he was, but he might've lost track of time."

They'd almost given up when Ash finally arrived, muttering his apologies as he squeezed into the chair next to India.

"How was the solicitor?" he asked, accepting the mug of tea India handed him.

Maeve sat up a bit, giving India a weary look. "You tell them, please."

"In a word, wild," India said. "The solicitor thought we'd come about Gav's bequest to Maeve."

Paul looked confused. "What bequest?"

"Gav left Maeve his share of the *Revenge* outright," India said, "*and* an insurance policy worth a quarter of a million quid."

Paul and Ash exchanged stunned looks.

"On purpose?" Ash asked, before flushing slightly. "I mean, did he just forget to change the beneficiary after he and Maeve broke up?"

"I suppose that's possible," Maeve said. The thought seemed to cheer her momentarily, but the cloud quickly settled over her features again. "Doesn't really matter either way as far as the police are concerned; it just gives me yet another motive for wanting to get rid of Gav."

Ash took the biscuit India offered him. "Did he always take out insurance?"

Maeve shrugged. "If he did, he never told me."

"Might mean he was doing it now because he knew his life was at risk for some reason," Ash suggested.

A Ghostwriter's Guide to Murder

Paul leaned over and put his empty mug on the nearest shelf. "If he did, he knew more than his friends."

Maeve shifted round to face Paul as he told them about his visit from the crew of Darty Deeds.

"Is that why we're meeting here?" India said. "You're worried they might be watching the pub?"

"Better safe than sorry," Paul replied.

Ash reached for another biscuit. "I didn't know you played darts," he said.

"Used to be pretty good," Paul admitted. "But I don't kid myself they asked me to fill in on the team for my skills. They came because they thought I might know something about who killed Gavin, but clearly they didn't."

"You said they knew I'd been arrested." Maeve frowned. "That means they must have contacts at the cop shop. If they find out about the insurance, they'll be sure I'm guilty. What if they decide to pay *me* a visit? I can't distract them with darts."

"I made sure they knew you were at the police station at the time of the killing," Paul said. "Gives you a clear alibi."

"I know you all seem comfortable with that, but if the police don't believe me, why would Gav's mates? I mean, the last thing I need is some guy named the Machine coming after me." Maeve planted her face in the Captain's fur again. "Three days ago I was living a relatively normal life. Now look at me. My life's a disaster."

India knew Maeve well enough to know that she was reaching the end of her rope. She leaned over and rubbed her back in slow circles. "I know it looks bleak at the moment, but that's because we don't have all the information we need yet. Like Simon at the midpoint of one of your stories. We need to start digging deeper." She looked to the other two for support. "Ash, what did you find out about Malik Ross?"

Ash swallowed the last of his biscuit before answering. "Obviously nothing that proves Foster stole money from him, but Maeve's assessment was spot-on. Ross is a big noise in the commercial real estate game. It took some digging, but I was able to pin him down as the controlling interest in Dawson Construction as well." Ash pulled out a sheet of A4 and rattled it at Maeve, who looked up and took it from him. "Given Ross's ownership interest, it's no surprise that his five most recent development projects have all been overseen by Dawson Construction and Foster's been a subcontractor on three of them, taking on more and more responsibility each time."

"There you go," said India. "That's got to mean something."

Maeve frowned at the notes in her hand. "I see it all on paper, but it doesn't make sense. Gavin's background is dripping sinks and bunged-up khazis. He didn't have the experience to take on plumbing for major commercial construction projects."

"You're not wrong." Ash acknowledged the assessment with a dip of his head. "But based on what I've read, quality was never a major concern for Malik Ross. He's all about the bottom line. He probably started using Foster because he was cheap."

"Now that *is* Gavin—cheap and cheerful," Maeve said.

"In the end I think Ross got a lot more grief than he bargained for," Ash said. "He put Foster in charge of all the plumbing on the Waterfront. A first for him, as far as I can tell." He reached for another biscuit.

"A few months after it opened, all hell broke loose," Ash continued. "Burst pipes and extensive flooding. Significant property

A Ghostwriter's Guide to Murder

damage and bad press. Ross is still making repairs and settling lawsuits."

"That would be a good reason to stop working with Gav, but not to kill him, surely," India said. "You'd get no restitution from a dead man."

"Might explain why Gavin had a quarter-of-a-million-quid insurance policy," Paul said. "Maybe his lawyer told him to get it, working on a project that big."

"But that would be a business policy, not a personal one," Maeve said. "A personal policy is just suspicious." She ran a hand through her hair. "Especially when he left it to me and not Vicky or one of his mates. Add to that the fact that he left the cash right next to the *Revenge*, it's almost as if he wanted me to be a suspect."

Neither Paul nor Ash seemed to know how to address that speculation, but India leaned in. "You think he was after some kind of revenge? *He* was the one that cheated, not you."

"I know it doesn't make sense," Maeve groaned, "but none of it adds up. I suppose I'm just being paranoid now, but it happens when you're being suspected of a murder you didn't commit."

India knew she needed to stop this downward spiral before it got out of control. "All right, let's cut the wild speculation and start looking at practical questions we might have a hope of answering."

The group sat in silence for a few minutes.

"I keep wondering how Gav knew exactly *when* to come back and retrieve his cash," Paul said. "Not like he'd be able to watch the boat twenty-four/seven on the off chance Maeve looked *inside* the dock bumper."

"I'd given that some thought," Ash admitted. "I think he must've had some sort of remote surveillance hooked up."

"You mean he's been watching Maeve?" The cheek of it made India angry. "Pervy little bastard."

"Not watching Maeve *on* the boat, watching the money *from* the boat. I think he may've set up a motion sensor camera and had it pointed at the dock."

"If he was tipped off remotely, then he could've hightailed it over," Maeve said. "I wasn't exactly quick at deciding what to do about the whole situation. He'd have had plenty of time to swoop in and reclaim the cash." Maeve shifted the Captain off her lap. "I'll bet he couldn't believe his luck when he saw me put the money back and head off."

"Obviously he didn't know someone else was watching *him*," India said.

"Sadly, no, but"—India caught a welcome hint of enthusiasm in Maeve's voice—"if he did have a surveillance camera on the boat and he grabbed the cash before he removed it, the camera would've still been recording."

Clever girl. India smiled. "And if we're lucky, we'll have a video of the killer in action."

Chapter Twenty-Three

"An espresso machine?" Paul said. "Quarter of a million quid and you'd buy an espresso machine?"

"A professional one," Ash insisted. "Wouldn't have to go out to the Costa. I could just sit in my own place and whip up a latte whenever I wanted. Simple pleasures, mate."

The gathering on the *Wayfarer* had broken up like someone had set fire to the place, and they were all now hustling along the towpath toward the *Revenge*. Video evidence would solve the crime, clear Maeve's name, and potentially leave her a quarter of a million pounds richer. All very much to be desired in her book. She felt jaunty for the first time in days.

"What would *you* get, then?" Ash directed at Paul.

"Sailboat," he said without hesitation. "A real cruising yacht. All teak and brass."

"Luxury flat for me," India added. "Something bigger than my current shoebox, and with a view."

Maeve didn't join in. She had more than enough on her mind at the moment without trying to decide on her heart's desire. *A book contract?* Simon suggested as they trotted along.

151

Maybe, although she might care a lot less about being published with a quarter of a million pounds in her pocket. The thought made her pick up the pace, and she was the first on board the *Revenge*. She climbed up to the roof and started poking around the various vents and storage spaces that might conceal a camera while Paul and India examined the hull from the towpath.

Ash stopped at the *Red Lion* to retrieve a ball of string, which he tied to what was left of the tire bumper. Once he had it affixed, he jumped onto the *Revenge* and stretched the string to see where the logical line of sight would be. He quickly settled on the roof of the main cabin. It made the most sense, but there wasn't really any place to hide a camera. Toward the bow end of the boat, the roof jutted out slightly, and Ash slipped his hand behind the decorative wood and felt about.

"Might have something here."

India came over and shined the light from her phone into the area. Ash continued poking around until his finger found a rough hole. "There's a place here that's been cut out. Something you did?" he asked, turning to Maeve.

"Not me. I'm not what you call handy."

"From the feel of the wood, it's a relatively fresh cut."

"Can I see?" Maeve asked. Ash stepped aside and let her move in.

"Whatever was there is gone," she said finally.

"I'm sorry." Ash looked almost as disappointed as she felt. "He must've taken the camera off first thing when he came to claim the money."

"That's it, then. No film, no proof." Maeve tried to conceal how devastated she was. She'd thought they'd found an answer.

A Ghostwriter's Guide to Murder

"It wasn't on the body, or the police would've found it, and we didn't find it in the water," Paul said. "The killer must have seen it and taken it with him. Odds are he'll have destroyed it."

"Or she," India said habitually.

"Or she," Paul corrected himself.

Their momentary high had evaporated. "All right, let's not stand around here looking like a bunch of wet cats." Maeve ushered everyone onto the *Revenge* and dug out the good whisky. The one she brought out when she was suffering a monumental case of writer's block. Maybe it would provide inspiration here. It would certainly give her some comfort. She passed around the paper cups she kept for visitors and let everyone help themselves while she fixed food for the Captain.

Paul looked at the bottle appreciatively and poured himself a large helping. "Disappointing outcome, but at least Ash was right. Gavin did hide a camera on board looking toward the dock."

"How did he manage to install a camera without anyone noticing?" India asked. "Ash works nonstop, but Rowan and Sage?"

"The ladies never really met Gavin, and if they saw someone with tools working on the outside of the boat, they'd probably just think it was some kind of repair." Maeve took a drink and looked around the cramped space. "Wish I knew what possessed Gavin to hide the money here." She held up her hand. "Don't worry, I'm not being morose, just practical, like India said. What if the authorities moved the tire for some reason? The cash would be gone. It was very risky."

"You said he had a lockup." Paul reached over to top up his paper cup. "He even bothered to come here and get the key. Makes you wonder why he wasn't keeping the cash there."

153

"Maybe he needed quick access. A storage facility would probably be a fair bit out of town." Ash took a sip of the whisky, looking surprised but pleased by the taste.

"True," Maeve conceded, "but far safer."

The Captain made short work of his kibble and wound his way through the crowd on his turf before settling on top of Maeve's feet. He liked this lot, but it was easier when they were at the pub.

"Maybe the tire was just short-term storage," India suggested. "He could've got the cash recently and stashed it here till he could move it somewhere safer. Could've been trying to hide it from his creditors." India was talking faster in her excitement. "You did say he was sued over the Waterfront, right, Ash?"

Ash nodded.

India's eyes flashed. "What if he was gradually moving all his cash assets into the lockup? Cash he and Vicky were going to take to Spain."

Paul swilled the liquid around in his cup and drank before entering the fray again. "Not sure about hiding assets. There'd be records from the project, and seems like Gav's creditors could still come after him for their money even in Spain."

"I suppose that's true." India looked disappointed.

"We've said it before, the cash Maeve found wasn't legal. Drug money or stolen money, that's still my vote." Paul leaned back and looked at the other three.

"I wasn't convinced at first, but I have to say I agree with Paul now," Maeve said. "Why else would someone murder Gav?"

"So, the real question isn't why was the cash in the tire, but where it came from," Paul concluded. "If we know where it came from, we might be able to figure out who wanted it back badly enough to kill for it."

"Right, then. Who else did Gav know, other than Ross, who might have that kind of money lying around?" Maeve asked the group in general.

"What about the fourth player on the darts team?" India asked. "The Mechanic?"

"The Machine," Paul corrected. "No one seems to know for sure where Toliver's money comes from."

"If Ash's drug squad friend is watching him, then it's not a wild leap to think his earnings are drug related." India reached out for a refill.

"I could see him being in the drugs trade," Paul observed. "The man had that kind of energy when he came into my place. A thug that's used to threatening and being feared. And as we saw, back and forth to the Continent regularly."

"If it is drugs, my friend's the one who can tell us more," Ash said. "He was reluctant to talk before, so I make no promises, but I'll have another go."

"I could revisit Vicky," India volunteered. "I'm convinced she knows more than she's saying. If she and Gav were running away to Spain together, he would've discussed things with her, right? I'm sure I can get her to talk to me. It might take a bit of finessing, but I'm willing to try."

"Worth a go," Ash said.

India turned to Maeve. "Have you ever met Vicky?"

"No. Never wanted to. Why?"

"Then you should come with me. You write witness interviews all the time. You know what you are doing."

"Not sure that's a good idea," Maeve said slowly. "What if the police find out I went to see her—won't they wonder why? Last thing I need is to give them any more reason to be suspicious about me. They've got too many already."

"As you say, they're already suspicious." India hesitated. "Maeve, we don't have the luxury of taking our time on this. We need answers—quickly—and I think you can help me get them."

Ash nodded. "We're at a critical point in this campaign; we can't retreat now. You two should go to Vicky's, Paul goes to practice at the Bell, and I'll see if I can find out more about the Machine."

Clearly, Ash was ready to go on the offensive. India and Paul as well. Maeve shouldn't be the one holding back. "You *really* think Vicky can help?" she asked.

"She can," India said. "I feel it in my bones."

Maeve poured herself some more inspiration. Simon would talk to anyone he thought might have information. *I do whatever it takes* echoed in the back of her mind. He would, and so would she.

Maeve raised her paper cup. "To digging deeper."

Chapter Twenty-Four

The sign on the door of the Ink Spot said *Closed*. Maeve stuck her head into the groomers next door and was greeted by the warm, damp smell of wet dog.

A girl with spiky pink hair stuck her head out from behind the curtain that screened off the back room from the entry area. "Can I help you?"

"We're looking for Vicky next door. Any idea where she is?"

"She doesn't usually open up if she doesn't have appointments. Did you check upstairs?"

"Upstairs?"

"There's a flat above the shop. Entrance's round the back if you wanna try an' knock."

Maeve and India walked to the end of the block and doubled back along the alley. A flight of steep wooden stairs that served as a fire exit led to a small platform outside a scuffed metal door. There was a narrow window in the door, but it was covered over on the inside by a curtain.

157

India knocked and waited. There was no sound from within. "What do we do now?"

"You should go to the coffee shop round the corner and wait for me," Maeve said, turning her friend back toward the steps.

"What are you going to do?"

"Just take a quick look around. I won't be long."

India stood her ground, holding on to the handrail for support. "The door's locked."

"I can deal with that."

India raised an eyebrow but made no move to leave.

"I went to a conference once sponsored by the Mystery Writers Guild. They had a bunch of speakers meant to help you add authenticity to your writing. One of them showed us how to pick locks. I can't do cars yet, but doors, especially old ones like this, are easy."

"Right, then, do your stuff, but I'm coming with you."

"No way," Maeve insisted. "I'm already in trouble and I have precious little to lose at this point, but you ought to keep your nose clean."

"Where's the fun in that?" India insisted.

Maeve was enjoying this new, more assertive India, and she had to admit she'd be glad of some help. "All right. But you're not going in—you can keep watch from out here."

Maeve wriggled the thin metal rod that hung from her key chain in the handle lock until they heard a soft click. She opened the door and stepped inside. India followed her across the threshold. Clearly Maeve possessed no natural authority. India stood behind the half-closed door, looking down toward the alley.

"I'll watch from here," she whispered.

A Ghostwriter's Guide to Murder

They'd entered a combined kitchen/sitting room, where a large tabby cat meowed from the back of a well-worn settee. There was a TV on the low dresser across from the cat and a desk at the far end of the room. Maeve approached the desk and sifted through the bills scattered across the surface—gas, electric, and a credit card. She looked at the statement to see what Vicky was buying. Streaming service, Costa most days, and vet bills for the cat.

The other pile of paper was customer invoices. In the stack she found India's; more expensive than she would have thought. India really was the best. Imagine paying that much for pain just to get information for her. She dug through the rest of the drawers, hoping to find something that looked relevant—a bank statement with a large deposit, directions to the lockup, a note from Gavin confessing his crimes. Unreasonable, but Simon would've found something significant. Sleuthing wasn't as easy as she made it seem on the page.

Turning back to the door, she found India at the kitchen counter stroking the cat. So much for being a lookout. "Come on, let's get out of here before we get caught."

As they started to make their way back down the stairs, India reached back and grabbed Maeve's hand. "It's her."

Maeve squinted at the woman approaching along the alley. She didn't know what she'd expected. Certainly not the petite woman with the short brown hair, no boobs, and a fair bit of padding on the backside. It was shallow, but she felt a tiny flicker of satisfaction.

"Can I 'elp you?" Vicky asked, approaching the bottom of the stairs.

"Hiya," said India. "You did my climbing rose the other day, remember?" She pointed rather unnecessarily to her own arm.

"Course." Vicky's eyes narrowed slightly. "Is there something wrong?"

"No, no, it's lovely. I brought my friend by, and the shop was closed so your neighbor said we should try round back. But obviously you're not here, you're over there." India gave a nervous laugh.

"Right. Well, why don't you go round to the front door, and I'll come let you in."

Vicky ushered them past her into the alley and then headed for her back stairs.

Good thing the cat can't rat you out, Simon whispered.

* * *

Inside the shop, Vicky brought out a book of designs and laid it in front of Maeve. "Take a look at this, and then we can chat. I'll just put the kettle on." She disappeared behind the curtain, and they could hear water running. Several minutes passed before she returned. Maeve noticed there was no mug in her hand.

Vicky stood leaning on the counter in front of her and looked back and forth between the two of them. "Right, let's start with you telling me what you were doing in my flat just now?"

India started to deny, but Vicky cut her off. "Don't even try. I have CCTV at the front and back doors. My man 'ad it installed. Not the best neighborhood 'ere. Girl can't be too careful." Vicky looked pointedly at the two of them.

Maeve knew they were caught. Ash was right, no retreating; it was time to jump in feetfirst. "It was my fault," she said quickly. "I was looking for something of Gav's, and I was impatient. I should've waited but I didn't. Sorry."

"And what gives you the right to break in an' start digging around?"

"It's complicated. Maybe we should start again." Anonymity was all well and good, but Maeve's instinct told her they needed to lay all their cards on the table if they were going to get any help from Vicky. "My name's Maeve Gardner." She could see that the name registered with Vicky immediately.

Vicky looked her up and down, taking in the ripped jeans and the oversized jumper. "Not exactly what I expected," she said, pulling a pack of cigarettes out from under the counter and lighting one. Maeve noticed that the lighter shook ever so slightly.

"Me either," Maeve agreed, catching Vicky's eye and holding it. She wasn't sure how to start this conversation. She could write this exchange for one of her characters, but playing the scene herself was unnerving. For better or worse, she'd have to make it up as she went along.

"So, wot you looking for?" Vicky exhaled puffs of smoke as she spoke like a dragon sending up signals.

"A lockup."

"What lockup?"

"Well, we all knew that Gavin had money stashed away, right," Maeve said. She and India had agreed that they should start by trying to sound like they knew more than they did.

Vicky cocked her head to one side, not breaking eye contact, but she didn't say a word. Maeve tried to gauge whether she was playing along or if she knew there really was money.

"The fifty thousand at the dock was just the tip of the iceberg," Maeve bluffed. "Gav told me there was a lot more in a

Melinda Mullet

lockup he kept. I want to get the money out before the cops do. I have the key. But I don't know the number or the location."

"And you think I do?" Vicky laughed. "If I did, why the 'ell would I tell *you*?"

"I'm willing to make a deal." Maeve ignored the smoke and leaned forward. "Tell me where the storage is, I'll give you a cut of the cash."

Vicky took a deep drag on her cigarette until the tip glowed. "'Ow do you know that Gav didn't 'ave more than one key? I might 'ave the cash already."

Maeve gave that one some thought. "Believe me, if you had that kind of money, you'd be long gone by now." It wouldn't hurt to let Vicky think there was a huge amount of money at stake.

"Why should I trust you?" Vicky demanded.

"Gavin did." Maeve paused for emphasis. "And I know he trusted you. Things may've been different when he was alive, but now he's gone, we're both in the same boat. We gave up a lot in our lives for him. He'd want us to be provided for."

Vicky gave a loud snort. "You never gave up anything for 'im."

It hadn't occurred to Maeve that Gavin might've talked about their relationship with Vicky. For some reason that ran-kled. "You know what men are like. They don't always see what we do for them. I *did* sacrifice for him. More than he knew."

"She really did," India chimed in. "You both gave so much to that man."

Vicky seemed to think about that for a minute. "Never was very good at saying thanks, was 'e."

"No, nor very tidy," Maeve added.

162

A Ghostwriter's Guide to Murder

"God, the socks everywhere. It was like 'e 'ad ten feet, not two." Vicky gave a watery smile. "There's a lot of Gav's things I 'aven't 'ad the 'eart to go through yet. Not sure I want to do it for you, but if I did, what exactly would I be looking for?"

"Receipt from a lockup rental. Should have a unit number on it. Maybe a canceled check to a bank."

Vicky still looked dubious. "All right," she said finally. "Give me a day or two. If I find the paperwork, then maybe we can talk again. I'd want at least 'alf of what's in there, mind."

"That's not happening." Maeve sat back and fixed Vicky with a Simon Hill stare. "I figure Gav slipped you the fifty thousand before he was killed." It was a wild accusation, but Maeve was improvising on the fly. "What makes you think you're entitled to half of the rest?"

"*At least* 'alf. Without the location, your key's not worth shit, so *you* need *me*. As for the fifty thousand, I 'aven't the slightest idea where it is; in fact, from the questions the police 'ave bin askin' me, sounds more like you've got it." Her voice rose sharply. "Maybe you even killed 'im for it."

Maeve continued to look Vicky in the eye, meeting the challenge head on. "I didn't get the money either, and even if I had, I'd never have killed Gavin over it." She thought fleetingly of the things she'd written about him as recently as last week and felt ashamed. "We were finished as a couple, but I'm not heartless. I'd never want to see him dead. He was a good bloke." As she said it, Maeve realized it was true. All she felt now was sadness at the waste of a life.

Vicky's shoulder's sagged as if the weight of being in control had suddenly become too much for her. "It was awful." She shuddered. "They made me identify the body. 'Is poor 'ead."

India leaned over and patted Vicky's hand. Always the comforter. "Must've been dreadful, luv."

Vicky sniffed. "Can't believe anyone who knew 'im could kill 'im. 'E was such a charmer. Why kill 'im? Why?" She looked to Maeve as if she might have an answer to give.

"You've seen more of him over the past few months than I have; if anyone would know, it'd be you," Maeve said softly. Quite unexpectedly she found herself feeling profoundly sad for the brokenhearted woman in front of her. She'd loved Gavin. Maeve's loss paled in comparison. "Was there someone he might've crossed? Someone he'd been worried about?"

"You know 'im, everything's rosy. Always said 'e 'ad a special plan for a rainy day, thought we were golden." Vicky reached for a tissue and wiped her eyes being careful not to smear her liner. "Maybe that's what's in the lockup," she added.

"Where'd he get his rainy-day fund from?" India asked.

"Never said it was money, did 'e, but 'e 'ad something up 'is sleeve."

"Did he ever talk about a bloke named Malik Ross?" Maeve asked.

Vicky shook her head no.

"You said he was looking at retiring to Spain. Was that what the cash was for?" India prompted.

Vicky gave her a sour look. "An' I thought you were so sweet. You were just trying to get information out of me, weren't you?"

"No. Well, not entirely." India looked embarrassed. "I am truly sorry about what happened to Gavin. I knew him and I liked him. We both want to know who killed him, and I know you do too."

A Ghostwriter's Guide to Murder

India's words seemed to strike a chord. Vicky disappeared into the back again and came out with a tray, a kettle, and three mugs with tea bags. "'E always said you were clever. I suppose if anyone can figure out who killed 'im, it would be you."

Gav's vote of confidence threw Maeve. He thought she was clever. It was hard to get her head around.

"I never stuck my nose into the money side of things," Vicky was saying. "That was 'is business." She poured water into each of the cups in turn and handed them round. "Gav never talked much about work. Now I wonder if 'e was just trying to protect me. Coulda thought what I didn't know wouldn't hurt me."

Maeve had to admit that was the kind of thing he'd do. Protecting the little woman. "Do you feel safe?" she asked. It was a loaded question, but the answer could be telling.

"I don't know anythin'—why wouldn't I be?" Vicky looked at her guests as if seeking reassurance. "'E never talked business in front of me. Just darts. Mind you that one bloke, Mac, always made me a bit nervous. They called 'im the Machine. Could be 'cause of the way 'e played darts, but if you ask me, it was something else. When you looked into 'is eyes, there was no emotion. 'E was a real cold bugger."

"What did you know about him?" Maeve asked.

"Less than any of the others. Roy and Jimmy worked with Gav sometimes, but not the Machine."

"Think the Machine could kill someone?" India looked surprised at herself for throwing the question out there.

"Without thinkin' twice, I'd say."

"Could he have killed Gavin?"

Vicky hugged her cup to her chest for warmth. "'E could've, or maybe someone 'e worked with, but God I 'ope not." She looked at the two of them wide-eyed. "'E knows where I live."

Maeve had gone from hating the woman to being genuinely concerned for her safety. Truth was stranger than fiction. Could Vicky really be in danger from the man they called the Machine? And what about Paul? Was he in danger? She felt a slight chill. He was heading into the lion's den with no backup.

Chapter Twenty-Five

"Hands down the best cheese toastie on the planet," Ash insisted.

"I'm not denying it, mate, just a bit pricy for me," Paul said regarding his plate.

"Worth every penny." Ash took another bite and chewed, relishing the crunch and the tang. "Real all-natural British cheddar, topped with onion jam, slipped between two homemade slices of bread and grilled to a crispy perfection." He gave a contented sigh. Friday night was cheese toastie night, and Ash was breaking the pattern for no man.

He'd run into Paul as he was making his way toward Camden Market, and in a rare rush of camaraderie, he'd invited Paul to join him. Toastie night was a usually a solitary event, but Paul was on his team. Paul had even started a tab for him at the Anchor, just like Maeve and India had. Ash was starting to feel like a part of their company now; after all, they were on a quest together.

Paul and Ash sat at the bar counter of the Cheese Shop looking out the window at the market at Camden Lock. To their left was the bronze statue of Amy Winehouse, the community's lasting tribute to the ephemeral spirit of Camden Square. Across the North Yard was an entrance to the warren of market stalls in Saddle Row. In the 1800s, when Camden Lock was the city's major transport hub, these buildings had housed farriers, feed suppliers, and harness makers. With the rise of the railroads and the decline of horse-drawn barges, the old artisans had been made redundant and slowly faded away. In more recent times, the area had been revitalized, the former shops and stables now taken over by a sprawling new food and craft market. Most of the stuff on offer was cheap tat, but a few vintage shops remained with the odd treasure to unearth. Nothing like the antiques in the market at Portobello Road, but the food here was far superior and a rebellious spirit still filled the passageways in spite of the daily tourist infestation.

"Any pointers for going in undercover, as it were, before I hit the dart team practice tomorrow?" Paul asked.

"No." Ash was lost in his own head, and the question had taken him by surprise. His negative response was fierce and emphatic.

Paul looked taken aback. Ash reminded himself that none of his new friends knew about his past, nor would they understand his sensitivity to the undercover remark. It hadn't been a jab on Paul's part, simply an honest request for information.

"Sorry. Undercover work was hardly my area of expertise." Ash tried to smile but suspected it wasn't convincing.

"Just thought they may've talked about it in the general police training." Paul reached for his beer and took a swig.

Ash shook his head.

"What about the Machine? Find out anything I ought to know about him before tomorrow?"

A Ghostwriter's Guide to Murder

"I put out a couple of feelers, but my contact hasn't got back to me." Ash wondered if the Doc had decided he'd already said too much.

Paul nodded. "Disappointing. If there's anything to know, I'd like to know *before* I head to the Bell."

Ash wiped the cheese grease from his fingers and contemplated ordering another. It was tempting, but it was a cholesterol nightmare. He'd best leave it.

The stalls were closing for the night. The square in front of them grew dim as the last of the light in the sky struggled to penetrate between the grimy-looking brick buildings. Glancing over at Paul, Ash noticed he was squinting at the entrance to Saddle Row. All Ash could see was a tall, muscular bloke in a denim jacket hurrying away from them.

"I think I just saw Mac Toliver," Paul said, getting to his feet. "Wait here, I'll be right back."

Ash watched as Paul took off at a fast walk, crossing the cobbled yard and heading after the man they called the Machine. He was at a loss for what to do now, but the sight of Paul disappearing alone into the shuttered market made him nervous. In any campaign it was crucial to have your teammate's back. Ash hesitated for a fraction of a second, then tossed the necessary cash onto the counter before setting off in pursuit.

Paul had picked up his pace, and Ash had to trot to try to keep him in sight. It would be easy to lose him in the dark. At the cut through to the Horse Tunnel Market, Ash paused and looked both ways. There was a flicker of movement at the farthest end of the passage and Ash ran after his squad mate, his feet echoing off the brick ceilings of the narrow passage. Paul paused at the Coach House, and Ash caught him up, panting slightly.

"You didn't need to come," he said.

Ash ignored him. "Which way did he go?"

"I don't know." Paul turned slowly in a circle. "I think I've lost him."

The two made their way along Paddock Lane and then through the lower stables, looking for signs of life, before turning back up Haybarn Lane. At the far end, Ash caught a glimpse of the man in the denim jacket again. He watched as the Machine looked to the left, then shot off down the passage to the right, quickly pursued by two men in hoodies and trainers. Ash hung back, unsure of his next move. But Paul rushed after them without hesitation.

The crowds had thinned now, concentrated in the food halls in the West Yard, and the market itself was eerily quiet. At the end of the right-hand lane they could hear raised voices. The metal roll-top door of the last stall on the left was raised a couple of feet off the ground—enough to allow a grown man to duck under.

"Keep out of sight," Paul whispered, stepping into an alcove reserved for the fire department connection and pulling Ash in beside him.

Ash froze. Outside the world of video games, he was not a man of action. His breath came in shallow gulps. The blood rushed from his head, he felt dizzy, and his fingers tingled. He tried to focus on the breathing pattern the police therapist had taught him. In for five, hold for five, out for five, rest for five.

"I'm going to take a look," Paul whispered. Ash wanted to call him back, wanted to help, but he couldn't get the air. He watched as Paul crouched down and peered under the door at the men inside. To Ash's relief, Paul quickly scampered back to join him in hiding.

A Ghostwriter's Guide to Murder

"Three men. One of them is Mac Toliver. He's outnumbered, but if I step in now, I'll tip my hand."

Ash nodded. "Did you catch what they're saying?"

"Not really."

Paul edged forward again to get a better vantage point. Ash felt ashamed. So much for being a ninja. Paul was ready to jump into the fray, but he was panicking and hiding like a coward. He straightened his shoulders and forced himself to move up next to Paul.

"You've been talkin' to the cops." The voice was South London and nasal. Not forceful enough for the Machine.

"One of my best mates was found dead in the canal." A deeper voice this time. "Course I'm talkin' to the coppers. I want to know who killed him."

That had to be the Machine.

"Rumor goin' round it was you," South London said.

The Machine made a snorting noise. "There's always rumors flyin' around. Wasn't me. Never would be."

Ash heard a scuffling noise, then, "Take it easy." South London was sounding a bit less cocky now. "Don't mess with the messengers."

"If you've got a message, pass it on and get out," the Machine growled.

"Boss is worried you're runnin' a side gig. You keep getting' yourself in trouble, he'll drop you hard and you don't want that, do you? Osami's a bad enemy to have."

"If the boss is worried, he can talk to me himself."

"He'll be wantin' some proof you wasn't involved," the third man in the room chimed in. Ash knew that was foolish.

"I was tendin' to me own business," the Machine snarled. "You should tend to yours."

The sound of a fist hitting flesh was followed by scuffling noises, and in spite of being outnumbered, the Machine seemed to have the upper hand. He was still talking, at least. "You tell the boss I have witnesses. Me and Malik were out at the new site by the river. Meetin' with two idiots from the zoning board. Neither of us were anywhere near that canal when my mate went in."

His proclamation was met with silence.

The thumping noises continued for a few more minutes before the Machine ducked out from under the metal door.

Ash and Paul flattened themselves against the wall and breathed a sigh of relief as the Machine sauntered away in the direction of the North Yard without looking their way.

Once they were sure they were alone, Paul and Ash crept to the stall entrance and peered underneath. The two hooded men were lying sprawled out across several stacks of vintage T-shirts, looking more than a bit worse for the wear. Both had blood trickling from their noses, but they were moving. Not dead, but they'd be angry when they made it to their feet.

Paul raised a finger to his lips and dragged Ash away down the dim passage at a determined pace.

"Where are we going?" Ash whispered.

"I need a drink," Paul said. "And this is a night for Dingwalls—blood and beer. That's right up their alley."

It was dark when they emerged from shadow of the market. Paul led them past the back side of the West Yard kitchens and along to the edge of the canal. They slipped in under the low-beamed ceilings of the Lock 17 waterside bar. To the locals it would always be Dingwalls, breeding ground of the punk revolution in the late seventies—all petty violence and counterculture heroes. The music of the Clash and the Sex Pistols still echoed from the walls.

Ash slid into one of the dark-blue pleather booths facing out onto the water, and Paul headed to the bar to get the drinks order in. He came back balancing four pints. Ash looked around for others but saw no one.

"Service can be slow," Paul explained, placing two pints in front of each of them. He took a long drink before looking across the table at Ash. "Sounds like Toliver isn't our killer."

"If he's telling the truth," Ash pointed out.

"Easy enough to check," Paul conceded. "More importantly, it seems he's working for two masters. Never a good move."

"I know of the bloke they mentioned—Osami. Lord of the local drug scene. Definitely not a good one to anger."

Ash attempted to keep pace with Paul on the beer front, but he was starting to feel rather overwhelmed.

"Do we think Foster was connected to the Osami lot?" Paul asked.

"Maybe, but since Osami's thugs didn't seem to know who killed Foster or why, I'd guess not."

"Can your former police colleague tell us more?"

"He could, but only if he's willing to trust me. I sent a message but haven't heard back. I really didn't keep in touch with any of the crew at Camden Road when I left," Ash said. "Just the one bloke, and we hardly worked together. We just gamed together. Still do."

"Has he had anything to say about Gav's death?"

"Like I said, we never talk shop. We just game. That's the only reason I still have any contact with him. It's . . . complicated."

173

Paul drained his second pint and waved to the bartender for another round.

Ash hadn't drunk this much in ages. No work would be done tonight, that was for sure.

"You've never told us why you left the Met," Paul observed.

Here it came. Ash wanted to leave. To run away. Maybe get another cheese toastie; something to soak up all the beer swishing around in his innards. He fidgeted with the beer mat in front of him. He was trapped in the booth with Paul looking across at him. Suddenly the focus of attention, a position he hated. But from the look on Paul's face and the two new beers in front of them, they weren't going anywhere soon, and Paul was expecting an answer of some sort.

"Screwed up an undercover job," Ash mumbled finally, studying the foam on the top of his beer intently. There. He'd said it.

"Really? You're all about the details. That doesn't seem likely."

"Wasn't up to the job." Ash continued fiddling with the beer mat.

"Come on, Ash. What happened? Sounds like a real adventure."

Ash looked down at the table. He didn't want to tell the story, didn't want to fall in Paul's estimation, but the story would come out eventually. Telling his own version was probably the lesser of the two evils. He took a deep, steadying breath.

"CID was seconded to help with a case for the Drug Squad," he began slowly. "I was sent in posing as a computer specialist in a money-laundering operation."

A Ghostwriter's Guide to Murder

"Shouldn't have had any trouble convincing folks of that," Paul said.

"I was convincing enough at first, but then things started to go sideways. Someone figured out I wasn't who I said I was, and the next thing you know the guns came out and people started shooting." He tried to sound casual, but he knew it wasn't ringing true.

"So, your leg, not a bike accident, I'm guessing?" Paul said.

Ash nodded. "Suppose I was lucky. The bullet went in above the knee. Tore things up in there, but at least I came out alive. Two other agents weren't so lucky."

"Why'd you lie about your injury?"

"Wasn't the proudest moment of my life. Still don't know how, but I must've tipped my hand, and because of that people died." *Game over.*

"Sounds like it might have been a bit more complicated than that," Paul observed. "Was it a big operation?"

"I suppose so, yes."

"Then there must've been any number of places where the mission could've been compromised."

"Didn't feel that way at the time," Ash muttered, plowing through his beer in hopes of shoring up his plummeting self-esteem. "By the time I got back from medical leave, I was the butt of every joke in the office." He realized he was starting to slur his words. "Wa'n' worth stayin' in the end, was it? I left and good riddance." Ash crossed his arms defiantly. "That's ancient history now. Me and the *King of the Red Lions* are all the team I need."

"Well, you've got me and Maeve and India on your team too, like it or not," Paul said. "We're your friends—flesh-and-blood friends, not virtual ones." Paul raised his glass. "To friends."

Melinda Mullet

Ash joined the toast. Even in his increasingly bleary state, he realized how good it felt to have friends again. He did his best to finish the last of his beer, but his eyes were drooping and he felt he might just fall asleep in the corner of the booth.

"Come on, mate," Paul said. "Looks like it's time to get you home to bed."

"A quest for rest," Ash giggled. Why had he giggled? He never giggled. Paul must be right: It was time to call it a night.

176

Chapter Twenty-Six

India stood out in the cold with Maeve, waiting for the guys to arrive. Paul's voice down the phone suggested that something was up with Ash, but he hadn't elaborated. Maeve's lock picking skills probably could've let them in, but it seemed an invasion of Ash's privacy, so they chose to wait with the Captain sitting on the side of the *Revenge*.

They'd almost given up when they finally saw the lads coming from the direction of the Saint Pancras Bridge. Paul was moving slowly to keep pace with Ash, who was weaving down the towpath singing a tone-deaf version of "Love Hurts." Paul took his key off him as they approached and let them all into the *Red Lion*. India had thought Ash might resist, but he looked as if he was well past caring.

"Hello, girls." Ash bestowed a fuzzy smile on the two.

"What've you done to him?" India demanded.

"Long story," Paul said. "First, we need tea."

On board the tech-laden boat, India set to rummaging in the cupboards, looking for tea bags. She found some that were out of date. *Out of date*—who kept tea bags that long? She finally

177

Melinda Mullet

found some fresher ones in the bread box and made them each a cup of tea.

Paul settled Ash in the bright-orange gaming chair next to his keyboard, his head leaning against the wall behind him. Maeve perched on a box labeled *Games* while Paul gave them the abbreviated version of the evening. India was certain he was leaving something out, something about Ash, but she didn't push.

"Long and short of it, looks like Toliver has an alibi for the time of Gavin Foster's death," Paul concluded.

"But he *is* involved with the drugs trade," Maeve said, "and he was close friends with Gavin. He says he knew nothing about the money, but he could be lying. What if it was his and Gavin was hiding it for him?"

"Or Gavin could've simply stolen the money from the Machine," India said, handing round the mugs of tea. "From what you've said, the Machine doesn't seem like a man that would tolerate that sort of thing. He may not have killed Gavin, but he could've sent someone to do it for him."

Paul ran a hand through his hair. "Seeing him in action tonight, I'll admit Mac the Machine Toliver has a dark side, but from what I've heard, Toliver the darts player has been like a big brother to the members of his team. I can't really see him having one of his best mates killed."

Ash picked up his tea and eyed it for a moment before rising and staggering out the door to the stern. The sound of retching carried in on the breeze.

Paul raised his voice to be heard. "What did you get from Vicky?"

"More willing to talk than I would've been," Maeve said.

A Ghostwriter's Guide to Murder

"She was a bit edgier with you around," India observed. "But I believed her when she said she doesn't know who killed Gavin and doesn't know where the money is. Not only that, when we talked about the Machine, she seemed genuinely frightened."

"I agree," Maeve said. "I think she's in over her head, but she didn't look surprised when we told her there was money hidden elsewhere. I'll lay odds she's still not telling the whole truth. She admitted Gav told her he had something put by for a rainy day."

Paul frowned. "More money, you think?'

"Nothing more useful for a rainy day," India observed.

Ash returned, looking pale. India reached for his cup and added a couple of spoons of sugar before returning it. "But it wouldn't have to be money he's storing away," she continued. "It could be information, right? Something that he could use to blackmail someone. Based on the folks he's been hanging around with, that would be smart. But it would also give more people a motive for wanting to kill him."

"Sounds like finding his lockup should be the priority." Paul said.

"Agreed." Maeve glanced over at Ash.

India saw he'd downed his tea and was now leaning against the wall, snoring softly.

"I think Vicky can help us with the lockup. Whether she knows it or not, Gav must have some record. Maybe at your old flat."

"I'm not going back to the flat. That's a bridge too far," Maeve replied, moving to put her mug in the sink.

"No need," India said. "I'll keep on her. Make sure she's looking."

Melinda Mullet

India put an empty plastic bin next to Ash and covered him with a rug. He called her their healer. Initially she was a bit offended, another mum role, but the more she thought about it the more she liked the idea. He'd definitely need a spot of healing in the morning.

She turned back to the others. "He'll be fine, but we should all get some sleep. My gut tells me things are going to get worse before they get better."

Chapter Twenty-Seven

Maeve knew India was right about things getting worse, and she'd been waiting for the other shoe to drop since they left Gavin's solicitor. Two hundred and fifty thousand pounds was just too much motive for the police to ignore once they were aware of it, and sure enough she woke in the morning to the sound of a loud knocking on the roof of the *Revenge*. The Captain began barking and running in circles. She pushed him back inside as she made her way out on deck in a T-shirt and a pair of flannel joggers.

Two uniformed officers stood on either side of DC Gray, and farther back along the path, DS Dixon was leaning against a retaining wall, smoking a cigarette. Almost as if he were trying to distance himself from the operation unfolding around him.

Gray looked up at her from the towpath. "Maeve Gardner, I'm arresting you for the murder of Gavin Foster."

An eerie sense of déjà vu flooded over her as Gray plowed ahead with the usual warnings. "Can I at least change out of my pajamas?" she demanded.

Gray looked unsure.

"Where am I going to go?" Maeve growled. "It's a boat, for Christ's sake."

"All right, make it quick," Gray conceded.

Back on the *Revenge*, she grabbed her mobile and texted Ash. He'd be feeling rough this morning, but she knew she could count on him. *I've been arrested . . . again.* She considered adding an emoji, but which one? Fear, anger, exasperation? She couldn't decide which was leading the swirling parade of emotions in her head, so she left it. *There's a key under the potted geranium on the port side. Can you please come and take care of the Captain? I'm leaving him here. He hates Rowan's cooking and I trust you to look after him.* She sent the message, then added *Let him bring his stuffed dragon. It comforts him.*

Her hands shook as she moved to get changed. The first time had been bad enough, but something inside told her this time she wouldn't be allowed to walk away. This time she was really facing down a charge of murder.

* * *

At the station she was allowed a call, and she reached out to Julian. If his enthusiasm previously was anything to go by, getting his attention might be tricky, but he picked up immediately.

"Have you been charged or merely taken in for questioning?"

"Charged."

"I'm on my way."

* * *

To his credit, Julian was prompt and much more engaged this time, and she felt comforted as he sat by her side facing off against DS Dixon and DC Gray.

A Ghostwriter's Guide to Murder

"You recently paid a visit to the offices of Hutton, Wallace & Stoat. Can you tell me why?" Gray asked.

"Whatever the reason, it would be covered by attorney-client privilege, which DS Dixon knows full well even if you don't," Julian replied before Maeve had a chance to open her mouth.

Dixon conceded the rebuke with a faint nod of the head. "Were you aware that Gavin Foster made you the beneficiary of a life insurance policy in the amount of two hundred fifty thousand pounds?" he asked.

Maeve looked at Julian and got an encouraging bob of the head. "Not until two days ago," she replied.

"Why do you think he made you his beneficiary?" Dixon continued.

Maeve shrugged. "We were in a long-term relationship."

"Were," Dixon stressed, "but not now."

"True." Maeve didn't need Julian to tell her that she couldn't be asked to speculate; she'd picked up that much writing Simon.

Dixon referred to the notes in front of him. "Foster's partner at the time of his death was a woman named Vicky Shaw."

Maeve said nothing, fervently hoping that the police weren't aware of her visit to Vicky's the day before.

"In fact, Foster changed the beneficiary on his insurance policy a couple of weeks before he died to Vicky Shaw."

"Then she gets the money," Julian responded. "The insurance policy has nothing to do with my client, and this line of questioning is just digging for dirt."

"The change was made effective on the first day of October," Dixon said quietly.

Maeve felt the bottom drop out of her stomach.

183

"Gavin Foster was killed on the thirtieth of September," Dixon continued. "Seems rather convenient, doesn't it?"

Yet another nail in what Maeve was now envisioning as her coffin.

"Courts don't lay much stock by convenience." Julian was impassive. "Do you have proof that my client knew about the policy, and more significantly that she knew the policy was changing at the end of the month?"

"Can your client prove she didn't know?" DC Gray shot out.

Dixon raised a hand slightly in Gray's direction. She must know that wasn't the standard of proof, or she should. Even Maeve knew that—again, thanks to Simon.

"We have your client's prints on the murder weapon. We have fifty thousand in missing cash, an insurance policy issued in her name that would've gone to someone else the following day, and a collection of lurid descriptions of the man's demise on Ms. Gardner's computer. That's motive, opportunity, and a very vivid portrait of her state of mind." Gray looked smug.

"Those were nothing more than private ramblings," Maeve began, but stopped at Julian's soft shake of the head. She knew he was right. They wouldn't believe her, and in this case, probably the least said the best. Dixon hadn't raised the issue, only Gray. Maybe he accepted the dark prose for what it was: a simple catharsis penned by a jilted lover.

At this point Dixon stepped in, removing the file folder from in front of Gray and taking charge. "Let's go through the morning of Foster's death one more time."

Maeve looked for Julian's approval, and he nodded, so she began once more.

A Ghostwriter's Guide to Murder

It was like reliving a bad dream. The two-hour run-up to Little Venice and back, finding the money, debating what to do with it, putting it back, going to the police, and coming back to find the disaster that had brought them to this juncture.

"You have my client's fingerprints on her own steering pole that she used that morning by her own admission. Beyond that you have no witnesses to this alleged crime. You are presenting no CCTV footage to suggest that my client did anything other than what she suggested on the morning in question."

"The cameras were damaged," Gray said sulkily.

"She came to the police to report finding the money," Julian insisted.

"Not very quickly," Dixon noted.

"I wasn't aware that there was a statutory time frame with respect to discovering and reporting found money." Julian ignored Gray and focused on Dixon.

"She wrote about decapitating the victim and placing his head on a pike on the College Street bridge," Gray fumed, refusing to be cut out.

"We're convicted based on what we do, not what we think." Julian's tone was icy, and Maeve had a childish desire to add *snap* to the end of his sentence, but she kept her mouth shut. "I'll be petitioning to have her released immediately."

Dixon nodded. "Be my guest."

Maeve felt sure she wouldn't be leaving here anytime soon, but at least her lamb of a lawyer was proving to be quite the lion.

Chapter Twenty-Eight

After the adventures of the night before and hearing Ash's undercover nightmare, Paul was feeling more than a bit edgy about joining the darts team, but when he entered the Bell, Jimmy and Roy Boy were there alone, enjoying a pint. Paul ordered at the bar before coming across and settling in the corner with his new teammates.

"Where's Toliver?" he asked, not really comfortable referring to the man as the Machine and uncertain whether that was a privilege extended only to friends.

"'Ad some business," Jimmy said. "'E'll be 'ere soon."

Based on what he and Ash had seen and heard last night, his business could be all sorts, but as Paul was here to find out more about Toliver's relationship with Gavin, his absence was a plus.

"Right, cheers," he said, raising his glass to the other two. Best to start on relatively neutral ground. "How long've you guys bin playin' as a team?"

"Since we was in school," Roy said. "It's always been the four of us. Good times an' bad."

"Gav's death is definitely the bad," Paul observed.

A Ghostwriter's Guide to Murder

"Aye, but Mac'll look after us," Roy said. "Like always."

Jimmy smiled. "That's right, Roy Boy. 'E will."

"When we was in school, there was two types of blokes," Roy said earnestly. "Those that was Mac's friends and those that wasn't. Three of us weren't daft—we made friends with the top dog. Mac's proper loyal to 'is mates, and 'e's always done right by us."

"That 'e 'as," Jimmy agreed. "You always want the Machine on your team, don't you, Roy." He drained the rest of his drink and held up the now-empty glass. "Why don't you go get us another round before we get started. Put it on my tab."

Roy wandered off happily in the direction of the bar, and Jimmy turned back to Paul. Paul sensed Jimmy was trying to get rid of his friend for some reason.

Jimmy rubbed the back of his neck with his hand as if it pained him. "Couple of things you should know before we get goin' 'ere. Family business, if ya like, but as you're joinin' the crew, even for a short spell, 's worth mentioning." He paused as if searching for the right words. "Roy's a good lad, but 'e's the odd sarnie short of a picnic. 'Ad a rough go of it as a kid. 'Is Dad was a right bastard. 'E'd beat the 'oly 'ell out of Roy just for the sport of it. Left a mark— inside and out. Roy took off from 'ome at fourteen and never went back. We've bin 'is family since, and we look after our own."

Paul had seen that rough life in Roy's eyes from the first. Poor kid. "He's a brilliant darts player," Paul observed. "That's enough for me."

Jimmy nodded. "Second thing. Maybe I shouldn't say, but"—he looked toward the door before continuing—"Mac's proper cut up by this business with Gav. Never seen 'im like it before. 'E's always bin protective of us and 'e's convinced 'e failed

187

Gav somehow. It's really got under 'is skin and 'e's bin in a bit of a mood lately, so mind your step."

Paul didn't need to be told twice. He wasn't about to rattle the cage of a man called the Machine. "Gavin's a grown man," he said finally. "Not like anyone could've watched over him all the time."

"I've said as much, but guilt's a powerful thing."

Was Maeve right—did Toliver have Gav hiding money for him? Had he been caught in some kind of cross fire? It might explain Toliver's guilt, Paul thought. "And he really has no idea why Gavin was killed?" As long as it was just him and Jimmy, it was worth a direct question.

"None. And even less idea where the bloody money came from. It's a mystery, but we try not to upset Roy by talkin' about it too much."

"I understand." Jimmy might not know where the money came from, but did Toliver? Paul glanced sideways at his companion. Was Jimmy just trying to get him to stop asking questions? He was generally good at the subtle signals that emanated off people. You saw the full range of human emotion in the confined spaces of a ship out on float. He'd developed a knack for telling who was stressed, who was lying, and who was reaching the breaking point. The subtle cues of hands and eyes and shoulders that told the story.

Jimmy was a man resigned to his fate. His shoulders drooped, and his gray eyes showed little or no animation. In the grand scheme of things, he was a man defeated by life, but his concern for his friends seemed genuine, and Paul sensed he was being truthful. Further conversation was cut off by the return of Roy and the drinks.

A Ghostwriter's Guide to Murder

Paul caught Jimmy's eye to show he was cooperating and switched to a safer subject. "I hear everyone on the team works for Dawson Construction?"

"Well, Jimmy and me do," Roy said. "Mac got us jobs there. 'E knows one of the top guys from somethin'. Not that me an' Jimmy got much in the way of skills, mind, but we pick things up along the way and we get by."

"Jack of all, master of none," Jimmy agreed.

"And Gav worked for Dawson too?"

"Sure, but Gav was different. 'E 'ad 'is own business." Jimmy sounded proud. "Got licensed as a plumber an' all. Worked for 'imself for a bit, then 'e started subcontractin' for Dawson. They put a lot of work 'is way 'e wouldn't 'ave bin able to get otherwise. That was down to Mac too."

Paul was struck by the fact that all three men seemed to owe Toliver a lot. It would give him power over them. Was he abusing it, or was he the protector Jimmy would have Paul believe?

"What about you," Jimmy asked. "'Ow long you 'ad the Anchor?"

"'Bout five years now. Got it at a bargain. It was in pretty rough shape when I took it over."

"And before that?"

Paul hesitated. You couldn't ask questions if you weren't willing to answer them. "Navy diver for nearly ten years," he admitted. "Repair and rescue."

Roy's eyes grew wide. "'Ow deep d'ya go?"

"Hundred fifty feet's usually the max."

"See sharks?" Roy asked.

"All the time." Paul sensed he'd gone up in the lad's estimation.

"Takes bollocks that," Jimmy said, tilting his glass toward Paul.

"What does?" Toliver's deep voice rumbled behind them as he approached the table.

"Diving with sharks," Roy said with a grin.

"Very James Bond," Toliver agreed. "Remember the movie with the bloke they exploded in a decompression tank. Ever seen somethin' like that?"

"Can't say I have." Paul tried to remain open and friendly, but face-to-face he couldn't help seeing the man in a different light. A harsher light.

Toliver sat down next to Paul as Jimmy went off to get him a beer. He came straight to the point. "Heard anythin' new from the cops about Gav?"

"They still don't have the killer, and honestly, they don't seem to know their arse from a hole in the ground." Paul decided to try again. "I've said it before and I'll say it again, you probably have a better idea of who might want to kill him than they do."

"Well, things went tits up with some bad pipes," Roy began, but he was cut off by a side-eye from Toliver. Seemed the Waterfront wasn't a subject for public discussion.

Toliver took his pint from Jimmy as he returned and moved toward the dart boards, indicating it was time to begin. "We'll find out who killed Gav," he said over his shoulder. "And when we do, they'll wish they'd never been born."

As they played, Paul studied Toliver. There was a confidence to him, a swagger that glossed over any physical cues he might offer, but in Paul's experience the one thing you couldn't hide was your eyes. Paul was reluctant to make eye contact with the man for too long. Like facing down a vicious dog, he didn't want

A Ghostwriter's Guide to Murder

to appear challenging in any way, but in Toliver's eyes he saw anger and a lot of it. Anger at the loss of a friend, or a simmering rage that boiled over into violence? It was hard to tell. Like Jekyll and Hyde, Toliver was two different men. One beating the lackey of his drug lord boss in a show of power, the other a protective brother to his childhood friends. Which one had Gavin seen last?

Toliver demanded precision from his teammates, but as he coached Jimmy and Roy on the finer elements of his strategy, he showed patience and an unexpected kindness. He was less familiar with Paul but equally considerate in his instruction. Paul held his own, even learned a trick or two, and thought he was well in, but as he was leaving Toliver put out a hand to stop him.

"You did well, and you're almost a full member of the Darty Deeds now."

"Almost?" Paul was suddenly wary again.

"We need a bit of help moving some furniture tonight. Easy stuff, just wants a bit more brawn."

Paul hesitated. He knew he should make an excuse to avoid what he suspected would be a highly questionable outing. Joining the darts crew after hours was probably reckless, but if he was going to figure out the puzzle that was Mac Toliver, he needed to commit. "I'm not all that brawny, but I can try," he said.

Toliver hardly registered the remark. It seemed his invitation had been more along the lines of a command than a question.

"Meet me and the boys after closing time tonight. Jimmy'll send you the address."

191

Chapter Twenty-Nine

Ash found himself engaging in a very unprofessional level of panic.

He'd woken after midday to a pounding head and a nauseous stomach. Good thing he'd checked his texts right away and gone to retrieve the Captain. The problem was he had no experience with dogs at all. He'd Googled what dogs can and cannot eat: no pizza, no grapes, no raisins, no chocolate, no onions, no garlic. Living as he did on a steady diet of pizza, tea, coffee, and biscuits, chocolate and otherwise, this could be a problem.

His guest was now sitting on a pile of old tech journals by the port hatch, a stuffed dragon at his feet, looking forlorn. Ash hadn't found where Maeve kept the dog food, and he felt uncomfortable digging around in her things. Searching through his cabinets, he found a couple of tins of chicken he kept on hand for emergencies. Amazingly, they were still in date. That would be a start at least until he could get to the shops.

Ash scraped both tins into a cereal bowl, and the Captain wolfed it down without stopping to breathe. He looked happier having been fed and padded over to rest his head on Ash's lap. Ash reached down and stroked the silky fur of his ears, finding

A Ghostwriter's Guide to Murder

the warm, steady presence reassuring. Maybe he should try talking to the Captain instead of the *Red Lion*. No better chance of an answer, but at least he wouldn't look quite so daft.

"You like dragons, do you? I do too." Ash picked up the rust-colored toy. "What's he called? Smaug, maybe? I like Smaug."

The Captain's only response was a heavy sigh.

"I know how you feel, mate. I miss her too."

Ash wondered what Maeve was doing. Getting a lousy meal and feeling alone, he suspected. He shifted in his chair and leaned down to stroke the thick fur along the Captain's back but felt him stiffen and begin to growl deep in his throat. Ash's first thought was that he'd done something wrong—already—but the Captain rose and made his way to the stern, his hackles standing on end as he stood with his paws on the rear steps looking toward the *Revenge*. Ash leaned over him and peered out the rear hatch toward the neighboring anchorage. There was a man stepping onto the boat and inspecting the roofline.

Ash hesitated. Was it one of Toliver's people? Was it the killer? *Don't be stupid,* he chided himself. Why would the killer return to the scene of the crime? *Someone's just being nosy.* Press, maybe. He made his way up the aft steps, glad that his new canine companion was sticking to his side. The Captain was a cream puff, but his growl sounded vicious and his fifty-pound body weight was intimidating if you didn't know him.

"Can I help you?" Ash called from the towpath.

The man turned toward him but didn't look fazed. He reached into his jacket pocket and pulled out a warrant card. "DS Dixon," he said. "You Ashley Warren?"

Ash would have preferred not to answer, but he knew it would only forestall the inevitable. "Yes."

193

Melinda Mullet

"Got a minute to answer a few questions?"

Ash inhaled deeply. "I gave a statement to your men already." The Captain moved to stand in front of him. A protective gesture, it seemed, but he'd stopped growling and was simply regarding Dixon curiously. Dogs were reputed to be good judges of character. Ash exhaled and unclenched his fists.

"We appreciate your help, but I have a few questions of my own." Dixon stepped off the *Revenge*, and Ash reluctantly gestured toward his own boat.

They seated themselves in the two deck chairs at the bow of the *Red Lion*. Ash chose the chair closest to the galley entrance. In any battle, you should always know your closest point of retreat. The Captain settled at his feet, watching their visitor.

Dixon pulled out a notepad. "According to your statement, you were here on board the morning of the murder." He looked up to confirm Ash's nod. "The *Revenge* is less than ten feet off your stern, yet you heard nothing?"

"I told your PC, I wear noise-canceling headphones when I'm working. Helps me concentrate."

"And you didn't see or speak to your neighbor at all that morning?"

"No." Dixon didn't break eye contact. He clearly wanted more. "I heard Maeve take the boat out around half nine. The noise woke me up."

"You always work from home?" Dixon asked.

"Most of the time."

"And you don't keep regular hours?"

"They're regular for me," Ash said.

"Still in bed at half nine on a weekday?" Dixon looked at him with a raised eyebrow.

194

A Ghostwriter's Guide to Murder

"No law against that, but as it happens, in my line of work there's no such thing as weekdays or weekends. I work when I need to. A lot of things I do, I do in the middle of the night when businesses are closed—upgrading, running scans—all easier when there is less traffic."

Dixon nodded, seeming to accept the rationale. "How well do you know Maeve Gardner?"

"Well enough to know that she's always been a quiet, respectful neighbor, and for the record I don't think for one minute she killed Gavin Foster."

Dixon looked out at the sunlight shimmering on the surface of the water as two ducks drifted by, enjoying a lazy Saturday swim. "It's very peaceful here," he remarked.

Ash had no response for that, and they sat in silence for several minutes.

"I'm inclined to agree with you," Dixon said finally, folding up his notebook and putting it back in his pocket. "About Maeve Gardner, that is."

Ash leaned forward. *Could this be the break they needed?* "Then why've you arrested her?" he demanded.

"You were with the Met." Dixon tapped his fingers on the arms of his chair. "Won't come as news to you that there's a lot of politics involved."

"Are you saying her arrest was politically motivated?"

"Nothing quite that unscrupulous, I hope, but I will say management's keen to see cases cleared up quickly, and when an obvious answer presents itself, there's a lot of incentive to run with it."

The Doc had been right about the politics, and if he was right about the pressures from above, CID would be an extremely stressful place to work. Ash didn't envy Dixon having to deal with DSI Bolton every day. Then again, if Dixon was unhappy enough, he might be open to sharing. Ash decided it was worth a try. He rose and went belowdecks, returning with some beers. He handed one to Dixon, who hesitated only fractionally before saying, "Thanks."

Ash opened his beer, ignoring the roiling in his stomach, determined to nurse the drink this time. "You seem like the kind of man who isn't happy with the obvious answer," he prompted.

"Maybe I've just been on the force too long," Dixon replied, "but somehow this all seems a bit too convenient to me."

"How does the rest of your team feel?"

Dixon gave a soft snort. "My 'team' is one young woman keen for promotion and anxious to please our masters. She's raised arse kissing to an art form, just not mine."

"At least you're taking this seriously." Ash was glad, but he was also wary. He knew this visit could be a trap designed to get him to open up. He'd need a bit more from Dixon before he could believe him, let alone trust him. Ash rested his hand on the Captain's side as he lay by his chair and felt the easy rise and fall of his chest. He wasn't concerned, and that made Ash fractionally more at ease.

Dixon continued to look out across the water. "Can I ask you a personal question?"

Ash took a sip of his beer before responding. "You can ask, but I may not answer."

"Your skills in the tech forensics department are legend."

Ash stiffened. Clearly he remained the butt of jokes if he was still being discussed around Camden Road.

"I'm guessing you tapped into the database and had a look at Gavin Foster's sheet," Dixon continued. "I'm not complaining, mind. I know it would be easy for you to get ahold of. What I want to know is did you notice anything odd?"

Ash was glad he wasn't being asked to take another trip down memory lane. "He seems to be a legit businessman now," he noted. "Has quite a slick brief. Brought in for questioning a couple of times, but he's been Mr. Teflon."

"True enough," Dixon agreed. "He was questioned on stabbing and extortion charges recently. You know what those two events have in common?"

Ash shook his head.

"Bloke named Mac Toliver. Foster's nearby when these things go down but claims to have nothing to do with anything. Next thing you know, Toliver's lawyers swoop in and pull him out."

Toliver's lawyers, Ash noted, not Malik Ross's. He wondered how much Dixon knew about Toliver's real boss. "How can Toliver afford a solicitor like that?" he prompted.

"He runs with some big dogs. They have power and connections everywhere."

"What kind of big dogs? Drugs?"

"Seems so, and Toliver's the top man's driver and bodyguard."

"He's a gun for hire?"

"Haven't seen any evidence that he's an enforcer. More protection."

"Is Toliver transiting drugs? He's back and forth to the Continent a lot."

"Team's been stopped at the border several times coming back from tournaments, but nothing."

Dixon was being forthcoming. Ash felt he should return the favor. "From what I've heard, Toliver didn't kill Foster."

"How do you know?"

"Can't say, but I've heard he was at a meeting with Malik Ross and a couple of members of the zoning board at the time. Might be worth confirming."

"Good to know, thanks." Dixon took a drink of his beer and went back to watching the ducks. "Things have changed a lot since you left Camden Road."

"They needed to," Ash replied.

"For the worse, not the better, I'm afraid. It's not just the slick lawyers. That's galling enough, but between you and me, we have bigger problems—witnesses that suddenly refuse to talk, evidence that conveniently goes missing from the custody locker."

"You think you've got problems *in-house*?" Ash asked.

"Seems likely. There was a thin inquiry, and it was put down to clerical error. Someone in the ranks screwing up."

"But you don't believe that?"

"Let's just say it's not that simple. Pay's lousy for your average copper and the current work environment is rotten. For the right money it wouldn't be hard to find someone willing to cooperate."

The news wasn't that surprising to Ash, but it could complicate things for Maeve. "Is Maeve Gardner getting caught in the undertow?"

"Hard to say at this stage."

"Why were you on Maeve's boat earlier?"

"Checking out a theory."

Ash handed Dixon another beer, still cradling his first. "What theory?"

A Ghostwriter's Guide to Murder

"Not really something I should be talking about with a friend of our chief suspect."

"But you don't believe she *is* your chief suspect," Ash pointed out.

"True." Dixon leaned forward in his chair. "We need to look at every angle. It's proper procedure, but no one's focusing on the money that was found. I want to know where it came from and how Gavin Foster knew that it had been discovered."

"I figured he was keeping watch on the boat. Surveillance on his hiding place," Ash admitted. "A remote device with some kind of motion sensor."

Dixon tipped his bottle toward Ash. "We think alike. But whatever was there is gone."

Ash nodded. They were ahead of the police on that point at least. "And what's your theory on the source of the money?"

"Every time Foster's been in trouble lately, Mac Toliver's been around. I'd say odds are good he's involved. The money's his, or he at least knows where it came from."

"If Toliver's people have a cop on payroll, pursuing them will be nigh on impossible. Especially if they've decided to frame Maeve for Foster's murder."

"True. *My* hands are tied." Dixon looked pointedly at Ash.

"Seems you could use some help, then." Ash sensed that their quest might have gained another ally. A nonplayer character yet potentially a source of critical information. "If you have any hope of finding the real killer, you're going to have to work outside the usual channels," Ash said. "Are you willing to do that?"

"Do I have a choice?"

Ash smiled. "Not from where I'm sitting."

Chapter Thirty

❧

Maeve had been many things in her life—reckless, cocky, even stupid at times—but she'd never been a victim. So why was she feeling so royally victimized? Trapped in a jail cell charged with the murder of her former lover was a good start, but it was more than that.

Julian had assured her that the police evidence, damning as it was, was circumstantial at best, and certainly not enough to take her case to court. Not yet anyway. It was the *not yet* that terrified her. She'd always thought that if you were innocent, you'd be vindicated. In books it always worked that way. Simon Hill would find the missing link that broke the case wide open. The real killer would be caught and punished. All neat and tidy.

Stuck here alone on a Saturday night in the Camden Road nick, there was no missing link. They'd tried to dig deeper and found snippets of information but no smoking gun. Her friends were doing their best, but it was her future on the line. She stood and began to pace off the length of the holding cell, shaking her hands up and down to burn off the nervous energy coursing through her body. Ten steps forward, ten steps back—an apt metaphor for her current situation. "We aren't finding the answer, Simon." She could hear the strain in her own voice.

Then you're looking at things the wrong way round came the reply.

Was that her fault? She'd come into this narrative as the jilted lover. Gavin cast as the cheating bastard; her as the victim. She paused in her pacing. Ah, well, that answered that question at least. *She* was the one victimizing herself. Even before he was killed, she'd been allowing Gavin to make her feel like a victim. It occurred to her that subconsciously she'd been hating him for that as much as, if not more than, any of the rest. She'd allowed her emotions to take over. Concocted those savage death scenarios for him in her writing journals. Cathartic at the time, but now they'd come back to haunt her.

It was time to make a change. Time for a little perspective. The role of the woman scorned didn't suit her, and in fairness, it wasn't all that accurate. Reality check number one: By her own admission, she and Gavin had a one-dimensional relationship. It'd been fun while it lasted, and in the wake of the breakup, she'd lost sight of that fact. It'd been great fun at times. Maybe not enough times, but often enough for her to stay on board for four years.

Reality check number two: The Gavin she knew wasn't a bad person. He was unsophisticated, rough around the edges, but not the villain the police were trying to make him out to be. And in this situation, she reminded herself, he was the literal victim. In fact, he seemed to have been trying to clean up his act, keen to move away from his misspent youth and his foray into the drugs trade. He had a woman who clearly loved him. Maybe because of that, he'd found ambition. He believed that being a businessman would give him standing in the community and a bit of respect like it had Malik Ross.

Start with what you know before what you think, Simon chimed in.

All right. Toliver as the bad guy was tempting, but that was speculation. What did they *know*? Gavin was working for Dawson Construction. Malik Ross controlled Dawson Construction; that meant Ross had control over the projects Gavin was given. Ross claimed to have mentored Gavin. Not strictly true, she was sure, but Ross was the kind of guy who'd enjoy having a groupie. Someone impressed by his business savvy and keen to emulate him. Had Ross taken advantage of Gavin's enthusiasm and ambition and made demands on him? Asked him to do something shady? Was that where the odd run-ins with the police came from? She couldn't know that for sure, but since it was Ross's firm of attorneys bringing Gavin's get-out-of-jail-free card, it seemed logical that Ross was the one responsible for getting Gavin in trouble in the first place.

She started to feel a bit of sympathy for Gavin. Was Ross threatening Gavin? Demanding things that put him at risk? Was that why he'd taken out insurance on his own life? Was that why he'd wound up dead in the canal by her boat? Speculation again but based on actual events.

If Gavin was getting tired of Ross's demands, it would make sense that he might decide it was time to get away. Time to make a fresh start in Spain with Vicky, and to do that he'd need a chunk of money. Fifty thousand wouldn't be enough, but it would be a good start. So, where had it come from? With all their digging and debate, Maeve and her friends were still no

A Ghostwriter's Guide to Murder

further ahead with that crucial question. All they could agree on was that money found in a tire was somehow dodgy.

Gavin had been bringing in more money of late. According to Ash, he'd been doing bigger projects for Dawson Construction, including the swanky new development at the Waterfront. She'd had some time to think about it now, and she remembered him talking about the project. He'd been so excited when he landed the contract that he'd brought home a bottle of wine that didn't have a screw cap. For the man who loved a bargain, it was a real departure. That was what stuck in her memory, but she struggled with the rest of the conversation. She remembered the nonverbal part of the celebration and felt warm in spite of the drafty conditions in the cell.

Come on, Maeve, focus, Simon insisted.

Gav had been going on about how doing the plumbing work from start to finish would give him the credibility he needed to take on more large projects. It was a big deal to him. A lucrative one that would set him up. The Waterfront project meant more money coming in, but that would be on the books, not fifty thousand in cash hidden in a tire.

She was going around and around in circles.

The Waterfront had been a big break for Gavin, but it also looked like it might've damaged his reputation. The litigation surrounding the plumbing was a right mess, and she couldn't see a man like Malik Ross taking the fall if there was someone else who could. Ross would want to blame Gavin, saying he'd taken on more than he could handle. That felt right.

Reality check number three: Gavin wasn't the world's greatest plumber, but he'd done well in his training courses. He was

203

inexperienced but hardly incompetent. In fact, the complaints Ash described focused on the condition of the pipes, not the way they were installed. It might be semantics, but it suggested this wasn't an installation issue.

The parts, maybe? Gavin's business plan was uncomplicated. Cheap components plus cheap labor equaled maximum profit. What was the maxim he was always spouting? *Minimum in, maximum out.* He was always looking for the cheapest parts—the screw-top option. Maeve stopped midpace.

Of course. He'd gone looking for the cheapest supplies, and someone had convinced him to buy their crap pipes. Suddenly she was quite sure she knew where the money had come from. The missing link.

Oh, you silly boy.

Chapter Thirty-One

Paul found himself standing on a street corner on the Isle of Dogs in the pouring rain. Stupidly, he'd left his umbrella behind, and now he was huddled in the doorway of the off-license like an addict. It was gone eleven, and he was starting to feel like a right prat for having agreed to meet the Darty Deeds crew for a bit of moonlight moving. Surely anything legit could be done during the daytime, but Toliver had insisted and the others hadn't looked concerned.

So he was here, and he assured himself he needed to be. He couldn't break cover. Look what had happened to Ash. Better to stay the course and keep his head down. Be one of the lads. His instincts said Toliver had accepted him at face value for the moment: useful darts player and potentially useful source of information. That was what they needed, and he was determined to use it to Maeve's advantage.

He was starting to wonder if the whole thing was off when Jimmy turned up, whistling off-key and sporting a big grin. "This is gonna to be fun," he said. He was dressed for the weather in a black waterproof jacket with a hood and oversized mittens.

"Fun for you or for me?" Paul replied. As suspected, their little project wasn't going to be quite as mundane as moving furniture. He'd been wanting a bit of adventure in his life. Hopefully this wasn't going to be too much.

"Aw, don't be like that. Just a bit of a lark."

Paul wasn't at all sure Jimmy's idea of a lark and his would be the same, but it was too late to abandon ship now, as Toliver and Roy were coming down the street toward them. The Machine was wearing a baseball cap pulled low over his eyes and a scarf knotted around his neck. Paul wished he'd thought to be a bit more discreet himself. This was a business area and there'd be CCTV all around. The best he could do was look down. He scrunched his head into the neck of his coat like a turtle and stepped out from under the awning to follow the rest of the team.

The Machine made his way without hesitation to the rear door of a high-rise office building and used a key card to swipe them in. They took the goods elevator to the twenty-fourth floor and followed their leader to a nondescript door that looked like it might be the back door to one of the swankier offices down the hall. No pass card this time; the Machine pulled out a skeleton key and picked the lock with ease before ushering them all in ahead of him.

If Paul had any question about where he was, it was quickly dispelled by the wall of framed photos and magazine covers, all featuring the same smiling face—Malik Ross. *Entrepreneur Monthly*, *Cigar Aficionado*, and dozens of photos of the real estate mogul with various political types. He was a man who relished his power and his position and liked to remind himself and everyone else of who he was.

A Ghostwriter's Guide to Murder

"Get a load of this one," Jimmy said, scanning the wall for the photo he wanted. "'Ere." He pointed at a picture of Ross and a famous pop star in a see-through outfit. "Now 'er I'd like to meet. The rest of this lot"—he gestured at the politicos—"what a load of wankers."

Roy leaned in to look at the picture of the singer. "'E looks short, or is she just wearin' tall shoes?"

"Never met 'im," Jimmy said. "Just stood out 'ere cooling my 'eels one time waiting for Gav, lookin' at the pics."

The Machine led them through a doorway and into a personal gym with a treadmill that looked out over the lights of the Isle of Dogs and down the river toward Canary Wharf. Their leader ignored the view and plowed on through a second door to a dressing area that led into the most ludicrous bathroom Paul had ever seen. There was a giant shower with four showerheads: one in the ceiling and three more on the walls designed to service various other parts of the body. A man like Ross probably had a lot to wash off.

As impressive as the space was, the focal point of the room was the throne, and what a throne it was. Paul had never seen a gold-colored lav before. Gold colored but not actually gold, he presumed. Malik Ross surely didn't have the kind of disposable income that could support even a ten-karat loo. That was Russian oligarch money, not London real estate magnate money.

"Got your tools, Roy Boy?" Toliver asked.

"On it."

Paul watched as Roy unhooked the lav from the water supply at the wall and popped off the anchor covers. As Roy worked, Paul stepped back and found himself leaning on a marble-topped table that had a stack of loo rolls underneath and, he realized too

207

late, a pile of papers on the top that slipped to the floor. He supposed if you had a lav like that, you might spend a lot of time on it. Catching up on your reading and such.

Paul gathered the papers and put them back on the table. He moved slowly, hoping he might see something of interest, something with Gavin's name on it, perhaps, but that was foolish. All he had in his hands were profiles of buildings for sale.

"Must think 'e's a real king, sittin' on that throne," Jimmy said. "Bet they don't even 'ave a bog like this at Buck 'Ouse."

"Well, the king's about to be dethroned." Roy chuckled, pleased with his own joke. Unhooking the toilet from the floor, he gestured to Jimmy, and the two of them hefted it off to the side.

"Right, lads, heave-ho." Toliver indicated Paul. "Come on. You're here for the extra muscle. Roy's good with his fingers, but there's no strength in 'im."

Jimmy put his hands under the bowl and looked to Paul, who reached under the tank and lifted. It was heavier than he'd expected, and he struggled to speak. "Can I ask why we're stealing a man's bog?"

"You'll see when we get there," Toliver said.

Paul was pleased that so far their adventure seemed to be falling more in the category of a lark than serious criminal activity; nonetheless, he was anxious to get away from the scene of the crime. They exited the building and shuffled off round the corner as quickly as they could move, carrying the glistening bog. It was hard enough inside the building but almost impossible once the rain got it wet. They nearly dropped it twice, and Paul's back was screaming at him by the time they arrived at a dark-blue 4 × 4 parked by a loading dock down the alley. Toliver opened the hatch, and the throne was loaded inside.

A Ghostwriter's Guide to Murder

Paul should've been worried about where they were going, but he was so relieved to finally have a chance to sit down he simply closed his eyes and willed his back to stop cramping.

When he opened his eyes again, they were south of the river on the A2 taking the exit for Vanbrugh Park. Toliver swung the car into a respectable-looking residential street and pulled up in front of the last house in the row. They all piled out, and once again Paul was wrestling with the golden bog, this time along a side street and through a smaller gate into the house's back garden.

It seemed a long way to go to surprise someone with an unwanted piece of garden statuary, but he was past complaining now.

Toliver directed them to an area of shrubbery in the back corner of the yard, where a standpipe was apparently awaiting the new arrival. Roy pulled his tools out once more and began the hookup process. Soon there was a trickle of water spouting into the air from the center of the bowl, making a rather pleasant tinkling sound. If you could forget you were looking at a lav, it almost made a charming water feature. Almost.

"Well done, Roy Boy." Jimmy patted Roy on the shoulder. "Y' learned a lot from Gav over the past few years."

"You'll 'ave to polish it up a bit time to time," Roy said rather sadly. "May look like gold, but it's brass and it'll go green on ye."

"Blend in better with the yard," Toliver said. "Maybe me wife won't kick up such a fuss."

Toliver disappeared into the adjacent shed—his shed, apparently—and emerged with a bottle of whisky and some mugs. He poured a generous measure for each of them and passed them around. "To Gav."

Melinda Mullet

"To Gav," they echoed back.

Paul wasn't sure how he'd come to be standing in a criminal's back garden, toasting a murder victim over a fountain made from a brass bog, but here he was, now apparently a full-fledged member of the gang. There was a warmth here. A sense of camaraderie. As Jimmy said, they were family, and Toliver was the patriarch.

In this moment Paul felt certain that Toliver hadn't been involved with Gavin's death. If there had been an issue between the two men, he would've worked it out, not killed his friend.

They finished their drinks, and Roy and Jimmy loaded the tools back into the car. Toliver drove back to the city, dropping the lads at the Tube at Rotherhithe. Paul tried to exit at that point, intending to catch the bus home, but Toliver insisted on driving him all the way back to Camden.

Paul was nervous and struggled to make conversation. "What made you think of a lav as a memorial to Gavin?"

"He was a plumber, wasn't he?" Toliver grinned, and Paul forced what he hoped was a genuine-looking smile.

After a few more minutes of silence, Toliver glanced across at him. "It also sends a message. Don't tell the lads, it'll only upset 'em, but between you and me, I suspect the lav's owner had something to do with Gav's death."

It had been an entertaining evening but not really useful until now. Paul thought he might've just struck gold. Toliver had *his* sights set on Ross as the killer. Did he know something they didn't? He tried to sound casual. "Malik Ross? What makes you think that?"

"I've seen how he operates firsthand. He has the morals of an alley cat. If Gavin got on the wrong side of him, he'd take steps."

A Ghostwriter's Guide to Murder

"Would Ross go as far as killing him?"

Toliver stared at the road ahead. "Wouldn't put it past him, but as far as the lads are concerned, this was just a lark in memory of a mate. Gav would've loved it." He shot Paul a glance out of the side of his eye. "You were just there as extra muscle, and if you go flapping your mouth about this, I'll remind you your fingerprints are all over that bog and, as luck would have it, all over those papers in Ross' bathroom. Cause any trouble, I won't hesitate to tip him off."

Paul realized with a sinking heart that he was the only one who stupidly hadn't been wearing gloves tonight.

"It'd be hard to explain what you were doing in his private office, and he's not the kind of bloke that would really want to listen to an explanation anyway."

He might be on the team but clearly wasn't a part of the family. Toliver's loyalty and protection wouldn't extend to him, but his gut told him it had always extended to Gavin.

God help the man who'd killed him.

211

Chapter Thirty-Two

India was convinced Vicky still had things to tell them, whether she knew it or not. Paul was well in with the darts crew, Ash had his own set of mad hacking skills, but taking on the emotionally distraught Vicky was a task that fell squarely in India's wheelhouse. She wasn't sure exactly how she was going to tackle Vicky, but she was confident that wine was the way to begin. She clutched the bottle of chardonnay she'd picked up at the Tesco down the block and pressed the buzzer outside the block of flats.

"Hello," came a fuzzy voice.

"Hiya! Vicky? It's India." She held the bottle up toward the camera above her. "Got time for a quick drink?"

There was a bit of a pause and India wondered if she should've got a more expensive chardonnay, but before she could say anything more, she heard a buzzing noise and the voice said, "Two fourteen."

Vicky wasn't waiting at the door when she arrived, and India had to knock. If the flat above the Ink Spot was anything to go by, Vicky had really come up in the world when she moved in

212

A Ghostwriter's Guide to Murder

with Gavin. The Islington flat was a real find. Lovely location and closer than India remembered, no more than a twenty-minute walk to the *Revenge*. If Gavin had been monitoring his cash from home, he could've made it over to Maeve's pretty sharpish.

Cooling her heels in the hall, she thought she might have to give up on Vicky, but she eventually came to the door holding onto the frame to steady herself.

"I 'aven't found any paperwork, if that's what you're 'ere in aid of," she muttered as she led the way into the lounge.

India shook her head and handed the wine to Vicky. "Nah, I wasn't here to hassle you about the papers. Really just wanted to apologize for the other day at the studio. It wasn't right." Vicky didn't acknowledge the apology, so India moved on. "Have you heard they've arrested Maeve?"

"Gav's lawyer told me." Vicky handed her a large glass of wine from an already open bottle. The glass was nearly filled to the brim. She'd need to pace herself. "'Bout time they found the killer"—Vicky raised her own glass in salute—"and I couldn't be more delighted that it's 'er."

"But she's *not* the killer!"

Vicky shrugged. "You say she's not, but the solicitors aren't convinced, and they tell me 'e left the insurance money to 'er. It's what they call motive."

India could see the anger flashing in her eyes. "That was just horrible timing. He'd made the change, Vicky. Gavin meant that money to go to you."

"*Meant to* won't pay the rent on this place," Vicky snapped, looking around at the mauve walls and the minimalist Ikea furniture. India didn't have an immediate response for that. She

Melinda Mullet

hadn't thought Vicky would be aware of the insurance situation yet. It was going to make her job tougher.

Vicky seemed suddenly restless. Jumping to her feet, she started to pace unsteadily around the room. "Bastard. 'Ow could 'e do this to me?" Her voice was brittle. Clearly she was moving into the anger stage of her grieving process.

She spun around and looked at India. "Was I a fool? I mean, was our whole relationship a lie?"

India started to reply, but Vicky wasn't pausing for a breath.

"Bet they were just laughing at me behind my back. Stupid little tattoo girl. Not like 'er. The posh writer. The clever one. Guess I was just nothin' but a pit stop along 'is way to the top. Once 'e'd made it, 'e'd want someone like 'er beside 'im."

"No, Vicky," India said, cutting in firmly. She put her glass down on the table to use her hands for emphasis. "Come on. Gavin was many things but not a liar. A woman's instinct should tell you that. *He loved you.* You know that in your heart. He and Maeve were done."

Vicky stopped pacing and looked at India. "If they were done, she wouldn't care. And if she didn't care, then she wasn't the killer—but she 'as to be the killer," she concluded with a whisper.

"Why would she go to the police about the money if she killed Gav?" India was taking a stab at the logical approach, though Vicky might be too far gone at this point. "She'd want to stay as far away from the cops as possible, right?"

"No." Vicky voice was now tinged with panic. "She 'as to be the one. She '*as* to be."

India wasn't following the rationale here—if there was a rationale. "*Why* does it have to be her?" she insisted.

A Ghostwriter's Guide to Murder

"Because if it's not 'er . . . then the killer's still out there." Vicky crumbled at that point, sobbing into the cushions on the couch, the bitterness and anger dissolving into fear. Vicky was clearly afraid of someone or something. Was it the Machine?

India sat down beside her on the settee and gently stroked her hair until the tears ran their course.

Finally, Vicky sat up, drying her cheek with the back of her hand. "Bloody ridiculous, the whole thing." She broke away from India and made her way unsteadily to the kitchen. In her absence, India leaned over and poured some of her own wine into Vicky's half-empty glass. She needed to keep a clear head.

Vicky returned with a box of tissues and blew her nose loudly before continuing to drink quickly and efficiently, oblivious to the size of her portion. India needn't have worried about the quality of the wine; clearly quantity was the only criterion at this point. The trick would be to get Vicky talking before she passed out.

"Have you told the police that you're afraid?"

Vicky gave a hollow laugh. "What do I tell 'em? That some mystery man, someone that killed Gav, might come for me?"

"Fair point." India nodded. "But what is it that makes you think someone might come for you?"

"They killed Gav over the money. I've seen cop shows. People like that don't leave loose ends."

"People like what?" India prodded.

"People that give someone fifty thousand quid."

"Do you know who gave him the money?"

"If I did, I'd know who to be afraid of, wouldn't I?"

"Did the money come from something illegal?" India asked gently. She didn't want to set Vicky off again, but the word *give* suggested the money wasn't stolen.

215

Melinda Mullet

Vicky shrugged. "I don't know what to believe anymore. Gav said it was just business. The way things work in the construction trade. 'E'd been so excited about the new projects 'e was workin' on. Felt like 'e was really starting to go places, you know. Then . . ." Vicky trailed off, her eyes starting to lose focus.

"Then what?" India prompted.

"Then the lawsuits came. More responsibility you take, the more blame you get. Suddenly it wasn't so much fun anymore. Gav was afraid the creditors would wipe 'im out and all the money'd be gone."

"Is that why he was thinking of moving to Spain?"

Vicky nodded. "Leave all this shit behind." She drained the glass in front of her and rose, padding her way across to the drinks tray and rummaging around the bottles. "Sorry, no more red, just a white." She grabbed an opener from the tray on the top of the cabinet and made short work of the cork. Pouring herself another full glass, she placed the bottle on the table within easy reach of her guest.

Drunk Vicky was far more willing to share, but India was worried it wouldn't last long. She took a sip of her wine and caught Vicky's eye. "I have to ask, why the hell would Gav hide money in a dock bumper along the canal? Seems . . ." She wanted to say *daft* but went with "*very* risky."

Vicky rose again, steadying herself on an armchair as she went to the sideboard and pulled out an envelope. "Found this when I was looking for the lockup papers." She flopped back down next to India and handed her the envelope.

Inside was a sheet of paper with a message scrawled in red pen across the middle. *Return the cash or you're a dead man.* No postmark, no signature, no indication of its source. The note

A Ghostwriter's Guide to Murder

gave no hint about the source of the cash, but if it was stolen, the owner obviously didn't feel able to involve the police, and as far as India was concerned, that spoke volumes.

"He never told you who was threatening him?"

"No, 'e never talked about the money except to say 'e didn't want to keep that kind of cash at the flat."

Smart move. The flat would likely be the first place someone would look. "I suspect he was trying to protect you, luv," India said, hoping the thought would comfort Vicky in some small way.

The words brought fresh tears to Vicky's eyes. Not the violent sobs of earlier, just a silent misery. Vicky slumped back and leaned her head on India's shoulder. "I don't know why I'm telling you all this. I think it's 'cause you remind me of me mum, God rest 'er."

I remind everyone of their mum, India thought ruefully. *The healer.* She patted Vicky on the knee. "We'll get this sorted and make sure you're all right. I promise."

Vicky sniffed. "Why?"

"Because you're a good woman in a bad situation, and because I have a soft spot for a strong woman doing her best to fight the good fight."

Vicky gave her a watery smile. "Thank you."

India felt Vicky still knew more than she was saying, or more accurately, more than she realized. "Gavin was watching his hiding place, wasn't he?" India said gently. "I mean, how else would he know Maeve had discovered the cash?"

"Not 'im, me," Vicky said. "I 'ad a screen in the back of the shop showing the camera 'e 'ad focused in close on the tire. If anyone came messing with the cash, I was to let 'im know. The

217

Melinda Mullet

day 'e died, I saw someone take the money out and then put it back. I called Gav, and 'e headed over to move it before anyone else came to stick their noses in."

Suspicions confirmed. "You were watching the cash, and someone else was watching Gavin," she mused. "Whoever sent this, I presume." She indicated the paper in her hand. India couldn't help feeling frustrated by Gavin's ineptitude. "Why on earth didn't he keep the money in the lockup? It would've been far safer there, and maybe none of this would've happened."

"'E needed to keep it 'andy," Vicky said softly. "We'd found a cottage in Spain, and Gav'd been negotiating with this bloke for a couple of months. It's a tough market for 'ouses. Good ones anyway. 'E'd left the money by the boat so 'e could 'ave it for puttin' a cash deposit down quick when 'e needed it. Any day now, 'e'd said. We were so close." Vicky's voice was fading. India needed to push ahead before she passed out.

"You said Gavin had something put aside for a rainy day; was that it? The cash at the dock?"

Vicky shook her head slowly. "It's like when you know a secret and you figure the person who 'as the secret owes you one." She was slurring her words. "Like me sister Gwen." Vicky pointed to a photo on the side table of a woman and a young girl.

"Gwen 'as a beautiful little girl. Sasha. Love 'er to bits, but *I* know that 'er Dad's not really 'er father. Gwen was messin' about with this bloke from the express delivery service. She got a package all right. 'Course she didn't tell 'er 'usband, but she told me."

"You blackmailed your own sister?" India wondered if she'd been too hasty in her good-woman assessment.

218

A Ghostwriter's Guide to Murder

"Never asked for money or nuffin' like that, but boy when I need a favor does she 'op to it. It's not blackmail, just a bit of an edge." Vicky yawned.

India leaned in closer. "And Gavin had something that gave him a bit of an edge?"

"'E was a clever boy," she murmured sleepily.

India gave her a gentle nudge. "That information could tell us who might want to kill Gavin. Have you looked through all his files?"

Vicky gave a half snort, half laugh. "Did Gav look like the kind of bloke that kept files? 'E's got shoeboxes—dozens— chockablock with receipts and paperwork. 'E used to say that's why we made a good team. I bought shoes and 'e needed boxes."

"Where does he keep the boxes?"

Vicky waved her glass in the direction of the hall, sloshing wine on the floor.

"Maybe I can help look."

Vicky seemed unable to focus now and gave up with a shrug. "'Elp yourself. Closet's there." She lay back on the settee and stroked the cat, who'd appeared out of nowhere.

India was hoping it was a small closet, but it turned out to be more like a pantry. Inside were dozens of shoeboxes. Some contained shoes: trainers, hiking boots, steel-toed work boots. The others were full of papers.

India opened the lid of the nearest box. Receipts, dozens of them. All about five years old. She carried a stack of boxes back to the lounge and sat on the floor, sorting through all the scraps of paper. By the time she'd finished the second one, Vicky was snoring softly with the cat curled up by her side. India headed back to the closet and began rapidly flipping through each box.

219

Melinda Mullet

Sod's Law she was nearly three-quarters of the way through when she found what she was looking for. A receipt for a lockup in Tottenham, paid up through the end of the year. The space was rented in the name of Lou Masters, but the receipt was here with Gavin's things, and she was sure space 419 belonged to him. Finally, something concrete to work with.

She tidied up the lounge and took a snapshot of the threatening letter Gavin had received to show the others before tucking it back in the sideboard. She couldn't help but feel sorry for Vicky. Such high hopes, and a genuine affection for Gavin. What a waste. India grabbed a blanket off the bed and draped it over the sleeping woman.

"We'll find the answer," she whispered. "For Maeve and for you."

Chapter
Thirty-Three

✎

"Do you think that's wise?" Ash asked from the driver's seat of the Fiat he'd rented to get them to Foster's lockup. Paul was tossing Wotsits over his shoulder to the Captain in the back seat, who was catching the cheese puffs like a frog snagging flies.

"You wanted to cheer him up," Paul said. "He's happy. Wind in his fur, road trip snacks, what else could he want?"

Maeve came quickly to mind. In spite of being new to dog minding, Ash could tell the Captain was distressed by his owner's absence, and it was worrying him. India insisted he simply needed a change of scene, and having nothing else to offer, Ash had brought him along on today's outing. The Captain and Smaug were settled in the back seat with India, and he did seem happier.

"Easy, Paul," India said. "I don't need him being sick back here."

"Right," Paul conceded, offering the bag to Ash instead.

"I've got sweeties too, if anyone's interested." India rattled a box of Quality Street toffees.

It wasn't a long drive, but it had already taken on the air of a family outing to the seaside. A half hour in and Ash was weary of the traffic and weighing his words carefully, keen to avoid an outbreak of juvenile squabbling in the car. They'd discussed Toliver's conviction that Malik Ross was behind Gavin's killing. Ash conceded it was a reasonable theory, but it was only *one* theory, yet Paul seemed to be taking it as gospel. Paul was clearly being influenced by Toliver's personal magnetism, allowing what seemed to be a budding friendship to block his rational view of the man as a thug.

"We saw your pal the Machine in action just two nights ago—up close and personal," Ash argued. "And Dixon says it's *his* lawyers getting Gav out of trouble, not Ross."

"Doesn't mean it wasn't Ross that got him into trouble. I'm sure Toliver's just protecting his mate."

"Or Toliver's covering up his own involvement by directing your attention to Ross," Ash insisted.

"Why would he?" Paul flipped another Wotsit over his shoulder. "I haven't told him we're investigating on Maeve's behalf. He just made an educated guess, and because of me we got to hear it."

Ash checked the rearview mirror to see if the chip found its target. "You may not have told him you're investigating for Maeve, but he knows he'd never convince you that she's guilty, so he's throwing out Ross. Anything to steer you, and hopefully the police, away from him and his cronies."

"Toliver wouldn't hurt Gavin. I feel it in my gut. They were like family."

Ash scowled. *His* gut told him the Machine was the villain in this piece. Covering for the real killer and likely framing Maeve into the bargain, but his views wouldn't sway Paul. Not yet. Not without more proof.

India handed them each a toffee from the back seat. If Ash didn't know better, he'd say she was hoping to silence them.

A Ghostwriter's Guide to Murder

"Theories are fine, but we need tangible proof if we're going to help Maeve." India waved her phone in the direction of the front seat. "If we can find out who sent this note to Gavin, then we might get somewhere."

Ash knew she was right. The threatening note was critical data, but proving who sent it might be impossible. All they could do at this point was hope that Foster's lockup could give them a much needed in-game hint.

* * *

As they'd anticipated, the storage facility was largely deserted on a Sunday morning, and following Ash's strategy, Paul and India approached the kid at the front desk and asked to look at one of the larger storage units. As the indifferent young man went to get his keys from the back room, Ash and the Captain slipped ninjalike through the side door and into the gated area unseen. The padlock on 419 was slightly stiff, and Ash spent several minutes wiggling the key Maeve had given them in the stubborn lock. He was starting to think the whole trip might've been a waste when the lock finally yielded with a reluctant click.

It was pitch-black inside the storage space, and Ash had to rely on his phone's flashlight function till he found a shop light on a shelf near the door. He flipped it on and revealed a row of floor-to-ceiling metal shelves filled with boxes. Not shoeboxes this time but proper file boxes. The Captain made a circuit of the room, sniffing with interest. As Ash approached a stack of plastic containers in the back corner of the unit, he heard a slight noise at the door and spun around to see Paul and India slipping inside.

"What happened to your guide?"

"He got bored with us," India said with a grin.

"India started debating whether we could get both settees in the space." Paul rolled his eyes. "Had me pacing the length off along all the walls. Then started talking through each item of furniture in our imaginary country house in detail. Poor kid looked like his head was about to explode. He bolted. Left us to finish on our own." Paul picked up the shop light and moved it closer. "What've you found?"

"Nothing yet. I just got started."

They wandered about, poking into boxes at random. The dated boxes were largely comics and football souvenirs from Arsenal's undefeated 2003–2004 season. India opened a plastic storage box and held up a sizable Transformer figure and a Lego model of the *Millennium Falcon*. The Captain stuck his head inside and tried to make off with a Han Solo action figure.

"Boys and their toys," India muttered, retrieving the bounty hunter and returning the box to the shelf. "What about this?" She pulled out another cardboard box simply labeled *Misc Stuff*. Inside were a dozen or so manila envelopes. She handed one to Ash and one to Paul and opened a third herself.

"Not sure what I'm looking at here," she said.

Ash had spread the contents of his envelope on top of a box labeled *Incredible Hulk 1994 and Aquaman 1986*. "This one looks like records for council flat conversions in Ilford. Two sets of books." Ash kept flipping through the papers. "Hardly radical news that Dawson Construction was overcharging the council for the work they were doing."

"At Malik Ross's direction, we presume," said India.

"Here's another project, and more accounts." Paul was flipping through the contents of his envelope. "And another."

A Ghostwriter's Guide to Murder

Ash looked up. "Is that all there is?" He'd hoped for something more incendiary. Cheating the local council on third-party contracts was more of a hobby for those in the building trade than an egregious criminal act. If Foster tried to blackmail Ross with what he had here, he'd be laughed out of the room.

"This one's a list of the council members in the various boroughs," India said. "A dozen names highlighted and an attached list of cash payments." She handed the sheet to Ash. "Bribes?"

"Looks like it," Ash agreed. "You can see the same names signing off on various site plans and inspection reports, but we'd need to find bank statements to support the payments. So far, I haven't seen any. Looks like he was hoping to blackmail Ross but hadn't got what he needed. Certainly not the leverage Vicky thought he had." *And nothing on the Machine,* Ash fumed silently. Disappointing all around.

India continued to hand around manila envelopes. "This one's different." She laid a photocopied list of accounts on the table in front of her.

Ash came to read over her shoulder. "Gambling records. Bets placed, wagers won and lost." He pointed to the header—*MTM.* "That's a name Ross operates under when he thinks he's being slick. He used it as a bookie and then again later when he wanted to hide his ownership in Dawson." Ash pointed to the bottom of the list. "Look at the last few entries. Relatively recent loans. Seems Ross isn't completely out of the lending game."

"What's the number in red at the end of each row?" India asked.

"The cumulative amount you owe for advances or loans."

"Some big numbers there," Paul noted. "But Ross isn't stupid. He's not using names, just client numbers. Not much use without a reference sheet."

"Then there must be a reference sheet here somewhere, or why keep all this?" India said, continuing to rummage through the envelopes. Ash wished they could simply file search for what they needed; it would be so much faster. But true to form, India's persistence paid off. She looked up with a triumphant smile and handed over a spreadsheet with more than forty names cross-referenced to a list of four-digit numbers.

"That's it, India. Brilliant." Ash spread out the loan records and started comparing the client numbers to the client names. "There's a few here that are still blank, no name to the number. The largest amounts. Probably his most influential clients."

"He'd likely be most protective of their identities, wouldn't he?" India said. "I mean, as a practical matter, Ross'd want to be sure *he* was the one with leverage over them, not anyone else."

"True." Trust India's common sense to bring her swiftly to what had to be the right conclusion. "Unfortunately, those clients are the most important from our perspective. The individuals with the most to lose. The ones most likely to do Ross's bidding to protect themselves."

"I'll keep looking," India said, turning back to the boxes of paper. "Someone here will have motive; it's just a matter of finding the right person. Someone vulnerable enough to need to appease Ross."

"It wouldn't have to be someone with a specific connection to Foster." Ash paused. "Then again, it might be. Take a look at this." He turned the lists to face his companions, pointing to client 6749—*Roy Malloy (£10,000)*.

Chapter
Thirty-Four

Maeve was pulled from her cell and brought along to the interview room again. She squared her shoulders, ready to put up a fight, but DS Dixon entered the room alone, carrying a handful of papers.

"Looks like you're in luck." He slid the papers across the table to her. "Sign here and you'll be free to go."

"What?" Maeve thought she must have misheard. "I mean, great, but why? Have you found the real killer?"

Dixon extended a pen. "Look, I'm following orders from above. Do you want out or not?"

"Definitely out." She signed her name and followed Dixon down the hall to the door of his office.

"Wait here and I'll bring you your things."

He disappeared through a set of double doors and left her alone in the open-plan office area. It was empty. Not surprising for a Sunday, but it was disappointing to see that no one was working overtime on her case or any other. Short-staffed as Ash said.

She paced around the floor, anxious to be gone. Most of the desks she passed were piled high with files, but the desk closest

227

to Dixon's office was unusually neat. A single file alongside a framed photo of DC Gray and her cat. Why was she not surprised that Gray was a cat person. The two creatures shared the same supercilious air. She'd have thought a busy detective would have a messier desk, but then again, Gray struck her as the kind of woman who was precise and rigid. A rule follower. Likely her perspective on the world and its foibles was narrow and unimaginative too. Not ideal for a police detective. Maybe that was why Dixon always looked irritated by her presence.

The lone folder on Gray's desk drew her eye. Even from a slight distance, she could see her name on the cover. She looked around again to be sure she was alone before approaching. She picked up a pencil and flipped open the front cover of the file without touching it. The movement caused a half dozen loose photos to fly out and land on the floor. So much for avoiding fingerprints. She scrambled to gather them up and saw that they were all pictures from the *Revenge*. Exterior shots plus a number of close-ups of her workspace.

She stuffed the photos back in the folder, taking a closer look as she did so. No wonder she stood out as a suspect: all those story cards pinned to the wall with detailed descriptions of death and revenge. The top sheet in the file seemed to be a final report. She scanned it quickly, hoping to see the name of an alternate suspect or at least a reason for her release, but instead the final recommendation that jumped off the page was *referral to the Crown Prosecution Service.*

Her newfound sense of relief vanished as quickly as it had come. They didn't think she was innocent. They weren't letting her go because they'd found the real killer. The realization struck her like a physical blow to the gut. Not only did they still think

A Ghostwriter's Guide to Murder

she was guilty, they were moving forward with the case. So why let her go? It made no sense, but she wasn't about to question it. She just wanted out and she needed to talk to Julian. Maybe he could explain things.

She could hear footsteps coming down the hall, and she skittered quickly back to the spot where Dixon had left her. He scattered the contents of a brown envelope on a nearby table and she gathered her things together, replacing her smartwatch on her wrist and grabbing her phone and keys.

She couldn't look at him. "Is that it?" she demanded.

"Sign for your stuff and you're out of here." He seemed to hesitate. "Just mind yourself out there."

* * *

Back at the *Revenge* she was disappointed to find no one around. Not even the Captain. He must be with Ash. Maybe they were with India and Paul? Off trying to help her or just off having fun? It was an uncharitable thought, but she was experiencing an uncharacteristic wave of bitterness. She sent a text to Julian and waited to see if the response might be immediate, but of course it wasn't.

The boat seemed so empty without the Captain. She desperately needed his comforting presence, and without him she felt frightened and so alone. She curled up in a tight ball in the middle of her empty bed and began to cry. Throughout this whole nightmare she hadn't cried, and she desperately needed the release. She cried until the tears were spent, then closed her eyes tightly to block out the horror of it all. When she opened them again, she registered the number on the clock and realized she had fallen asleep from pure exhaustion. Now it was getting dark. She sat up hurriedly and sent a belated text to India, receiving a GIF of a dancing sheep blowing a party horn in return.

At the Anchor came next. *With Julian.*

* * *

As she stepped across the threshold of the Anchor, she was assaulted by the Captain, who spent the first five minutes licking every available patch of bare skin. The whole crew was settled in the Nook and Cranny, including Julian.

They made room for Maeve in the largest of the armchairs, and the Captain scrambled his way inelegantly onto her lap, pinning her in place and whimpering softly with joy.

"Tell us what happened," India said. "Smarty-pants here said there was no way they'd let you out for at least another two or three days."

Julian shot his sister a dirty look over the top of his beer. "I filed for you to be released immediately, but I never thought for one minute they'd let you go. What did they say when they let you out?"

"Not much. Dixon had me sign the release papers and sent me on my way. His parting words were 'Be careful,'" Maeve said. "Hardly inspires confidence, but that wasn't the worst of it. My file was laying out on his DC's desk. I took a quick peek while I was alone, and the case is being referred to the CPS."

Julian frowned. "You're sure?"

"Absolutely. It was right there in black and white."

"Dixon's not a careless man," Ash said slowly. "If he left you alone with your file, he meant for you to see it."

Maeve was dubious but noticed Paul nodding in the background. They must know something she didn't.

A Ghostwriter's Guide to Murder

"Turns out we have an ally in Dixon," Ash explained. "He thinks you may not be guilty."

"May not be," India snorted.

"Leave out the semantics, India. He *believes* you're innocent," Ash confirmed.

"Then why does he keep arresting me?"

"There's a lot of politics in policing as well as evidence. You're the easy answer, and there are people senior to him that only care about clearing up the case log."

"Even if they're wrong?" Maeve demanded. The Captain sensed her anger and turned to lick her on the nose.

"Even then."

"So, what do we do next?" India looked back and forth between Julian and Ash.

"Keep looking for proof of Maeve's innocence and find the real killer," Ash replied. "We have someone on the police force who'll support us if we find the right evidence, and at the moment that's more crucial than you can imagine."

"How long do we have before they refer the case to the CPS?" Paul asked, looking to Julian.

"It'll go over in the next couple of days," he said. "It'd be great if you could have some proof of Maeve's innocence to offer by then, but that means you'll need to hustle."

"Thought you wanted us to stay out of this?" India challenged.

"Loath though I am to admit it, you lot seem to have a knack for finding things, and as the police aren't, there's not much else for it, is there?"

"You heard him, folks, we have a flair for this." India grinned. "And we've not been idle in your absence," she continued, turning to Maeve.

231

"India had another go at Vicky last night," Paul said, "and clever girl that India is, she came up with the address for Gavin's lockup."

Maeve leaned forward. "Please tell me you found something helpful."

"Mainly boxes full of Gavin's old toys and comics."

"That's all you found?" Maeve could feel the disappointment like a pressure in her chest.

"No, no," India went on. "Gavin was keeping information on Malik Ross' shady business practices."

"But not really enough proof to effectively blackmail him," Ash added.

"We did find out that he's still loan-sharking on the side," India added. "Roy Malloy is one of his clients, and he owes Ross more than ten thousand pounds."

Paul brought Maeve a large gin and a packet of crisps. "Kind of money Roy might be dead anxious to wipe off the slate."

"And it's a link to Paul's friend the Machine." Ash looked quite chuffed by this.

"You think Roy might have killed Gavin to get the money to repay Ross?" Maeve asked.

"If he knew Gavin had that much money, it might've been really tempting for him," India said. "And it's as good a motive as we've been able to come up with so far."

Paul scowled at them from behind the bar. "I don't buy it. Not for a minute. Roy worshipped Gavin, and like all the darts crew, they were fiercely loyal to each other. If Roy needed money, and he knew Gavin had some, he'd have just asked."

"Maybe he did and Gavin said no," Julian said from the corner.

232

A Ghostwriter's Guide to Murder

"Maybe it wasn't even planned," Ash said. "Maybe Roy was with Foster, saw the money, and took his chance. Or maybe Foster had tried to blackmail Ross and Ross pressured Roy to kill Foster in return for canceling his debt."

Paul shook his head. "Roy just doesn't have it in him. From what I've seen, the kid's not all there mentally."

"That would make him easily manipulated," Ash pointed out.

"If he'd done it, then Toliver would know," Paul insisted, "and he wouldn't be asking questions and drawing attention to the crime. He'd want to protect Roy."

"Best way to shield Roy would be to frame someone else for the murder." Ash turned to Maeve. "Dixon told me all of Foster's recent run-ins with the police have one thing in common— the Machine. He's always at the center of the storm, and Dixon says it was the Machine sending in the lawyers to dig Foster out, not Ross."

Maeve thought Ash had a reasonable point.

"Professionally, Toliver runs with some tough blokes," Paul agreed, "but he's doing his best to keep his friends out of it. Trying to *protect* them. That's real loyalty."

Ash rose from his seat, and Maeve saw his hands were shaking slightly. "You can't just discount the man as a suspect because you like him. You keep telling us he'd do anything for his friends. Wouldn't that include sacrificing an innocent woman to protect Roy from a charge of murder?"

There was an undertone to this argument that seemed almost personal. As if Ash was feeling threatened in some way by Paul's friendship with Toliver. The last thing they needed was division in the ranks.

233

Melinda Mullet

You need a diversion, Simon prompted.

"I think I know where Gavin got the money from, and if I'm right, it may open up some other suspects," Maeve interjected loudly.

India smiled. "That's a girl. What've you got?"

"When we asked Vicky about the money last time, she insisted it wasn't stolen, but she didn't elaborate. I think it was *given* to Gavin, and I suspect she knows who by."

"By whom," India corrected absent-mindedly.

"Really? Now?" Maeve said.

"Sorry, but you're on the right track. When I was there last night, she clearly said Gav was given the money. She just didn't know by whom."

Maeve shifted the Captain off her lap, and he went to lean on Ash's leg as if sensing that he was the one now in need of comfort. "We were still together when Gavin started the Waterfront project. He was so excited because it made him feel like one of the big boys. Ash told us Gav was the only subcontractor for the plumbing part of the project. Not just installation but procurement too. It was a massive project. Suppliers would be courting him, trying to get his business."

"You think he was taking kickbacks from the supplier of the faulty pipes?" Julian asked.

"Wouldn't be unusual, would it? Seeing how lousy their product is, it was probably the only way they could get any business. Ross hinted that Gav hadn't been in the game long enough to know who to trust and who not to."

"Would make sense of this as well," India said, pulling up the photo of the threat Gavin received on her phone. "Vicky showed me the actual note. With all the litigation over the Waterfront

A Ghostwriter's Guide to Murder

project, everyone must be scrambling to find cash to pay awards and legal fees."

"Our firm's doing some of the litigation on the Waterfront," Julian said. "The pipes that failed were supplied by a company called Patterson Plumbing out of Croydon. Father-son operation. They've been forced into bankruptcy by all of this."

"If they gave Gavin fifty thousand pounds to secure a deal, they can't be thrilled at the way it's turned out," Maeve pointed out.

"Return the cash *and* you're a dead man," India noted.

"We might finally be getting somewhere," Paul said. "Certainly a much better suspect than Maeve, or Roy for that matter, but I wouldn't completely discount Malik Ross."

Ash rolled his eyes. "Because the Machine says so."

"No," Paul insisted. "Because he must be furious about the bad PR and the money he's had to pay out to injured tenants. And there's still more lawsuits brewing. If he got Gavin to admit he took money from the Pattersons, Ross might've demanded Gavin give him the money to offset his losses. If Gavin refused, he could've sent someone after him."

"Maybe even someone from Patterson's," Maeve said, "but there's only one way to find out. Looks like I'm heading for Croydon in the morning."

"That's a bridge too far," Julian said quickly. "If you're right, it would be dangerous, and besides, how would you justify asking a load of questions about alleged bribery and threats?"

"I'll think of something," Maeve said. "The police won't go, so who else is there? It's down to me."

"I agree with Julian. It's too dangerous," Ash insisted. "I'll see if Dixon can help."

Melinda Mullet

"We don't have enough evidence to bring Dixon in, and he's made it clear we don't have much time." Maeve glared round the circle of faces. "I'm not asking you to get involved. I can go by myself."

"Oh no you can't," Paul replied. "You go nowhere alone."

Maeve could even hear Simon agreeing in the background on that point. "All right. Then we go together."

236

Chapter Thirty-Five

Patterson Plumbing was hardly a bustling hive of industry. The gates to the side yard were padlocked and a seizure notice had been hung on the fencing.

Maeve and Paul approached the dilapidated trailer that served as an office and knocked. There was a light on inside but no answer. Paul attempted to peer into the high window, but the shades had been drawn, and Maeve was starting to think it might be a wasted trip. The place was eerily quiet, and she wished they'd brought the Captain along, but when she'd left this morning, he'd been happily watching Ash cooking sausages for him aboard the *Red Lion*. She hadn't even known Ash could cook. *Traitor.*

"Oi. Clear off," came a voice from behind them. "No more press. Can't you bloody vultures understand. *No interviews.*"

They turned to see a burly man with a shaved head and a tattoo of the Madonna on his arm. Older than Maeve would have expected but still fit. Patterson Senior at a guess.

"Go on, get out." He gestured back toward the street with his coffee.

237

"We're not press," Maeve said. They'd discussed it at length on the trip over, and after scrounging through her back log of Simon scenes, they'd decided that insurance adjusters would be as good a cover as any. They'd researched some terminology, but she wasn't feeling supremely confident. "Insurance," she said vaguely.

"Had enough of your bloody lot too." He sighed. "But I suppose you'd better come in."

He settled in a folding chair behind a table that was serving as a desk and gestured to two stacks of boxes set out to approximate stools.

They balanced themselves gingerly on the makeshift seats, and Maeve noticed that Patterson reached for a miniature bottle of Dewars and added it to his coffee.

"Out of sugar," he muttered, giving the concoction a stir before looking at them expectantly.

"We are trying to finalize an assessment of the payouts due to the injured parties at the Waterfront," Maeve said, hoping she sounded as if she knew what she was talking about. "Before we can do that, we need to be sure we've accounted for any necessary offsets." She stumbled over the unfamiliar word.

"Moneys that were fraudulently transferred out of the company around the time of the claim," Paul added.

Paul was a quick study. Compared to her, he was a natural. "According to our research, a rather sizable payment was made to a Gavin Foster during contract negotiations over the Waterfront project," Maeve continued, doing her best to sound professional. "We intend to recover that revenue or deduct it from the overall payments made with respect to the claimants."

"If the money isn't refunded, of course, it would leave you open to lawsuits from the impacted residents," Paul added.

"Bring it on," Patterson said. "Can't get blood out of a stone. And as for these supposed payments, you'd have to prove they were made. Foster's dead. Good luck getting him to tell you 'owt." He leaned back and crossed his arms.

Before they could respond, the door opened behind them and a younger man entered the room. The spitting image of his father, only leaner and rougher. He vibrated with rage and energy. He scowled at the two of them.

"Wot now?"

"Insurance," his father said.

"As if we'll see tuppence."

"Less than that," his father replied. "These folks here have decided that there was a sweetener paid to Foster and they'd like it back."

The young man made an elaborate show of being surprised. "Never heard of such a thing."

"Must not have been in this business long," Paul challenged.

Maeve wasn't keen to see this conversation devolve into a full-on fistfight and decided to try placating the men. "We're just saying you might want to request a refund from Gavin Foster's estate under the circumstances. He took all that money from you and then landed you up to your neck in it. Hardly seems fair." She was wildly improvising, but there wasn't much else for it.

"Haven't seen Foster since we delivered the pipes," Patterson Senior said. "Good pipes, too. He's the one that buggered things up. That poncy developer knows it too. First, he was all over blamin' Foster, but now he's died, the bastard's tryin' to shift the blame onto me and the lad."

"Was Malik Ross aware of the payments you made to Mr. Foster?" Paul asked.

"What payment?" Patterson Senior sat back again with a scowl.

"And you never went to talk to Foster about the pipes? Recently, maybe?" Maeve asked.

"Not ever," Junior snapped.

"Never went to ask for your money back?" Maeve pressed.

"Told you. No money to ask for," Senior insisted.

"Might be inclined to put it on record that we believe you if you have an alibi for a week ago today," Paul said.

"Matter of fact, I do." Patterson Senior leaned in again. "I was in court giving a deposition about all this shit. You can check with my lawyers."

Paul looked at Junior. "And you?"

"Aye. Me too." His face was red, and he looked like he was about to come to the boil. "Not enough drivin' us out of business, you lot want to take every pound of flesh you can strip off the carcass." He made a move toward Paul, and his father got to his feet.

"All right, Micky. Calm down," Senior said. "Not going to help us if you get sent up on an assault charge. Blood out of a stone, lad, I keep tellin' you. They can dig all they want, they can't get money we don't 'ave." He caught his son's eyes and held them.

Maeve wasn't sure if he was simply encouraging the lad to stand down or reminding him that they already had their money back and they shouldn't cause a fuss. Either way, Micky backed off and stormed to the other end of the trailer, slamming the filing cabinet on the way past. The noise reverberated through the metal box like a gunshot.

A Ghostwriter's Guide to Murder

Maeve rose, and Paul followed suit. "Clearly this discussion has been counterproductive." She moved toward the door. "Someone from the legal team will be in touch soon."

Paul and Maeve retreated hastily, putting the deserted yard behind them.

"Lad with a bit of a temper," Paul said.

"And I'd say he's lying. Easy enough to prove that Dad was in court, but I'll lay odds Micky boy wasn't."

"I could see him bashing someone over the head for fifty thousand. Fifty thousand that they could clearly use right now. Going through insolvency's no picnic, especially when you're losing a family business," Paul noted.

"I like Micky Patterson as a suspect, especially when you see the threats that were made toward Gavin," Maeve said. "Seems just his style."

"Might mean Ross wasn't involved after all," Paul said.

"I wouldn't count him out yet," Maeve said. "We've always known Ross wasn't the killer. He'd have hired someone else to do the dirty bits."

Paul looked down at her and smiled. "Writing for Harlan's given you a real flair for this."

Maeve appreciated the sentiment, but it was Simon nudging her along. "Ross is a vindictive man, one who wouldn't appreciate being made a fool of by Gavin's mistakes. Why not come to an arrangement with Micky Patterson—retrieve the fifty thousand, get rid of Gavin, and I'll make your legal problems go away."

"You might have something there."

In the back of her mind, she heard Simon's soft *Bravo*.

241

Chapter Thirty-Six

"This lot's all mouth and no trousers," Toliver was saying in the team huddle before the match began. "Just keep your heads down and focus and we'll be straight through."

The Rose was a swankier pub than they were used to. No fruit machines, just plush seating areas filled to the brim with punters even on a Monday night, and the menu on the blackboard in the main room was adorned with artistic renderings of crabs and prawns done in multicolored liquid chalk. A gastropub, for God's sake. Paul shook his head sadly.

The team captain for the Rose approached, wearing a navy-and-cream sweater vest and an attitude. The rest of his team wore the same woolly vests, and they looked as if they were hosting a cricket match, not pub darts.

"Standard rules, and Louisa here'll keep score." He pointed over his shoulder at a smiling woman in a lavender cardy.

Toliver shrugged. "Long as she knows what she's doin'."

The first round had Jimmy up against a brash luxury car salesman. Roy was cheering Jimmy on from the sidelines, so Paul took his beer and joined Toliver at a high-top table a few

A Ghostwriter's Guide to Murder

feet from the rest of the crowd. After the first few darts flew, Toliver seemed to be content that Jimmy had things well in hand, and he sat back and gave Paul his full attention.

"I hear your mate's out of jail."

Paul wondered briefly how he knew, but he supposed, working for a drug lord, there wasn't much Toliver didn't know if he wanted to.

"She's out but not clear. They're referring the case to the CPS," Paul said.

"Wouldn't put it past 'em. Not much chance they'll be looking further if Malik Ross is behind it. He'll have his friends at the Met tying this up in a neat little package."

"Ross really has that much influence over the police?"

"He's a right twat, but he's mastered the art of manipulation. He has a long list of people with secrets—addictions, debts, all sorts. He collects them like shells on a beach and uses them as he needs them. He didn't get ahead in the real estate game on his brains alone."

Paul considered mentioning Patterson but was reluctant to give too much away. For all Ash thought he'd gone native, he didn't fully trust Toliver and some things were better kept to himself.

"I think Gavin might've been keeping records on some of Ross's more creative enterprises. We found papers when I was helping Maeve sort through some of the stuff he'd left in storage."

Toliver displayed the shadow of a smile. "Bright lad, our Gav."

"I suppose if Ross found out, it'd be solid motive for wanting to get rid of Gavin." Paul tried to sound as if the thought had just occurred.

Toliver nodded thoughtfully and continued to drink his beer while watching Jimmy close out his match. He clapped heartily

243

and turned back to Paul. "One thing we know for certain is that Ross didn't have the bollocks to kill Gav himself."

"Then who would he use?"

"Any number of highfliers I can think of that owe him favors. People in debt to him. With Ross the payback is always far less important than having something to hold over a client's head."

"Not all of his clients are highfliers," Paul said softly. "Did you know Roy owes him money?"

Toliver placed his glass back on the coaster in front of him, aligning it precisely in the center before looking into Paul's eyes. "I do, but how do you?"

"It was in Gav's storage stuff. Made me a bit worried for Roy."

Toliver moved in very close, and Paul thought he might've blown it. "Roy did owe Ross. To be honest, it was mostly Roy's old man. He told me a few months back, and I gave him the money to clear the debt—get him away from his dad's mess. Whatever you're thinking, Roy didn't need that money, and even if he did, he wouldn't have taken it. And he damn well wouldn't have killed Gav. We clear on that?"

"Absolutely. And glad to hear it," Paul added.

Toliver sighed heavily. "I do my best to keep an eye out for these lads, but it's not always easy."

Paul turned back to his beer. Roy might've owed Ross money, but Paul had never really seen him killing anyone, especially Gavin. That brought them back to Patterson or possibly one of the other names on the list of Ross's clients. Ash was steering Dixon toward Micky Patterson, which left them to focus on some of the larger debtors on Gavin's list. There were still names they didn't know, and it would take time to identify them, even with Ash's skills. Maybe more time than they had before Maeve's case was referred to the courts.

Ash would hate it, but the fastest way to find the real killer and get Maeve off the hook would be with Toliver's help. Paul was confident Toliver knew the players better and had sources of information they didn't. Maybe even sources the police didn't have. He was keen to take advantage of that. He believed Toliver when he said he was determined to find the real killer; that resolve could work to their benefit. "Okay, so how do we figure out who was in deep enough to be willing to kill for Ross?"

Toliver cocked his head at Paul. "We?"

"Finding the killer's the only way to clear my friend Maeve's name, and although I didn't know Gavin as well as you all did, I stole a memorial bog for the man, and I guess feel invested in getting justice for him as well."

Paul registered a flicker of a smile crossing Toliver's face.

"We, then," Toliver conceded. "I think I can get Ross to talk. He's the first one to throw someone else under the bus if it means protecting his own skin. We just have to make him feel the heat."

Paul felt his pulse quicken. This was what they needed: decisive action. "You'd be willing to take Ross on?" Paul felt the need to clarify. "Even though he's your boss?"

Toliver snorted. "Ross isn't my boss. He's a hustler. A wannabe. I just do the odd security gig for him so I can keep an eye on Jimmy and Roy. Make sure he's not takin' advantage of them."

That explained why Toliver kept hanging around Ross—to keep an eye on the boys. Helpful for Jimmy and Roy and helpful for him.

Toliver downed the rest of his beer. "I should've been watchin' out for Gav better an' all. But whoever Ross sent to kill him is not gettin' away with it."

Paul could see that Toliver had no loyalty to Ross. He wouldn't hesitate to take him down if he needed to; his drug lord boss was far more powerful. The kind of man you didn't mess with. The kind of man who could probably afford a real gold loo.

Throwing his lot in with Toliver wasn't the ideal situation, and the others wouldn't like it, but for now Paul had no better plan.

"What do you have in mind to get him to talk?" Paul asked. Toliver and his people used methods that were likely quite brutal. The thought made him uncomfortable, but how else could they tackle Ross head on when the police wouldn't? Proving Maeve's innocence had to take priority over his own discomfort and anyone else's concerns.

"No need for you to worry about how we get him to talk just yet. When the time comes, maybe you can help me, we'll see." Toliver pointed toward the woolly-vested competitor waiting to take Paul on. "Meantime, you're up. Start slinging some arrows."

Chapter Thirty-Seven

Maeve sat at her desk, pretending to write. This involved sipping her wine every couple of minutes and repeatedly clicking the end of her pen.

She wasn't used to writing longhand, but as the police still had her computer, she had no choice. She stared at the board in front of her. Simon Hill was on the trail of a killer, a man who'd drowned his own brother.

Perhaps that was why she was having trouble returning to the story: Reality was just a tad too close to fiction in this instance. The vision of Gavin floating in the water still haunted her. Everyone was doing their best to help, and she appreciated it, but her brain was on overload. She needed a break, but maybe working on her Simon Hill novel wasn't the best diversion.

It had been a productive day. She felt sure they'd finally found out where Gavin's money had come from, and they'd unearthed another potential suspect in Micky Patterson. Ash had gone to share the news with DS Dixon, Paul was off at a darts tournament, and tomorrow they'd get their heads around the next step. But for now, she was trying to have one seminormal evening at home. She needed to step away from worrying about her own fate and focus on the fate of her protagonist.

She knew where the story was going, right down to the killer's remorseful suicide. A penitent Catholic punishing himself for the horrific crime he'd committed. The story was all there; she just needed to get the words down on paper.

She pushed back in her chair and looked at the ceiling, almost falling over when she heard the knock on the forward door.

"Yoo-hoo," Rowan called. "Can we come in?"

"Sure." For a change, Maeve was happy for the distraction.

"Welcome back," Sage said, breathlessly tottering down the stairs behind Rowan and collapsing her full weight on the narrow padded seat on the port side.

"Good to be back." Maeve didn't rise. The Captain was sitting with his head in her lap and hadn't even budged to greet the ladies.

He was staying as close to his mistress as possible. All these comings and goings didn't suit him in the least. If necessary, he'd physically pin her down to keep her where she belonged. He moved in closer and placed a paw on her leg.

"We made you some brownies." Rowan extended a square pan full of gooey chocolate goodness, still warm on the bottom.

"Marvelous. Thanks so much." Maeve accepted the gesture but wondered if she'd dare eat them. The Wiccans looked back at her as if butter wouldn't melt. "Drink?" she asked.

"Well, now, just a wee one to be social." Rowan smiled.

Maeve turned and stretched to retrieve the bottle of rosé from the fridge, grabbing the only clean glasses she had left, a juice glass and a coffee mug.

A Ghostwriter's Guide to Murder

Rowan took the coffee mug and poured a healthy portion before filing Sage's and topping up Maeve's. "To being free of the Man," she said, raising her glass.

"Are you really done with all the silliness now?" Sage asked.

"Not sure I am, but for the moment, I'll just be happy to sleep in my own bed for another night."

"We've had a few brushes with the law, mostly in connection with our horticultural endeavors," Sage said sympathetically. "So many ridiculous laws, not to mention all the licenses and forms to fill out."

Maeve couldn't help smiling. She would dearly love to immortalize the ladies in one of Harlan's books, but sadly they were not the kind of people Simon or his fans would appreciate.

"It's easier for us; we can play the doddery-old-lady card," Rowan continued. "'Why, Officer, I had no idea,'" she said sweetly. "You're still too young for that."

"I look forward to the day," Maeve said, taking another drink of her wine. Much more and any hope of writing was going out the window.

"Ash has been very dutiful with the Captain," Rowan said, smiling as he tried to climb onto Maeve's lap. "He's walked him two or three times a day while you were gone. Never seen him outside so much. He's a good soul for all his shyness."

"Oh yes, he has a lovely aura," Sage agreed. "Indigo, leaning more toward violet than blue, but still excellent. Means he's spiritually connected as well as curious and gentle. It's why he's so good at research, you see. He has the curiosity to keep digging and the intellect to know how."

"A girl could do far worse." Rowan raised her mug in salute.

249

Melinda Mullet

"He's got a thing for India," Maeve said. "I hope he makes a move before it's too late."

"Does he?" Sage looked confused. "How odd."

"I'll have to give him a nudge after I get this mess sorted out," Maeve said.

Sage smiled. "It might be best to let him find his own way, dear."

* * *

After the ladies left, Maeve made herself a cup of tea and sat down to look at the wall in front of her once more. The index cards pinned at eye level were orderly and everything was linked: scene to scene, action to reaction. Why couldn't life be more like that? Maybe that's why readers loved mysteries so much. A finite number of clues and between the covers a defined beginning, a murky middle, and a satisfactory conclusion. So unlike life itself. No satisfactory conclusions here.

Maeve looked at the last card and tried visualizing the finale in her head like a movie. She found it made the writing flow better, and she was quite proud of the scene she'd devised. Immersing herself in canal life over the last four months, she'd learned a lot about the movement of boats along the more than two thousand miles of waterways that ran the length and breadth of the country. She'd learned how the locks worked to raise and lower the boats as they moved up- or downstream, and the complexity of the inner workings of the lock system had given her an idea for a fabulous death scene.

Simon's quarry was a man who'd killed his own brother—drowned him in a fit of rage. Now, filled with a fierce sense of guilt, he was driven to drown himself to balance the scales of

A Ghostwriter's Guide to Murder

justice in his own troubled mind. Drowning yourself is not an easy feat if you intend to ever be found. Jumping overboard from a boat in the ocean with weights tied to your body is one thing, but then the body is lost at sea forever. In this case, Maeve needed the body to be discovered, so the drowning would have to take place in a more confined space, and a canal lock was a novel twist. Still, it was tricky. Drowning someone else was easy. Drowning yourself was much harder. The human instinct for survival overrode the best-laid plans of authors and murderers.

Maeve's eyes strayed to the brownies on the stovetop. They did look good. She wasn't going out again tonight, why not have a go? She soon found herself wiping the chocolate from her fingers and starting to write. Her brain had just needed to relax, that was all. A bit of Wiccan zen and the words started to flow. The suicide note was good, and the character's plan would be foolproof as long as Simon Hill didn't figure it out.

Maybe this time she'd been so clever he wouldn't.

Chapter
Thirty-Eight

"Absolutely not." Ash was doing his best to stand firm against not just Paul but Dixon as well. "Ross is a loose cannon and anything he says under duress, likely extreme duress in this case, would be inadmissible. You know that." He directed the last remark at Dixon. Of all people he should know better.

Paul had called them to the Anchor the morning after the darts tournament and explained Toliver's strategy for getting Ross to talk. He was going to execute his plan that evening, and he'd asked Paul to be there as a witness. Now that they'd discovered where Gavin's fifty thousand pounds came from, Paul had embraced the idea of Micky Patterson as a lone suspect, or perhaps a combination of Ross and Patterson if Ross'd convinced Patterson to do his dirty work for him. Either way, he said, Ross knew more than he'd admitted so far, and Paul was sure Toliver would be the perfect one to extract a confession if there was one to be had.

Ash could see the logic behind the Patterson theories, but he still wasn't convinced the Machine wasn't playing them all. He was a violent man with powerful and violent friends, and they

252

A Ghostwriter's Guide to Murder

ignored him at their peril. A potential traitor in their midst, but Paul was having none of it.

Dixon, for his part, had his back against the wall. He'd admitted the case was technically closed and the senior officers at the station were content to have it so. He had no other way of moving forward that wouldn't put his own job at risk. He was trying to check Micky Patterson's alibi, but it wasn't easy without attracting unwanted attention to his unsanctioned efforts.

"Look, I'm not thrilled by the idea," Dixon said, "but I don't have an alternative to offer. If Toliver can orchestrate some kind of trap to get a confession out of Malik Ross and he promises not to do any lasting harm to anyone involved, I'm willing to give it a go."

"And what if the whole bloody thing blows up in our faces?" Ash demanded.

"Then at least it's all on Toliver. None of us have our fingerprints on this scheme," Dixon replied.

"Fingerprints? Paul is planning to be *in the room*." Ash's voice shook with anger. "That makes us involved, like it or not." He didn't trust the Machine as far as he could throw him, and he didn't like putting the only shot they had in the man's less-than-clean hands. Moreover, they couldn't guarantee that any of this would help Maeve out of her predicament, and as far as Ash was concerned, that was the fatal flaw in the plan.

"Maeve is out of jail and safe at home for the moment," Dixon insisted. "That gives us a little time to try to get some real answers. We need to make use of it."

"But *why* is she out?" Ash demanded for what felt like the hundredth time. "It makes no sense. If someone's trying to frame her for the killing, then they should want her right where she was in police custody, not out wandering the streets. Something's wrong here."

"I agree," Dixon admitted, "and if we can get Ross to name the killer, then we can clear Maeve's name and the CPS will have to dismiss the case."

Ash stood up and paced the length of the bar. "How can you be comfortable using Paul undercover like he was one of your officers? He's not a cop, and no offense, Paul"—Ash directed the latter at his friend—"he doesn't have the training."

"Sometimes being undercover doesn't work out even if you do have the training," Dixon insisted.

Ash felt the sting of the remark. Before he'd been thrown in the deep end, he'd been given half a day's instruction on undercover operations from a junior officer who treated the whole thing as one big joke. A tech nerd—who'd even look twice? The anger on his face prompted a red-faced apology from Dixon.

"Look, Ashley, I'm sorry." Dixon backpedaled furiously. "That didn't come out the way I intended."

"Yes it did. I went undercover as a police officer and got myself shot. I screwed up."

"You went in as a security consultant. You were watertight. Someone blew that operation, but it wasn't you."

"Yet I took the blame, didn't I."

"No one emerged from that operation looking good. I don't think we were meant to," Dixon added grimly.

"How do we know Paul isn't being set up?" Ash demanded. "It's one thing to send a cop in, but Paul's a civilian. It's too risky." Ash knew what it was like to be alone and vulnerable in a situation where you weren't holding the cards. Paul might be their soldier, better able to fight than he was, but Ash didn't

A Ghostwriter's Guide to Murder

want to see his friend put in danger. He had few enough friends as it was.

"Do you have another option?" Paul asked, coming out from behind the bar. "I'm all ears if you do, but for the moment I think this is the best we've got."

Ash opened his mouth but realized he had nothing more to say.

Dixon looked between the two men. "I'll take some time off from work. I'll follow Paul, keep a low profile, and watch what's happening."

Dixon's presence was reassuring but hardly foolproof. Ash hadn't been alone when he went in undercover. There were other agents on the premises, but when push came to shove, it hadn't mattered. The thought made him sick, but he was clearly being overruled. His teammates were convinced they were playing off angle, using a risky maneuver to try to catch the enemy on his back foot, but Ash wasn't confident they were even taking on the right enemy. He felt betrayed. It was Maeve's freedom they were putting at risk, that and their own lives. He wasn't about to stand around and watch them do it.

With a wounded look in Paul's direction, Ash turned and walked out.

Chapter Thirty-Nine

Paul was starting to fret. Was Ash right about the risks of this scheme of Toliver's? He'd felt self-righteous after their argument earlier in the day, but the closer it came to the time to put Toliver's plan into action, the more nervous he felt. He stood outside a ropy-looking warehouse in Deptford anxiously waiting for Toliver to arrive—a disturbingly regular occurrence in his life these days.

Paul should've felt more confident knowing that Dixon was concealed down the alley behind a rubbish bin, but somehow even the two of them together seemed a questionable match for Toliver's alter ego if they reached a point where their interests diverged.

Speak of the devil, the man himself came striding along the road with a cocky grin on his face.

"Ready for some fun?"

Once again, Paul was pretty sure there would be a substantial difference in his idea of fun and Toliver's, but he'd been wrong before, and besides, it was too late to back out now.

"Let's do this," Paul said with more enthusiasm than he felt.

A Ghostwriter's Guide to Murder

He followed Toliver through a steel door on the side of the building, and as they entered, Paul noticed the door was left unlocked. It saved him the worry of trying to figure out how to get Dixon in. He could fend for himself. Inside they found Jimmy waiting for them.

"Ross'll be here in a few minutes. Let's get Paul settled." Toliver turned back to him. "I want you to have a good view and a chance to catch what Ross says. Bit echoey in here, so you'll need to be relatively close."

"Big space," was all he could think of to say.

"It's being turned into a James Bond experience. VR entertainment all themed to Bond movies. Martinis and good-looking birds catering to your every whim. And a casino, of course."

This was the project Maeve was writing about. Hopefully that was a good omen. "Sounds like a winner."

Looking around, Paul saw a collection of carnival mirrors on wheels spread along one side of the open space. As he walked toward them, his head and body shrank and stretched in bizarre contortions of his real self. In the half-light it was somehow more disturbing. At the far end Toliver led him past what looked like a mock-up of an old Wild West saloon, complete with a cowboy in a black hat poised on the far side of the swinging doors.

"Jimmy?" Toliver called. "You set?"

"You bet." Jimmy's face appeared from behind one of the larger rolling mirrors.

"Stay hidden and follow the action, just like we rehearsed. Ross likes Bond, he's going to get Bond."

Paul wondered why he was here if Jimmy was around to serve as a witness. Then again, Jimmy wasn't the most credible witness, he supposed. "Where did you get all this stuff?"

257

Melinda Mullet

"From my cousin," Toliver said. "He runs one of those party rental businesses. You know, rich folks puttin' a carnival in the backyard for the kiddies' birthday."

Paul had no idea what the Machine would do with it all, but before he could ask additional questions, Toliver rounded on him.

"No phone, right?"

"You said not to," Paul replied truthfully, hoping Toliver wouldn't decide to frisk him, as he did in fact have a phone strapped to his calf with flesh-colored gaffer tape at Dixon's insistence. It would be a nightmare to get off later, but that was the least of his troubles right now.

Toliver led Paul to a catwalk on the far side of the room. At one end was a metal storage box that would give him cover while he observed the scene from above. He caught sight of Dixon slipping in and concealing himself behind a rack of bright-blue coveralls parked to the left of the door. Luckily, Jimmy was busy rigging up a giant jack-in-the-box and didn't notice. Paul felt happier knowing he wasn't alone. "What's the plan?" he asked as casually as he could, as if cornering a criminal mastermind was an everyday occurrence for him.

Toliver wasn't going to be distracted. "Watch and see."

He went back downstairs and turned out all but one of the overhead lights before placing a lone folding chair in the center of the open area below. If Ross wasn't suspicious as soon as he entered, he was a fool.

Toliver posted himself near the door, behind a pillar less than three feet from where Dixon was concealed. Paul felt the hair rising on the back of his neck. Jimmy was behind one of the larger mirrors, and Paul knelt down, waiting for the action to begin.

A Ghostwriter's Guide to Murder

An agonizing ten minutes ticked by as Paul worried about scratching or sneezing or otherwise giving himself away. His nerves were stretched so thin he almost jumped out of his skin when the clang of the door opening announced the arrival of the guest of honor.

As Malik Ross stepped in and started to move toward the center of the room, Paul reached down and set his phone to record.

"Toliver?" Ross called.

"Right here."

Ross turned in time to see Toliver shut the door he'd entered through and lock it.

"Stop arsing about and show me what you wanted me to see." He was trying to sound cocky, but it wasn't quite ringing true.

"You'll find out soon enough." The voice was that of the Machine now not Toliver. He backed Ross toward the chair. "Have a seat."

It was a command, not a suggestion, and although Ross's first inclination seemed to be to continue blustering, he stopped short when he caught sight of the gun in the Machine's hand.

"Take a load off," the Machine insisted again.

Ross sat gingerly on the edge of the metal chair but looked ready to bolt at any moment.

"Brilliant idea, this Bond experience, you know. So much great material to work with." The Machine moved closer. "Wanna know my favorite 007 scene? Bond and Scaramanga in *The Man With the Golden Gun*." The Machine looked down at the weapon in his hand and shrugged. "Not quite a golden gun, but it'll do. Just the thing for an interactive playground."

Paul felt sure the gun was no prop, and he couldn't help thinking they probably should've listened to Ash. But it was too late now.

The Machine flipped a switch on the wall next to him, momentarily leaving the room in darkness, before switching on another overhead light that cast a red glow over the entire floor area.

"What are you playing at?" Ross demanded again, this time with a slight crack in his voice.

"You wanted an adult playground. Here it is. Welcome to your immersive nightmare." The Machine pointed to the wheeled mirror Jimmy was concealed behind. It moved seemingly of its own volition from the side of the factory floor till it sat right in front of the uneasy man. Ross found himself looking into a mirror that made it look as if there were hundreds of Rosses fading off into infinity and suddenly behind him an infinite number of Machines holding a gun pointed at his head.

The Machine laughed. "You'd have lost already. You need to move."

Ross stood and quickly looked right and left for a place to conceal himself and regroup. He ducked behind a large pillar, and Paul heard an exclamation as a wooden box sprang open to reveal a leering clown on a spring that lurched up and hovered over the top of Ross's head, bouncing alarmingly. Ross screamed in genuine terror. The Machine was certainly getting his money's worth from the rental folks.

"That's right, forgot you had a thing about clowns," the Machine said in a tone that suggested he very much had not forgotten.

260

A Ghostwriter's Guide to Murder

Ross scrambled away from the leering figure and ran toward the center of the room. He turned back toward the Machine. "What do you want from me?"

"The one thing you never want to give," the Machine said. "The truth."

"Truth about what?" Ross demanded.

"Gavin Foster. Did you kill him?"

"Don't be daft. He worked for me. I make a policy of not killing people that work for me."

"Change of pace from the old days, then," the Machine remarked.

The Machine continued to advance, skillfully backing Ross into another part of the room, where a motion trigger dropped a chattering skeleton at his right shoulder.

Ross swore. "Look, I told you I didn't kill him. Now enough's enough."

"But I think you know who did," the Machine insisted, herding Ross like a stray calf toward the corner with the cowboy. As they approached, the saloon doors swung open and the cowboy moved forward on his tracks, raising a six-shooter at Ross. Paul caught a flicker of movement. Jimmy was doing a good job of triggering the effects. They must have practiced all day.

The cowboy was only a dummy, but it was lifelike and, in the eerie red light, disconcerting. Ross was shaken, and probably stirred as well, and he seemed to have decided he needed to find a way to negotiate with this madman. Paul wondered if he'd even seen the sequence from *The Man With the Golden Gun*, an elaborate game of cat and mouse between Bond and the villain. Was Ross aware that none of Scaramanga's guests ever left the carnival room alive?

261

"Look, I didn't kill Gav. He was a good lad. But yeah, I may know who did."

"Thought you might," the Machine replied, moving closer to Ross, the gun still trained at his chest. "Go on then."

"Last time I saw Gav, I sent him to collect some money from a guy that owed me. Shoulda been a simple straightforward courier job. Pick up the cash and bring it to me, but I waited and waited, and the money never came. Gav wasn't answering his phone, so I called my client and said where's my money. He swore he gave it to my courier, but then they always do, don't they? I mean, it was only part of what he owed me, but fifty thousand's fifty thousand. Figured he was lying about my courier, so I told him I'd give him forty-eight hours to sort it. Two days later he came with the money, and I thought nothing of it. Figured maybe he'd just needed a couple more days to get the cash together."

"Liar." The single screamed word echoed off the rafters in the open space. Jimmy burst through the saloon doors behind the cowboy and rushed at Ross. "Gav gave you that money. I was with him that night. Heard you thankin' 'im an' all. Don't you dare try an' say 'e didn't." Jimmy looked poised to attack Ross, and Toliver hastily stepped forward, putting a restraining arm on Jimmy while continuing to point the gun at Ross.

Jimmy looked up at Toliver pleadingly. "You 'ave to believe me. I was there. Gav 'ad the money, all of it, and 'e gave it to this bastard. I was with 'im. We were on our way to that tournament in Surbiton."

"Oh, I believe you, Jimmy," Toliver said quietly, turning back to Ross. "Well now, maybe you'd like to rethink your little story." The Machine returned, his voice softly menacing. "Seems you received your money as requested, but you still sent someone after Gavin. Why?"

"Foster owed me money too," Ross blustered.

"I don't believe Gav owed you fifty thousand pounds," Toliver pressed. "I know he hadn't borrowed it, and where else would he get that kind of money?"

"Greedy bastard took fifty thousand in backhanders from that lousy pipe company in Croydon. Bloody fool should've known the stuff was shit if they were willing to pay that much to get rid of it. I call it an idiot tax. Least he could do was give the cash to me to offset all it was costing to fix that mess. Fair's fair."

"So you used one of the poor sods that owed you money to collect from Gav?"

"Yeah, my client's good at that sort of thing, and as luck would have it, he and Gav *both* owed me fifty thousand. He knew he'd given Gav fifty thousand, and when it turned out Gavin happened to have fifty thousand in cash lying about, he put two and two together and got five. He didn't know it was Gav's money he was taking, though; thought it was his."

Paul stood frozen in the rafters, calculating rapidly. So it wasn't Patterson; it was one of Ross's other clients. Someone they hadn't identified yet.

Ross was looking smug. "I got what they both owed me, didn't have to get involved. It all worked out pretty slick."

"Slick," Jimmy screeched. "Gav's dead."

Ross dipped his head in acknowledgment. "I'll admit, that was unfortunate."

"Unfortunate, was it?" The Machine moved closer, planting the gun squarely on Ross's chest.

263

Melinda Mullet

Paul felt panic rising in him. Things looked like they were about to go very badly downstairs. Would Dixon step in? Should he?

"Gavin turned up dead—think that was fair?" the Machine snarled.

"I didn't think my client was the type to go heavy-handed." Ross shrugged. "Figured he'd just get the money and we'd all be square."

"We're not square." Jimmy looked around wildly. "We'll . . ." He looked desperately at Toliver. "We'll call the cops."

"Good luck with that," Ross sneered. "My client *is* a cop."

264

Chapter Forty

Maeve was on her third glass of wine. Not wise maybe, but she was surrounded by her friends. India and Ash were there along with the ladies, and Julian had shown up as well. They were having a few drinks and pizzas had been ordered. The faces around her were bathed in the glow from the fire pit Rowan and Sage had dragged out onto the towpath. Ash swore they used it to heat their cauldron on a full moon. Everyone looked relaxed; everyone but Ash. She could tell he was worried. He made no bones about the fact that he was there to keep an eye on her, and she suspected he'd recruited Julian and India to help.

It wasn't that Maeve wasn't worried. She was. Her situation was little better today than it had been yesterday, but at least she wasn't stuck in the Met's cells, they'd figured out what kind of game Gav was playing, and she now knew she had at least one cop who believed she was innocent. She was putting a lot of trust in him, but for the moment she didn't have much choice. *Always look on the bright side,* she thought, taking another drink.

Paul and DS Dixon were off somewhere following a lead. Ash wouldn't say where or what was involved, and for some

265

Melinda Mullet

reason he looked angry about it all. Maeve could only presume the other boys hadn't asked Ash to come and play and he was feeling left out. She was doing her best to cheer him up, and she'd seated him next to her as she tried to show him how to cook sausages over an open flame. The Captain squeezed in between them, watching the proceedings with interest.

The sky darkened, and the circle of light around the campfire grew tighter and tighter until the world beyond faded to black. Maeve was happy to let it go—to forget about anything beyond the immediate circle of light and friends. She was safe here in her cocoon. India came over and stood by her chair, placing a hand on her shoulder.

"Any idea when Paul'll be back?" she asked.

"Don't even know where he is, so it's hard to judge." Maeve leaned her head back and looked up at India through slightly bleary eyes. The red glow from the fire now seemed to be lighting up the whole sky. Maeve dimly recognized that that shouldn't be possible.

"What *is* that?" India asked, looking down the canal in the direction of Camden Lock.

"Looks like a fire," Sage said. "And a large one at that."

India leaned to her right, trying to see around the curve in the towpath.

Maeve scrambled to her feet, climbing up to the roof of the *Revenge* and standing unsteadily on her toes. "Looks like it's coming from the area around the Anchor."

Julian and Ash jumped up at that and started off down the towpath at a trot. India followed them and Maeve grabbed the Captain's collar, handing him off to the Wiccans. "Can you keep him here while we see what's happening?"

266

A Ghostwriter's Guide to Murder

"Of course," Rowan replied. "Be careful, all of you."

Maeve put on a burst of speed to catch up and arrived at the Anchor just behind the others, who were watching in horror as flames spilled out of the rear window of the old building. The fire must've started in the kitchen. Maeve turned to follow India and Julian into the back courtyard, where Ash was fixing up a couple of hoses to spray down the roof and the walls of the stables. She'd never really thought of him as a man of action, but in a crisis, he was certainly stepping up.

"Someone's called 999," he said. "Might lose the pub if they don't hurry, but we can try to save the flats."

Maeve thought about calling Paul, but who knew how far away he was, and help was needed right now. It was down to them.

Maeve looked up the grass bank behind the converted-stable block. It rose up three stories to the street level, and a roof-high eight-foot brick wall kept the mud and grass from sliding down into the stable yard. The best vantage point for dousing the roofs with water would be the top of the wall. If Ash handed her a hose, she could spray water from above and hopefully keep the sparks from jumping across the narrow yard. In the distance she heard the sirens of the approaching fire department. With the help of the fire crew, maybe they'd be able to salvage something after all.

She took off at a run down the towpath to the stone steps that connected the canal level to the street above. The stairs were old, crumbling and dangerously varied in height and depth. An absolute menace after a few drinks, and she quickly reached for the handrail to steady herself. Halfway up she ducked under the rail and into the undergrowth, working her way toward the section that rose up behind the rear of the Anchor.

267

Melinda Mullet

Crouched on the wall, she tried to get Ash's attention so he could hand the hose up. She should've warned him of her plan before she raced off. Everyone's focus had shifted by now to the firemen, who were unrolling their hoses and starting to engage with the flames coming out of the windows nearer the front of the pub.

Maeve watched from her superior vantage point, finally giving up on getting anyone's attention and deciding to retreat back down to the level of the action. She clawed her way through the overgrown brush, catching her foot on the root system of an old tree and sprawling face first on the uneven ground. She picked herself up and pushed on toward the stairs.

As she went to duck back under the railing, she heard someone on the stone steps and straightened to find herself face-to-face with the senior officer from the police station. He'd sat in on her interrogation. She scrambled for the name in her head— DCI Bolton. That was it.

"Allow me." He extended a hand and helped her under the railing and back to the slightly more stable ground of the stairs with an amused look. "Just the woman I was looking for."

Surely she wasn't about to be arrested yet again. "What now?" she said, past being concerned about being disrespectful to a senior police officer.

"DS Dixon suggested I talk to you about the next steps in your case, but looks like we need to get that hand sorted first."

Maeve looked down and realized the fall had left her with a deep cut on her right palm. Her clenched fist had stemmed the blood, but now she'd opened it, the blood had started to flow and it was making a mess. She hadn't even noticed until her attention was drawn to it. The pain suddenly registered, as if her body had been waiting for the visual clue to respond.

268

A Ghostwriter's Guide to Murder

Bolton placed a hand under her elbow and began to steer her gently up the stairs. Maeve looked back over her shoulder. "The towpath's that way," she said, gesturing in the direction she'd approached from.

"I just came from there. The fire gear's blocking the way at the bottom now; we'll have to go around to the College Street bridge and down that way."

When they reached the road at the top of the stairs, Bolton gestured toward a dark sedan parked on a double yellow line. "Perks of the office." He smiled, opening the boot and pulling out a large white first aid box. He dug around inside and handed her the antiseptic cream. "Get some of that on your hand, and we'll wrap it up."

"Thanks." Maeve felt guilty being up here, tending to her wounds, and not down with the others. "I'm such a klutz."

"Happens to the best of us." He reached into the boot again and came up with a thermos. "That was a lot of blood. Have some tea, you'll feel better."

"Thanks." She took a sip and found the tea soothing and sobering. Just the ticket. She downed it as quickly as she could, then rose, anxious to return to the action. "Do you think someone set fire to the pub on purpose?" Maeve paused. There was a fire, wasn't there? Suddenly she wasn't sure. Her memory of being down at the Anchor seemed to be fading, and she was having trouble connecting how she'd got from down there to up here.

"Anything's possible," Bolton replied. "No doubt the fire department will look into it."

Maeve knew there was something odd that she was having trouble grasping. Like searching for the path beneath your feet in the fog. She frowned. What was bothering her? *Think,* she admonished herself. *What would Simon do? WWSD.* The thought almost made her giggle aloud, which was odd, because it wasn't funny, not really. She looked over at the man leaning on the corner of the boot, watching her. She shouldn't be here, or maybe he shouldn't be here? Concentrating on the question made her head ache.

"You all right?" Bolton asked.

Maeve tried to stand up. "I don't know. I feel fuzzy." Suddenly she knew she had to get out of here. Away from the smiling man with the first aid kit. She forced herself to try again, grabbing at the side of the car to haul herself to her feet. Her head spun and the ground lurched up at her. What was happening? It was as if she were in the middle of a nightmare. She tried to scream, but no sound came from her lips. The last thing she remembered was being tipped backward into the boot of the car and seeing the lid slam shut above her.

Chapter Forty-One

Paul was starting to think Toliver had missed his calling as a director. The man seemed to have reveled in the pure theatrics of making Ross squirm, not to mention his abject terror when Jimmy locked Ross in the jack-in-the-box crate with the clown. It hadn't made Jimmy any less angry. He was still spitting venom, but it seemed to have helped Toliver in some small way.

"It's the little things in life, innt?" Toliver said with a grin, and Paul had to agree. He hadn't been convinced that this stunt would pay off, but it had in spades. They'd sent Jimmy home to cool off and left Ross behind in the warehouse, not alone, as Toliver thought, but with Dixon waiting to take him in.

As they made their way back to Toliver's 4 × 4, Paul had to admit he was still a little vague about how the whole thing had come to pass. Ross clearly thought he'd been a clever boy, pulling strings behind the scenes to get what he wanted—getting a client to not only pay off a chunk of his own debt but retrieve money from Gavin as well. It wasn't clear to Paul whether Ross meant to get Gavin killed, but either way he had been, and by a cop no less. A cop who had to be one of the unidentified numbers on the

271

register of Ross's clients in the lockup, but Toliver was sure he knew exactly who it was.

"Ross had all sorts on his payroll. People willing to do whatever he asked to keep their positions, to keep their secrets from getting out. In this case, my money's on Jason Bolton. Has to be him."

Bolton. Ash had mentioned him. The man hustling Maeve's case to prosecution, supposedly in the name of boosting his solved-case record, but if Toliver was right, then truthfully to cover his own tracks. "Are you sure it's Bolton? Big accusation if you're wrong."

"He's round Ross's offices on the Isle of Dogs all the time. At first, I thought he was just one of the many lining up for a hand-out. A reward for keeping the wheels of Ross's machine turning. Lately, I decided he had to be part of Ross's collection of human seashells, a man with secrets. Face it, he'd be useful to Ross. A copper senior enough to make a difference but not senior enough to be obvious."

"Well, you were right about Ross," Paul conceded. "So what's the next move?"

"Doubt Ross'll be heading to jail, his lawyers will see to that, but the responsibility for Gav's death lays at his door. Clear as day. I'll find a way to pay that back down the road, but first, the man who actually killed Gav is answering to me."

Paul wasn't keen to be on hand for this part of the plan. Vigilante justice was not what was needed here, not if they were going to help Maeve. They needed the killer alive. To ensure that, he needed to warn Dixon that the Machine was going after one of his brethren. Would Dixon already know who the cop in question was? Paul had to think he'd have his suspicions. Dixon was no fool.

"I could testify against Ross," Paul said. *And Dixon will*, he thought to himself, but would it be enough? Belatedly he realized

A Ghostwriter's Guide to Murder

that likely wouldn't be the end of it. Not with Ross's legal team. Ash had warned them that a confession under duress would never stand. And with a crooked DSI in the mix, Dixon might be the one facing disciplinary action in all of this. Paul had a sinking feeling Toliver's theatrics might've been a waste after all.

"'Fraid it'll be your word against Ross's if you testify," Toliver said. "And you with a vested interest in what happens to Maeve Gardner." As they approached the car, Toliver looked down at his watch. "We need to find Bolton, but right now I'm worried about your friend. She's being framed for Gav's murder to cover up a copper's trail. She's a liability to Bolton now. He needs to close this case fast. He's identified a killer, and that killer needs to be a person that no one can question."

"How does he do that?" Paul was suddenly frightened to hear the answer but thought if anyone would have one, it would be the Machine.

"If it were me," Toliver admitted, "I'd want a dead killer with a full confession. I think that's why she was released from jail. Give her enough rope to hang herself, or enough to let someone else do it for her."

Paul stopped in his tracks as they reached the car and turned to face Toliver. "You think he's going after Maeve?"

"Bolton's a problem solver, and unlike Ross, it seems he's willing to do his own dirty work."

"Then Maeve's in real danger." Paul was suddenly glad to be with the Machine. He had the muscle and the savvy to deal with this kind of situation. "We have to find Bolton and stop him."

Toliver hopped into the driver's seat. "First, we find Maeve Gardner. When we find her, I'm betting we'll find Bolton."

273

Chapter Forty-Two

"Where's Maeve?" India asked.

Ash looked around the sodden chaos on all sides of them. The flames were out, and the men from the fire department were sifting through the smoke-damaged interior of the main bar, looking for any lingering sparks. "Maeve?" he called, spinning around in a circle. Raising his voice brought on spasmodic coughing.

"I don't remember seeing her since we were hosing down the stables." India was already heading down the towpath in the direction of the *Revenge*. "Maybe she went back to check on the Captain and the ladies."

"Not without us, surely," Ash said. He was now doubled over, trying to cough the smoke from his lungs.

India looked around for Julian and saw him across the yard, talking to the fire chief. Ever the lawyer. Ash began hacking again, and a medic approached. "Sir, please come see the medical staff." He gestured toward the emergency crew tending to one of the firemen.

A Ghostwriter's Guide to Murder

Ash tried to brush him off, but India intervened and helped steer him to a makeshift medical tent, where a tech stood with an oxygen mask and a thermal blanket.

"Just for a minute," the man said. Between them, they got Ash to sit down and put the mask on his face.

"Breathe a bit," India said. "I'll go check at the boat; I'm sure she's there." India could see that Ash was starting to panic and it was making the coughing worse. "I'll come right back and let you know one way or the other."

Ash moved the mask aside. "Be careful," he croaked out before another fit of coughing overtook him.

India walked briskly until she was out of sight of Ash before breaking into a close approximation of a run. Something felt wrong. Last thing she wanted was to get the Wiccans all in a dither, but she needed to assure herself that Maeve had simply slipped home.

They'd called Paul from the scene of the fire. He still hadn't explained what he was doing tonight, but wherever he'd been, he was now hustling back, and India was glad.

She puffed up to the *Revenge* and found Rowan and Sage still sitting outside, enjoying the dying embers of the fire pit. Sage was holding tightly to the Captain's lead to keep him from running off in search of the rest of them.

"Is Maeve here?"

Sage frowned. "No, dear. She was with you."

"We can't find her." India looked right and left, as if Maeve might be hiding somewhere in plain sight. "Could she have come back to the boat and you didn't notice?"

"Possible, I suppose," Rowan said.

India headed over to the *Revenge* and climbed aboard, calling for her friend. The place was empty. Rowan had followed behind her. "Surely the Captain would've gone mad if Maeve had returned," she pointed out. "He growled a bit earlier, but I thought he'd just heard the fox. We have several that are living in the undergrowth along the towpath."

India was looking at Maeve's desk. It was oddly neat, and in the center was a piece of school paper with several lines in her neat handwriting that said, *I can't keep living a lie. The guilt is too much. I must atone. It is time to cleanse myself with the same waters that took my victim.*

"Peculiar," Rowan said, reading over her shoulder. "What does it mean?"

India thought it was obviously a suicide note, and it was in Maeve's hand, but it made no sense. Maeve wasn't the type to commit suicide. Families said that all the time, but truly not Maeve. Not to mention she hadn't killed anyone. She'd have no reason to feel remorse. Maybe for the odd poorly conceived detective novel, but that was hardly her fault.

India picked up an index card that was protruding from under an empty tea mug. The pinhole in the center suggested it had been up on the wall before. No threats here, simply the musings of a writer on her denouement.

<u>Endgame</u>: Water = cleansing of spirit/conscience. Felix commits suicide by chaining himself to an iron ring in the water pipe that channels water into the lock system. When the next boat comes through and the water rushes in, he's submerged and drowns. Issues: would self-preservation kick in? Throw key out of reach. Or maybe a drug of some type to sedate himself. Research.

A Ghostwriter's Guide to Murder

India looked up at the wall. There were a few other macabre notes on autopsies and evidence, but mostly just a framework for the current PI novel, all in the same small, neat script.

Outside the boat, the Captain had started barking wildly.

"That's probably her now," Rowan said. The two women popped out of the galley and onto the deck in time to see Ash rushing toward them.

"Is she there?" Ash called out.

India shook her head. "Not here, but there is something odd on the *Revenge*." She heard the sound of more running feet coming from the other direction and was relieved to see Dixon approaching from the bridge side. "DS Dixon," she called. "There's something here we need you to see."

Dixon made his way onto the *Revenge* and bent over the note on the table in the salon. "What do you think?" she demanded. India noticed he hadn't touched the paper. Should she mention that she had? Her prints would be all over it. "I'm afraid I picked it up and read it. Sorry."

Dixon was now moving the mug with a pencil so he could see the entire index card. "Was this kind of note taking usual for her?"

"Well, I mean, normally she wrote on her laptop, but the police still have it."

Ash was watching Dixon closely from the doorway. "Well?"

"Strikes me as awkward for a suicide note," Dixon replied. He seemed more comfortable answering Ash's questions. "No reference to friends or the dog. Usually, final messages seek to absolve those left behind from guilt, and they often make provision for loved items or pets. This almost seems, I don't know—"

277

"Like an incomplete thought," India offered, unable to stay silent.

"Yes," agreed Dixon. "Like an excerpt from something."

India went over to Maeve's computer bag and brought it to Dixon. "There could be more in here," she said. "She'd been doing some work longhand on the book she was writing."

Dixon opened the bag and pulled out a pad of lined white paper. A dozen or so pages of dialogue and description, all in the same hand.

He passed it to India. "Recognize this?"

India scanned through the pages. "She didn't really share her work with me, so I can't say I recognize the text specifically, but it does seem odd to me that the writing ends at the bottom of this page midsentence and then the next page is blank."

Dixon took the pad and looked at the top edge under the light of the desk lamp. "Looks like a page has been torn out." He straightened and looked back at Ash in the doorway.

"How was she taking all this? Would you say she was suicidal?"

"Maeve? No. Not happy, obviously, but not in despair."

"Absolutely not suicidal," India concurred. "She hadn't given up hope, bleak as it all is." India returned to the desk and began to study the papers again, occasionally looking up at the note cards on the wall in front of them. "This is the latest book she's writing," she said for Dixon's benefit. "An old-time PI named Simon Hill. The cards represent an outline of the action in the story. From there she types up the scenes on her computer, or in this case writes it in her notebook. This card is clearly notes for the final scene." She gestured from the card on the table to the empty pin stuck in the wall at the end of the line. "The card

A Ghostwriter's Guide to Murder

before it says suicide note. Not hard to guess she'd have written one somewhere."

"And you think this is it?"

"Makes sense, doesn't it? The text's contrived, stilted even. Not what Maeve herself would say if she was desperate enough to write a suicide note. She'd never say *atone* or *cleanse*. Those are literary devices better suited to the 1950s world of her hero."

"So someone looked for the suicide note in her longhand text, then took it out, leaving it behind out of context to support the notion of suicide," Dixon said.

"If this is Gavin's killer, they were damn lucky that Maeve was writing longhand, and that the outline was on the board for anyone to see." India's hands began to shake. "This has to mean the killer has been stalking Maeve," India said.

"How would a stranger even know she had all these notes?" Ash asked.

Dixon ran a hand through his hair. "There were photos of her desk in the case files. The note cards with the outline on them, everything. We had them blown up on a board in my office at one point. Any number of people could have seen them."

"But only other officers, surely," India said.

"That's the problem." Dixon looked as if he'd aged in the last twenty-four hours. "It seems our killer *is* an officer."

"One of your lot killed Gavin?" India grabbed for the back of the chair next to her as her knees buckled.

"A cop?" Ash's face was chalk white. "And he's been here tonight, planning to kill Maeve by making it look like a suicide?"

"Dear God." India was trembling all over now, her mind racing. "She'd have researched her end scene meticulously. She

Melinda Mullet

always does. The scene could be re-created, and it would support the illusion that she'd planned her own death."

"Do you know who the killer is?" Ash demanded.

"I have a damn good idea, and we need to find him," Dixon said. "Quickly."

280

Chapter
Forty-Three

Maeve opened her eyes and groggily watched the gray clouds above her head skittering across the dark sky like smoke from a giant fire.

Fire.

She thought of the Anchor. It had been on fire. As the memories began to trickle back in, she registered that she was being carried. Why? She'd been up on the wall behind the stables. Had she fallen? Like Alice down the rabbit hole, images floated in and out of her head: trees, steps, cars. None of it seemed right. She tried to focus on the man carrying her. The policeman not there to help but to harm. Suddenly she remembered it all; this was wrong. Desperately, irreparably wrong.

She tried to move, to resist, but her limbs were heavy and the connection between her will and her ability seemed to have been completely severed. Bolton looked down impassively, as if he were struggling to carry a sack of potatoes, not a semiconscious human being.

"Almost there," he said, more to himself than her. She bounced up and down as he maneuvered a short, steep flight of

281

stairs. She looked as far left and right as she could, trying to figure out where they were. Rising up behind them was a block of flats. Familiar, but too far away for the residents to notice what was happening below.

The sound of running water told her they were at the Saint Pancras Lock. She'd walked here often enough with the Captain, ironically researching this very scene. As she thought of him, the tears welled up in her eyes. If the Captain was here, this wouldn't be happening to her.

At the bottom of the steps, they stopped, and she was dumped on the ground. She watched from the cold cement and saw Bolton grit his teeth before slipping into the canal that flowed beside them. The water trickling over the ends of the lock basin covered the noise of his movements. Bolton made his way across the ten feet or so to the massive water-balancing pipe that moderated the flow of water between the upper and lower sections of the canal. The pipe that would be flooded with water when the process of lowering the first boat began in the morning.

Bolton scrambled into the mouth of the pipe. Maeve couldn't see him any longer, but she knew what he was doing. She'd researched the area and taken dozens of pictures on her phone. Planned the end of book forty-three to perfection. Thought of every possibility. There was a metal ring hanging from the ceiling of the large pipe. He'd be throwing a rope over the ring and running the tail ends down into the water. He'd be struggling to stand because the floor of the cement pipe was covered in a thick coat of algae, enough to make getting a firm footing extremely tricky. With a rising sense of dread, Maeve knew with certainty that it wouldn't be long before he added her to the scene.

A Ghostwriter's Guide to Murder

A noose would be formed and slipped over her head. The other end of the rope would be attached to the ring in the ceiling. She'd be left sitting in the middle of the pipe, the frigid water soaking into her limbs, unable to move or speak because of the sedative she'd been given. Unable to pull the excessively tight noose over her head. Unable to stand without slipping on the slime that covered the floor of her prison. The rope just short enough that if she tried and fell, she'd hang herself. On the other hand, if she sat motionless and waited, the water would rush through with the first morning transit and drown her just as efficiently. From the outside a suicide. A very well-planned suicide.

If it wasn't so horrific, it would almost be funny. It looked like her greatest accomplishment as a writer was going to be penning her own death scene.

Chapter Forty-Four

"What's happening?"

Ash looked up to see Paul and the Machine striding along the towpath toward him. The rest of the crew were standing around outside the *Revenge* as Ash and Dixon pored over a map of the Regent's Canal lock system that Rowan had provided them.

"Maeve's missing," Ash said.

"That'll be Bolton," the Machine said without missing a beat.

"How can you be sure?" Ash demanded. He still wouldn't put it past this villain to be involved in some way.

Paul gave a succinct summary of what Dixon had already told them and the Machine's theory. The Machine remained unaware that Dixon had been present at the carnival scene and had come to the same conclusion. Independently, they had two votes for Bolton, but they still could be wrong.

"What's the plan?" the Machine asked, gesturing toward the maps.

"We've got this under control," Ash snapped. The last thing they needed was some brainless thug along for the ride.

A Ghostwriter's Guide to Murder

"Do you?" The Machine tilted his head to one side. "Bolton will be trying to fake a suicide. It'll close the case neatly and stop anyone questioning the evidence the police have on hand."

Ash was struck by the accuracy of the assessment, but it wasn't helping his anxiety about Maeve and her current whereabouts. "We know that, and we know how. We're just down to where—unless you can tell us that?"

Dixon ignored the tension in the air and called their attention to the maps. "According to Maeve's notes, there were two locks close by that she was considering using in the book: Kentish Town and Saint Pancras. Opposite directions, unfortunately." Dixon looked toward India. "You've been reading through her research, and I presume the killer did too. Any idea which one she was favoring?"

India shook her head. "No clue."

Ash looked at Dixon. "We can't gamble on going to the wrong one. We'll have to check both. You and I can split up and go in opposite directions."

"My car's just up the top of the bank," the Machine said. "Paul and I'll head to Kentish Town, you two take Saint Pan's."

"Make sure you stay in touch," Dixon insisted before turning back to Ash. "Let's go."

"You're not going without me," India said firmly.

"Do you drive?" Dixon demanded.

"Not often, but I can."

"Then come on. Take my car and get us to the Camley Street bridge."

India grabbed the Captain's lead from Sage's hand and headed after Dixon.

285

Melinda Mullet

Ash wanted to stop the Machine from taking off with Paul. But with Maeve in danger, they needed all the help they could get. You didn't always get to choose who went on a mission with you, and the Machine *was* a warrior. But deep inside Ash couldn't stand the thought of Maeve being rescued by anyone else. This quest was real and deeply personal.

He wanted to be the one who saved her.

Chapter Forty-Five

"This way," Toliver said, scrambling down a grassy hill over the top of a low wall covered in graffiti and onto the towpath below. He'd parked behind the Camden Boxing Club, landing them less than fifty yards from the lock.

A wrought iron railing separated the towpath from the canal's edge and from the wooden swing arms that controlled the flow of the water into the holding chambers. The two men vaulted the railings and hurried to the nearest tank. Paul pulled out his phone and shined the light around the sides of the wall. There was no sign of Maeve or Bolton. Toliver had switched on his own light and was directing it at the edges of the path at their feet.

"Doesn't look like anyone's been here disturbing things recently."

"Damn," Paul said.

"It's also not the quietest of spots. I wouldn't choose it," Toliver said, looking around. "Could be the other location, but honestly, if Bolton wants to get rid of her, he's likely done it already." The look on Paul's face must have prompted him to add, "Sorry."

287

"I'm not ready to give up yet," Paul said.

"Fair enough, but we can't keep guessing randomly. We need to find Bolton. Maybe we can get him to tell us where she is."

Paul knew Toliver was trying to be positive for his sake.

"If not, he needs to be dealt with for what he's done."

Paul didn't like the sound of *dealt with*, but Toliver was right, something had to be done, and at the moment they were getting nowhere fast. "Right, but how do we find Bolton?"

"I suspect he's a bit of a mess after dealing with"— Toliver paused— "this situation. He'll have gone to get cleaned up. Home, I'd think."

"Do we know where he lives?"

"No, but I can find out." Toliver picked up his phone and sent a text message.

Paul didn't bother to ask who he'd contacted, but he figured Toliver was taking advantage of his drug boss's connections to locate Bolton. Paul suspected they'd have someone like Ash who could provide all kinds of useful information when it was needed. They made their way back to the car and Toliver leaned against the boot, smoking a cigarette and keeping half an eye on his phone.

Paul couldn't bear just standing around. He was about to suggest they headed for Saint Pan when he heard a loud thwacking noise. Paul ducked instinctively, a moment of terror registering clearly on his face. Noticing that Toliver was on his phone, Paul realized it had been the sound of a dart hitting the cork at full force.

"Text notification," Toliver murmured.

Appropriate enough for the dart king, but in a dark side street at nearly one in the morning, it was unnerving.

A Ghostwriter's Guide to Murder

"We've got Bolton," he said. "Not far off; he lives in Finsbury Park." Toliver climbed in the car and tucked his cigarette into the mug holder before spinning the 4×4 out of the alley and heading north along the A503.

"Shouldn't we call the police?" Paul felt ridiculous as soon as the words had left his lips. What good would calling the cops do when they were after a cop?

Toliver didn't respond to the question; his thoughts seemed to be elsewhere. "I think it's best if you stay in the car when we get there."

Paul would certainly rather stay in the car, but he couldn't. The Machine had done well with Ross, who, according to his whispered conversation with Dixon, remained in the warehouse in Deptford. Dixon admitted he had no idea who he could trust to go and get him, and as more pressing matters had come to a head, he'd left the decision of what to do with Ross for the morning. The Machine's way of dealing with Bolton was likely to be much messier, and he feared it might wind up dropping Maeve right back in it. Paul decided to take the bull by the horns. "If Bolton's dead, how do we prove he killed Gavin and maybe Maeve?"

"What makes you think he'd be dead?"

"Well, not now, but maybe shortly . . ." Paul trailed off, not sure how to complete the thought.

Toliver shot him an amused look. "Don't worry. I'm not planning to kill him. We need him to talk if we have any hope of nailing Ross to the wall. Walking, though—that's optional."

Chapter Forty-Six

Ash knew India was having to think things through as she looked at the gear lever on Dixon's Ford Focus. But to her credit, once they'd loaded in, she peeled out with maximum velocity and minimum gear grinding.

He'd been assessing the situation as they headed for the car. The Kentish Town locks were largely manually operated; picturesque, but in the middle of an area with lots of cafés and restaurants. Not a good place for staging a suicide. Logic suggested that if Maeve was anywhere nearby, she was at Saint Pan.

He held on to the Captain and the seat in front of him as they careened around a corner. Not being adept at switching gears, India seemed to have decided that the best approach was not to. Taking advantage of the lack of traffic and the fact that she had a cop in the front seat, she made it all the way to the Camley bridge without fully stopping once. Dixon, Ash, and the Captain jumped out, leaving her to park the car. If Maeve was there, the Captain would find her.

The lock itself was surrounded by a low railing designed more to keep drunks from slipping in than to keep anyone out.

290

A Ghostwriter's Guide to Murder

Ash and Dixon climbed over the railing, and the Captain slipped underneath. Ash peered through the dark, searching for a likely spot to conceal a person. Based on Maeve's notes, her finale needed a sluice that came through a large pipe. It needed to be at least five feet across. Dixon was shining a flashlight up and down the sides of the lock. On the far side the beam hit a round opening in the cement. A small amount of water was trickling through it, but when the next boat came through to be lowered, it would turn into a full-on torrent. Just as she'd described. The Captain ran ahead of them down the short flight of steps to the lower level of the lock and stood sniffing at the cement. There was no sign of Maeve or her abductor, but as Dixon shined his flashlight into the tunnel, they caught sight of a dark figure in the center of the pipe. It was several feet inside, but it was recognizable as the hunched form of a person.

If there was any doubt it was Maeve, it was eliminated by the bark of recognition from the Captain, who jumped into the murky water without a second's hesitation, paddling his way to the far side of the canal and hooking his front paws over the edge of the runoff pipe. He was stuck there, scrabbling against the slippery sides, trying to hoist himself up into the space. Before Dixon could stop him, Ash followed the Captain into the freezing water and waded across the canal to the dog's side.

"Maeve. You all right?" he yelled, praying for an answer. When none came, he boosted the Captain up ahead of him into the tunnel. Dixon was shouting suggestions from the other side, but Ash heard nothing. His focus was on reaching Maeve before it was too late.

The Captain reached her first and began licking her face. Her head was slumped forward, resting on her chest, her eyes

291

closed. Ash pushed off hard from the bottom and landed on his stomach in the opening of the pipe. Crawling his way forward, he heard a faint moan in response to the Captain's attentions.

Not dead, thank God, not dead.

The words echoed inside his head. When he reached her, he realized that there was a noose fixed tightly around her throat. There were scratch marks above and below the rope line. She'd obviously tried to claw at it, but she was weak and there was no way she could've removed it without help. Her eyes opened fractionally and looked into his. "Bolton," she murmured before her eyes rolled back in her head. She was sedated, helpless and frozen from the exposure to the cold and wet, all because of that bastard Bolton.

Ash shined his phone light at the ceiling of the pipe and saw the other end of the rope tied tightly to a metal ring above their heads. He scrambled around, trying to stand up on the slick, rounded surface, but slipped and fell crashing into Maeve from behind. The force pushed her farther toward the opening of the pipe, leaving her choking on the end of the rope. He pulled her back as best he could and propped her against the Captain to take the weight off the noose.

He couldn't just dash around madly. He needed to think this through. If this campaign was going to be successful, he had to consider the terrain and make use of every tool in his woefully inadequate arsenal.

Before he stood again, he removed his jacket and laid it on the floor of the pipe to provide some traction. He was colder now but more stable. Crouching underneath the ring, he stuffed his phone into his pocket and worked by feel to loosen the rope that had Maeve strung up. Bolton had tied an elaborate series of

A Ghostwriter's Guide to Murder

knots that Maeve would never have been able to release. Ash continued to work on the rope despite his frozen fingers and an ever-rising sense of panic.

Dixon had waded through the water, and his, face pale in the moonlight, appeared at the opening of the pipe. "She still with us?"

"Yes," Ash answered tersely. "And she managed to say Bolton."

"I knew it in my bones." Dixon slammed his hand on the side of the pipe. "He won't get away with this."

He watched Ash struggling, but there wasn't room for two men inside the pipe.

"I've called for help, but you're going to need to get a bit of a move on there." His voice was tight. "Not sure we can wait for the professionals. India's been on the Waterway Commission's website, and apparently there's an automatic system flushing that takes place every night. Thousands of gallons of water will move through this pipe between now and two AM."

"How long do we have?" Ash demanded.

Dixon held up his watch. In the dark Ash could read *1:25*. "Not long."

293

Chapter
Forty-Seven

Toliver pulled the car up in front of a nice block of flats in Finsbury Park. Far too rich for the blood of a cop, Paul thought, even a DSI. The man was bent as a nine-bob note.

Grabbing a box of latex gloves from the back seat, Toliver handed a pair to Paul. Paul knew he'd been sloppy on their last outing, and apparently Toliver wasn't going to allow him to do it again.

They exited the car, and Paul followed him to the bin room. Security was sloppy and the outer door was ajar, though the door to the back hall of the flats was locked.

Toliver made short work of the interior door, and they were soon in the building, climbing the back stairs to the top floor. They walked softly along the hall to the door of Bolton's flat and found it unlocked. Careless for a man in his position, Paul thought. Toliver raised a finger to his lips, and they entered silently. The sound of raised voices drifted down the hall, muffled but angry. Paul watched as the Machine surfaced, removing the gun from the pocket of his jacket.

Paul put a hand on his arm. "No killing," he insisted in a low voice.

A Ghostwriter's Guide to Murder

"No killing, but I'm not walking in there without backup." The Machine reached the door to the sitting room and pushed it open silently.

Bolton stood with his back against the glass doors to the balcony, his hands spread apart, pleading with a man also pointing a gun at him. "Look, I'll give you whatever you want."

"I want my mate back."

Paul's heart sank as he heard Jimmy's anguished cry.

"'E never stole your money. 'E gave it to Ross, just like 'e said 'e did. I was there."

"Ross played you," the Machine agreed, moving into the room. "Never trust a glorified estate agent. He's just told us everything."

Jimmy flashed a glance back in their direction. "I 'ad to come. I know you told me to stay with Roy, but I couldn't let 'im get away with it."

"'S all right, lad, but how'd you know where Bolton was?"

"I told you. I was with Gav when 'e got the money. We came 'ere in the car on our way to the match in Surbiton, the big one where Roy got three hundred and eighty rounds. This is where the money came from, and we took it straight to Ross. Gav didn't cheat 'im. 'E'd never."

"I know," Toliver said soothingly. "I know."

The man in the window didn't look like a cold-blooded killer to Paul. He looked like—nothing. Nondescript in the extreme. Middle-aged, middle-weight, middle-height. A non-entity wielding power given to him by someone else, Paul thought, and yet, no doubt, he was convinced he was God's gift. Up close he was just a pathetic man trying to show a little swagger and failing miserably.

"Gav was a good bloke doing his best to make it," the Machine growled, moving closer. "Learned a few tricks from the likes of Malik Ross, tried to do what the big guys were doing, but just wanting to run a business and have a life. A life you took away from him"—he raised his voice—"for nothing."

"Not for nothing. He had something of mine, and I wanted it back," Bolton said. "Wasn't personal, just business."

"It wasn't yours," Jimmy sobbed.

Paul had been lingering in the doorway but now moved forward to stand just behind the Machine. "What have you done with Maeve?"

Bolton didn't answer.

In the silence, Paul's phone chimed, and he glanced down quickly to see a message from India flash across the home screen. *She's at St. Pan. Alive.* He felt some of the tension leave his shoulders, but he wasn't finished with Bolton. They needed to get some answers.

"How'd you know where to find the money?" he demanded.

Bolton remained tight-lipped.

"Did Ross tell you where it was?" Paul prodded.

Silence.

"Answer him," the Machine insisted, moving a step closer with his own weapon trained on Bolton.

Bolton looked back and forth between the three angry men in front of him, two of them armed, and seemed to decide it was in his best interest to say something. "Had a little chat with Foster," he replied sullenly. "I knew he'd pocketed the money I gave him, and I wasn't about to let him get away with it."

"And?" Paul pushed.

A Ghostwriter's Guide to Murder

Bolton fell silent again, and the Machine moved in even closer, his gun pointed squarely at the man's chest. "Out with it."

"Bloke denied taking the money, but Ross was riding my arse, so I told him he'd better get me my cash sharpish or I'd send someone after his nearest and dearest."

"But it wasn't your cash," Paul countered. "So what'd you do, follow him?"

Bolton dipped his head in acknowledgment. "I knew he was lying. He went for the money; I went for him."

"It wasn't your money," Jimmy wailed. "Why'd ya have to kill 'im?"

"Seems Gav was just hideously unlucky," Paul said, looking at Jimmy sadly. "Maeve found the money at precisely the wrong moment, and he was forced to move it. Ironically, to stop the police asking questions. And this bastard"—he gestured toward Bolton—"got crazy lucky. Gav didn't mean to, but he led him straight to the cash."

"Fate's a bitch." There was the slightest trace of a smile on Bolton's lips, and Paul was itching to see the Machine wipe it off.

"Perfect weapon to hand, no one around, and the canal to dump him in. Like it was meant to be."

"And you knew it was his girlfriend's boat?" Paul was working to fill in the gaps for Maeve's sake.

"No idea, but that was another piece of luck. She made the perfect killer. She had motive and opportunity. With her suicide and her confession, case closed. As you say, who's going to take the word of a glorified estate agent over clear evidence?"

297

Jimmy was shaking as he cocked the gun in his hand.

"No, Jimmy." Toliver's attention quickly returned to his friend. "Don't do it."

Jimmy looked despairingly at Toliver. "He *deserves* it. You know he does."

"He does, but you'd go down for murder. That's not you, Jimmy. Besides, there are other ways. Better ways." The Machine turned back to the man in the window. "Do you know what it's like for a cop in jail?" A cruel smile spread over his face. "There'll be no corner where you can hide." He moved close enough to whisper. "You'll find out that there are things worse than death."

"You sure, Mac?" Jimmy asked. "Doesn't feel right to just be 'andin' 'im to the cops. They'll cover for 'im. Sweep it all under the rug. Got their own interests to protect, don't they?"

"Plenty of people below him willing to talk." Paul thought about Ash's dislike for the man. "Police hate bent coppers, and the guvnor's already not a popular man."

"Don't count on it." Bolton's swagger seemed to have returned with the news he wasn't about to be shot.

"Doesn't mean you can't teach him a bit of a lesson your way, Jimmy," the Machine said, placing his gun on the table behind him. He looked across at Paul. "Did I mention Jimmy was the national bare-knuckle boxing champ when we were in school? Doesn't look like it, but he's right handy with his fists."

The Machine approached Bolton and grabbed him, pinning his arms behind him. "Bit of practice's always good for the lad."

Chapter Forty-Eight

Dixon had departed to try to find something in the boot of his car that might cut the rope as Ash continued to struggle with the cold and the damp. The wet rope seemed to have glued itself together, and the tension created by the connection to Maeve's neck was making everything worse. The scene in front of him was exactly the way Maeve had described it in her outline, down to the smallest detail. A credit to her imagination and her technical knowledge but no comfort to Ash.

Emergency services might be close, but Ash knew they couldn't wait. The Captain was clearly mystified that they weren't leaving, and he sat next to Maeve, whining softly.

To Ash, it seemed like he'd been clawing at the rope above his head for hours, but it hadn't been that long. The best thing to do was to relax for a moment and wait for Dixon to return with a tool that might make things easier, but every time he heard the slightest change in the sound of the water, he was terrified that the deluge was about to begin. He watched the sides to see if the water was rising even fractionally, and to his anxious eyes it seemed as if it were.

299

He could feel his strength fading—ticking down like a health bar in a game. It was a precarious balancing act, and being frozen there in limbo was stretching his nerves and his muscles to the breaking point.

For Maeve's sake, he forced himself to dig deep to find that extra bit of stamina. *You do this on-screen every day,* he chided himself. *Maeve's counting on you. Keep fighting.* His arms were shaking, but he went back to picking at the knots overhead.

It was dark in the tunnel, which made it all the harder, and he was relieved to finally hear Dixon making his way back across the canal, his figure outlined in the opening of the pipe.

"I found a pocketknife," Dixon said, struggling inelegantly to climb up into the tunnel. "Not sure this is wise. It's already cramped in there with the three of you, and I don't know how I get it back to you without unwedging Maeve."

"Let's see if the Captain can help." Ash knew his relationship with the Captain was new, but they said dogs had an instinct. Hopefully he sensed that they were all trying to help Maeve, not hurt her. Dixon extended the knife in his hand into the tunnel opening.

"Bring it," Ash said. "Go on boy. Fetch."

The Captain looked at him uncertainly. He didn't want to move away from his mistress. She needed him. He knew that much for certain, but the man in front of him kept waving the shiny thing at him and the nice boat neighbor with the sausages wanted it. He rose to his feet, stiff from sitting in the freezing water. He edged his way toward the man at the mouth of the tunnel and took the metal in his teeth. He looked back over his shoulder at the boat neighbor before turning slowly, his paws slipping and sliding as if he were on a sheet of ice. He moved

A Ghostwriter's Guide to Murder

cautiously, gingerly placing one paw in front of the other. The water seemed to be flowing faster, and it made him nervous.

Ash watched the Captain hesitate. It wasn't their imagination; the water was starting to flow more quickly now. What had been a trickle was now a stream. Ash looked at the side of the tunnel. The water was beginning to rise. With every second, less and less of the wall was visible. The Captain was frozen now, not moving forward or backward, and soon the decision would be taken away from him. At this rate the water would lift him off his feet and he would be swept away.

"You can do it," Ash pleaded, reaching toward the Captain with his free hand. "For Maeve."

He watched as the dog leaned in hard against the flow of the water. Too anxious to move but straining to reach Ash's hand.

The pocketknife was still just out of reach, and Ash slid his feet forward a few inches more, still holding on to the metal ring in the ceiling and struggling to stay upright. The water was now above his knees, and he saw Maeve being lifted from her position on the floor, her legs pushed straight by the force of the rushing water, her head thrown back, the noose tightening around her throat.

Ash lunged toward the Captain and grabbed the knife, bobbling it on the ends of his fingers for a moment. In a game, this was where dexterity points would carry you through. Ash knew he had none, but by sheer force of will he managed to close his fingers around the knife. He brought his two hands together and struggled to flip the knife open with his frozen fingers. The sight of the Captain being swept out into the canal by the water that was now flowing at full force down the sluice was enough to marshal every ounce of strength he had.

The blade flicked out and Ash attacked the rope with a vengeance, sawing at the fibers in a blind panic. The threads snapped one by one in what seemed like slow motion. All he could see was the rope and the knife, slashing over and over, cutting his own fingers as he went, then suddenly everything tipped upside down. The rushing water filled the tunnel as the last of the fibers broke free of the tether and he and Maeve and the trailing rope were flushed head over heels out of the tunnel on a wave of water.

Chapter Forty-Nine

He breathed in but found no air, only the foul, icy water of the canal filling his mouth and flooding into his lungs. The weight of the water pulling him down into a hell of his own making.

"There's the title, I think," Maeve said, pausing in her dictation. "*A Hell of His Own Making.* What do you think?"

"I could sell that," India replied. "You still cold?"

"A bit," Maeve conceded.

It'd been three days since they'd dragged Maeve out of the canal sluice and back to dry land, and she was still perpetually chilled. Partially psychological, no doubt, but India wasn't going to point that out; she simply dug out another fleecy blanket and tucked it in around her friend's legs. The Captain draped himself across her, doing his best to help with the warming process. India was glad to keep Maeve company, though truth be told, she was there to make sure she was quiet and resting per the doctor's orders. Three broken ribs, a broken arm, and any number of scratches and bruises. Not good, but it could've been so much worse.

With her arm in a sling, Maeve had convinced India to help her finish book forty-three, and so she sat taking dictation on the deck of the *Revenge* in the thin sunlight of an October morning. Rowan and Sage had brought over an herbal tea that might or might not contain actual tea, but Maeve seemed to be enjoying it and she had her hands tightly wrapped around the warm mug.

"We could take a break," India suggested.

"Not yet. I want to get all this onto the computer while it's still fresh in my mind. I'm sure it'll be all the better for my experience."

India settled back into the chair beside Maeve, giving the Captain's ears a quick scratch. "I'm happy to keep going, just don't go thinking you need to step to the brink of death to bring a dose of reality to all your books."

"Don't worry. I've had my fill of adventures for now."

India had wanted more adventure in her life, and she'd got it. Mercifully, Maeve was taking it all in stride, which made India feel less greedy for hoping they'd have more excitement in the future. Would she feel as keen for new adventures if this one hadn't turned out well in the end? Probably not. "Have you heard anything more from Julian?" she asked.

"Charges have been dropped, for a start."

"'Bout damn time," India said.

"True, but Bolton's involvement is apparently slowing the whole process. They've started an internal investigation, but it could be months with all the formal procedures."

"Surely they have enough to lock him up for life: murder, attempted murder, corruption."

"Should do, yes, but he's not making it any easier for them. He won't talk, won't admit to starting the fire at the Anchor to cause a distraction, and he hasn't admitted to coming aboard the *Revenge* to stage the suicide note."

"Do they need all that? Surely your testimony is enough to convict him."

"In the end it will be, but Dixon's trying to do things by the book. He suspects Bolton's guilty of a lot more than just killing Gavin and trying to kill me. Witness intimidation, evidence tampering, all sorts. They want to get him for everything."

"Dixon definitely seemed more cheerful the last time I saw him," India noted.

"I think he's finally getting to run his own department. And good for him. But come on, let's get Simon to finish this case. I'm ready to move on to a project of my own," Maeve said.

India clapped her hands together. "You're going to try writing for yourself again?"

"According to Julian, I'll have a bit of money coming in soon."

"A quarter of a million pounds," India sighed. "Still can't believe it."

"I felt flush enough to threaten to quit so I can focus on my own writing."

"What did they say?"

"They offered to publish an original Maeve Gardner if I continued writing the odd Simon Hill story. I've agreed, but only one Simon Hill a year; the rest will be me."

"That's wonderful. Will you be writing mysteries?"

"They say write what you know, so I'll start there," Maeve said.

India was happy for Maeve, truly she was, but she couldn't help feeling sorry for Vicky. She'd lost out at every conceivable level in this nightmare situation. The love of her life, the money, her fairy-tale future. Life was pain, but it still made India sad.

"What's bothering you?" Maeve asked. "Something is, I can see it written all over your face."

"Nothing, just a fleeting thought about Vicky. Poor woman."

"Not that poor," Maeve said. "I've told Julian to have the insurance proceeds split fifty-fifty. A day later and she'd have had it all, but a hundred and twenty-five thousand's nothing to sneeze at."

India leaned across and gave her friend a hug. "No, no it's not."

Chapter Fifty

Three Weeks Later

Winter was closing in, but as always in England there was the odd unpredictable spurt of clement weather. Global warming? Maybe, but whatever it was, they'd take it.

At the Anchor, Paul, Ash, and India were sitting outside, enjoying the evening air. Maeve moved to join them, helping herself to a large gin from the makeshift bar Paul had fashioned out of a shipping crate that had arrived with his new barstools.

The interior of the pub was still being repaired. Insurance would cover the bulk of it, as Dixon had quickly signed off on the report classifying the incident as arson and verifying that the owner was not involved. Bolton still wouldn't admit to starting the blaze, but his fingerprints had been found on a can of petrol discarded in the bushes near the pub. The unflappable Paul was taking it all in his stride.

Things were actually going faster than might've been expected, as Jimmy and Roy had been coming over to give Paul a hand on the weekends. Between them, Paul and the crew of the Darty Deeds had stripped out the burnt fixtures and wood and hauled it all away. The stone had been cleaned and repainted, and the boys were about to begin the process of replacing the wooden floors. The bottles of liquor that had survived the fire were still considered a write-off from an insurance standpoint, but Paul hadn't had the heart to throw them away. They were the spoils of war, and he'd had plenty of volunteers to help him drink them.

Maeve seated herself next to the others with her reclaimed gin. The Captain went to greet Ash, putting a paw on his lap and receiving an enthusiastic scratch. She never would've expected it, but their time together had blossomed into a real affection, and now that she was feeling stronger, the Captain often jumped across to Ash's boat for a visit, Smaug in tow.

"Room for one more?" DS Dixon asked, making his way toward them along the towpath.

"If you aren't going to fine us for drinking on an unfit premise," Paul said, gesturing to the bar crate, "then you're more than welcome."

"I'm off duty. I see nothing at all," Dixon replied, helping himself to a large whisky.

"We've got a darts tournament this weekend in Leeds," Paul said. "What are the odds we might have Toliver?"

"Don't see why not," Dixon said. "He's consented to being questioned a half dozen times over the past few weeks. He provided some useful information, and as you know he has a good brief. He didn't kill Gavin, and he didn't harm Maeve, so we won't get him on that, and the rest isn't my department."

A Ghostwriter's Guide to Murder

"No pushback for what happened to Malik Ross?" Ash asked.

"Toliver roughed up Ross, and Bolton for that matter, but neither one of them are inclined to file charges. They're too frightened of him."

"And what of Malik Ross?" Maeve asked. "Will he be facing charges?"

"Bit delicate, I'm afraid. He has a lot of powerful friends. Ross admitted that Bolton owed him money. He claims Bolton begged for an extension, then suddenly came up with the cash. Fifty thousand pounds' worth. Insists that's all he knows."

"What about the recording Paul made at the warehouse?"

"Not clear enough, and besides it would be tough to find a court that would allow it as evidence."

"And Bolton's still not talking?"

"Not about Gavin, so we'll have to see. In the end it comes down to the word of one crook against another—one wealthy and one not so wealthy. You do the maths."

"What about all the evidence Gavin had collected?" India asked. "Surely they can get him on corruption charges?"

"Most of the hard evidence Foster had was connected to Ross' business dealings. Accounting sleights of hand, other white-collar sorts of games. Foster had notes on the bribes being paid in the political arena, but no paper trail—no canceled checks or deposit records. Ross was too shrewd for that."

"So he's going to walk?" Maeve said. "Even after getting Gavin killed?"

"The only charge here would be accessory to murder, and the powers that be don't think it would stick. Too much circumstantial evidence."

Melinda Mullet

"That's rich—circumstantial evidence was fine for me but not for him," Maeve muttered. "As usual, with money you can buy your way out of anything."

"Bolton's not buying his way out of anything," Dixon said. "It's long overdue and he's going down. The force will be better for it, and the likes of Malik Ross will have lost their inside edge."

"I hope you're getting some credit for all of this," India said. "If you hadn't been willing to go rogue, none of this would be happening."

"Took a bit of grief for that, but in the end seems I'm up for a promotion if all goes well."

"Detective inspector?" Ash asked.

"That's right," Dixon replied. "Means I'll be well placed to push a bit more work your way." He raised his glass to Ash.

Three pairs of eyes turned in unison to look at Ash. "What kind of work?" Paul asked.

"Didn't he tell you?" Dixon said. "We've finally talked him into doing some freelance work under contract to the Met. We need him."

Paul grinned. "Thought you said you'd never go back."

"Well, things are a bit different now," Ash said.

"You're a hero," India said. "They should be honored to have you back."

Ash flushed, and it made Maeve very happy to see India praising him. It would be good for his confidence.

"He is a hero," Dixon admitted. "In fact, before we got sidetracked, I came by to let you know that Ash is up for a formal commendation."

"I'm not surprised," Maeve said. "He was amazing."

"Well done, mate," Paul added.

A Ghostwriter's Guide to Murder

India rose and walked over to give him a hug.

"Then celebrations all around," Paul said with a smile. "I'll get some champagne."

He disappeared into the pub and returned with a bottle of bubbly and an old wooden board. "I have something for you, Ash. Found this when we were clearing out the lower level after the fire. No idea how it survived the flames, but it did." He turned the board around and displayed a weathered pub sign emblazoned with a red lion. "Turns out the original name of the pub here back in the horse-and-barge days was the Red Lion. Thought you might like it for your boat."

India looked excited. "You should take it on the *Antiques Roadshow*. Bet it's worth a few bob."

Ash came closer to look at the sign and ran a hand over the image of the rampant red lion on the sign. "It's beautiful, but honestly, if I put one more thing on the boat, I swear she'll sink. Maybe we could put it on the wall in the Nook when it's rebuilt?"

"Sure. If that's what you want," Paul said.

"In honor of Ash and all of our hard work," India added. "What a fitting memento."

"We'll have to rechristen it the Red Lion Corner," Maeve said.

"I like that," India said. "Lions are fierce, and tenacious. Just like us. Maybe we could help you write your mysteries, Maeve. We do make a good team."

"That we do." Maeve looked around at the unlikely group of friends. They resembled a pride of lions, and she'd never have survived the last month without them. Not only were they her pride, they were her joy as well.

She raised her glass. "To us. To the Red Lions."

Acknowledgments

Here today, up and off somewhere else tomorrow! Travel, change,
interest, excitement! The whole world before you, and a horizon
that's always changing!
　　　　　　　—Kenneth Grahame, *The Wind in the Willows*

As a child reading *Wind in the Willows*, I dreamed of living on a houseboat along the banks of a river. Free to drift at will through the English countryside, answering to no one, and finding adventure at every turn. As is so often the case, the bucolic dreams of childhood eventually fade into the mundane realities of adulthood. My career led me to London, which I adored, and into the legal profession, which I adored less. Being a corporate lawyer is not a career path that engenders boundless joy or often even a vague sense of accomplishment. To those who knew me, it was no surprise that the lure of the always-changing horizon eventually set me on a new path.

As a budding novelist I wrote about things I loved—Scottish whisky, mysteries, longboats, London and a wide array of quirky characters. There were the odd moments of fear and anxiety, but through it all I am happy to say I have found boundless joy on this new journey.

Writing a story is a solitary endeavor, but a book is only brought to life through the efforts of countless committed

A Ghostwriter's Guide to Murder

people. I owe a tremendous debt of gratitude to all those who have helped to bring *Ghostwriter's Guide* to fruition. In particular, I'd like to recognize my agent, Abby Saul, at the Lark Group. Abby, you are a superlative representative, an endlessly patient, talented, and gracious editor, and a dear friend. Thank you for always keeping the faith even when I did not.

To the folks at Crooked Lane Books who have welcomed me so warmly into their literary family. I could not have asked for a more dedicated group of professionals with so much passion for the written word. My heartfelt thanks to Tara Gavin for embracing this project and to the amazing editing and marketing folks who have guided me through the process. Thaisheemarie Fantauzzi Pérez, Rachel Keith, Rebecca Nelson, and Monica Manzo, you have been amazing.

To my husband, Mark, for being so patient and supportive through all the highs and lows that come with being married to a writer.

To my daughters, Katherine and Amanda, for their love, support, and editing wisdom.

To my friends who buoy me along with wine, whisky, and laughter as the circumstances demand.

To my long-standing (far be it for me to say old) friend Ashley, who found himself named in this book through no fault of his own. He is absolutely as clever as his namesake, but he is *way* cooler than book Ash could ever hope to be.

And last of all, a special thank-you to my loyal fans, who have been along for the ride since the Whisky Business series launched and who will now, hopefully, set sail with me on this new adventure.